Daisy stuck her fists on her hips. "I see. You would rather do anything than get into a boat with me, wouldn't you?"

She pulled herself up to her full height. "Would it damage your masculine pride so much to allow a mere female to help you out? Yes, it would. Hah! I didn't think it of you, Ben. I thought at least you were... But I see I was wrong. You despise me just as much as..."

"No!" He couldn't let her think that of him. "Daisy, that isn't true! I don't despise you! I..."

Instinctively he darted forward. The breeze, which felt so balmy on the rest of his body, felt like icy teeth grazing over his thighs as he came out of the water, and it made him shiver.

"You would, in fact, rather freeze out here than be forced to sit within one foot of me for the short duration of the boat ride back to the mainland."

"No, Daisy..." He strode across the gravel to where she was standing, reaching her just as a flicker of lightning brought the entire scene into bright relief. "You haven't considered... If anyone were to see you and me, like this in a boat, in the dead of night..."

"Yes. You would risk being compromised into marrying me, wouldn't you?"

ANNIE BURROWS

A Scandal at Midnight

HARLEQUIN®
HISTORICAL™

Recycling programs
for this product may
not exist in your area.

ISBN-13: 978-1-335-40732-0

A Scandal at Midnight

Copyright © 2021 by Annie Burrows

For questions and comments about the quality of this book,
please contact us at CustomerService@Harlequin.com.

Harlequin Enterprises ULC
22 Adelaide St. West, 40th Floor
Toronto, Ontario M5H 4E3, Canada
www.Harlequin.com

Printed in U.S.A.

Annie Burrows has been writing Regency romances for Harlequin since 2007. Her books have charmed readers worldwide, having been translated into nineteen different languages, and some have gone on to win the coveted Reviewers' Choice Award from CataRomance. For more information, or to contact her, please visit annie-burrows.co.uk, or find her on Facebook at Facebook.com/annieburrowsuk.

Books by Annie Burrows

Harlequin Historical

The Captain's Christmas Bride
In Bed with the Duke
Once Upon a Regency Christmas
"Cinderella's Perfect Christmas"
A Duke in Need of a Wife
A Marquess, a Miss and a Mystery
The Scandal of the Season
From Cinderella to Countess
His Accidental Countess
A Scandal at Midnight

Brides for Bachelors

The Major Meets His Match
The Marquess Tames His Bride
The Captain Claims His Lady

Visit the Author Profile page
at Harlequin.com for more titles.

Chapter One

Lady Marguerite Patterdale pushed open the door of the library and breathed in deeply. The comforting smell of old leather and dust felt like a bosom friend, opening their arms and welcoming her home.

Home. Yes, even though she hadn't felt glad about anything so far today, here in the library she felt welcome. Accepted. Safe.

Pausing only to close the door behind her, she went over to her favourite shelf, the one that extended from the floor almost to the ceiling, and rested her forehead against the second and third volumes of *Clarissa*. And then, thinking that it wasn't fair to show such favouritism, she stretched out her arms along the shelf to embrace as many of her dear friends as she could.

How she loved them, all of them. Every single tome in this room had touched her very soul, in one way or another, and left something of themselves behind. Even the rather dull ones had taught her something of the world beyond Wattlesham Priory without her having to go to the discomfort of leaving her room.

But best of all, books didn't judge her by her pedigree, or her looks, or her wealth. They would reveal their treasure to anyone who delved into their pages. People didn't talk about 'an open book' for no reason. Books shared themselves freely, and transported their reader to a world of adventure, or learning, or imagination. They were the best companion any girl could have. Especially one who had no friends.

Oh, if only she could marry a book. No, a whole library. She couldn't choose just one book above all others, any more than she'd been able to pick one man out of all the supposedly eligible bachelors she'd met during her Season. Not that she'd wanted to pick any of them. Perhaps, if she'd gone to London actually wanting to find a husband there, it might not have ended so disastrously.

Marguerite shuddered as she recalled the dreadful things Mother had said that last day, after Lord Martlesham had slammed his way out of the house. Mother's disappointment had been hard to bear. But Marguerite simply hadn't been able to bring herself to explain why, in the end, she'd hadn't been able to accept his proposal.

Because Mother would have been even more disappointed than she already was. Because it would have meant explaining what she'd seen the night he'd been standing next to James, her oldest brother, which Mother would have taken badly. For Mother adored all five of her boys and would have been terribly upset if Marguerite had suggested…even hinted…that there could possibly be anything about their behaviour that had managed to give her an aversion to the entire male sex.

Mother would not understand why she couldn't just accept the fact that her only value within the family was her potential for marrying well. Which was to say, to a man who could either help foster the ambitions of at least one of her brothers, or support Father in his political aims. Mother just thought she should be happy to…to…*serve* her family in that way.

But even if she had wanted to get married, choosing a husband was not like choosing a book to read. Men were not like books. Men all pretended to be something they were not. They said things that weren't true. And, worst of all, they judged her for the way she looked, and the family from which she came, and the dowry she would bring to the union. And you could put a book back on the shelf when you were finished with it, or if you found it less interesting than you'd hoped. Whereas you were stuck with a husband for the rest of your life.

Still, her London season was over. And she was home. And she could…

The sound of booted feet, coming along the corridor made her raise her head. One of her brothers, no doubt. Accompanied by a few of his friends. For each of her brothers had contrived to round up a few friends while they'd been in London and invited them to spend the rest of the summer here.

As they always did.

Not that they'd come in here. The library was the one place she was safe. Not one of them could see the point of books, except perhaps for Ben Flinders, and that wasn't for the purposes of reading. They must be on the way to the billiard room, she supposed...

But, drat it, instead of marching past, the feet slowed as they approached the doorway, and somebody set their hand to the doorknob.

There was no way she was going to let them see her hugging a shelf full of books. Quick as a flash, she hitched up her skirts and shinned up the sturdy shelves, which, she'd discovered several years ago, were as easy to climb as a ladder. Even though she was older, and heavier, she was pleased to learn that she had lost none of her agility, managing to reach the top shelf and scramble over the ornamental scrollwork that crowned it before the door was fully open.

'We won't be disturbed by any of the other guests in here,' came the voice of Jasper, her second oldest brother. 'Nobody ever comes into the library.'

Certainly not the maids, to dust. Marguerite was lying on a veritable cushion of it. She clamped one hand over her nose and mouth to stop herself sneezing. The last thing she wanted was for Jasper, and his pestilential friends, to find out that she was so...well, in such a state of...well, that she couldn't cope with their brand of teasing, not today. If any of them said *one* thing about her coming home without a fiancé in tow, she'd...she'd...

Well, she hadn't even been able to bear her mother and father's presence in the carriage home, that was how sensitive she felt about her singular lack of success in securing a husband. She'd travelled in the smaller carriage with her maid, rather than spending two days cooped up with a mother looking at her with disappointment and a father with deep disdain. And neither of them, at any of the stops, during their excruciatingly polite interchanges in front of landlords and ostlers and waiters, had suggested her place was with the family, rather than the servants.

A surge of resentment swelled up against her brothers, all five of them. And their pestilential friends. They pursued her everywhere, ruining everything! Not only was she lying in a dust drift right now, but they had surrounded her like a pack of snarling, surly…guard dogs the entire time she was in London.

She'd done her best, in spite of her natural wariness when it came to the male sex, to fulfil the family's hopes for her Season. But how on earth was she supposed to find a husband when they all hedged her about wherever she went, repelling all other males with the same kind of zeal they'd shown for their games of Christians and Saracens through the ruins in the grounds when they'd been schoolboys? And had Mother and Father taken any of that into account? Had one word of censure ever passed their lips about her brothers' behaviour during her Season?

No. *She* was the one who had disappointed them. *She* was the failure who, in spite of all her advantages and the money expended on bringing her out, had, yet again, failed to live up to their expectations.

'We'll be private in here,' she heard Jasper say, 'and there's something I want to say to you all particularly, which nobody else must ever know.'

She would have groaned if it wouldn't have meant giving herself away. Not only was she stuck on top of a shelf but she was now about to overhear some sordid scrape Jasper needed to confide to his friends. And it had to be something bad for him not to go to James, the oldest of the brood, or even Father, who never seemed to bat an eyelid at anything his sons did, no matter how disgraceful she thought it. Instead, he'd just bail them out, with a few remarks about high spirits, or some such rot.

So much for finding safety in the library. There was nowhere, at the Priory, or London, where she would ever be free from her brothers. Which opinion was confirmed when the next words her brother spoke were: 'It's about Daisy.'

Daisy. Ooh, how she hated the nickname her brothers had given her. And not merely because it was a mocking reference to the flower after which she'd been christened. It was bad enough that they likened her to the common weed that was related to the beautiful, showy flower to which her mother had compared her mere moments after she'd given birth to her. Even though daisies were low-growing flowers, and her brothers kept on about how she shot up like a weed because she had the misfortune to take after Father's side of the family, who were all tall and skinny.

No, it was the fact that *everyone* called her Daisy nowadays. Even Mother and Father, who would never dream of calling Jasper Gem, or Jeremy Germ, let alone Joshua the Trumpeter.

But there, that was the way things were in this family. The boys had all the respect. All the fun. All the freedom. While she was nothing more than the butt of everyone's jokes.

Ben's spirits sank. They hadn't been here five minutes, and from the sound of it Gem was already planning to drag them all into some sort of folly that he'd describe as a lark, or a spree. And if Ben tried to say they were surely now all past the age for such folly, the others would accuse him of being a marplot. The best he could do would be to hear what Gem was planning, and then make sure that they didn't all come to grief over it.

'It's about Daisy,' said Gem.

At the mention of her name, the hairs on the back of Ben's neck prickled, the way they did before a sortie. Surely Gem wasn't going to suggest they all play some kind of practical joke on her, the way they used to when they'd been schoolboys? She didn't deserve that. Well, she'd never deserved it. The only thing she'd done to make all her brothers pick on her so unmercifully, as far as he could tell, was to be the one girl in a family of boys.

And in the library, of all places. A place she thought of as a sanctuary. A place he identified with her so much that he swore he could smell her scent. That light, floral, summery scent he'd inhaled so deeply the night he'd secured a dance with her and had the privilege of being her partner for one tortured half-hour. No, he had to be honest with himself, if with nobody else. The torture had lasted far longer than that half-hour. Every night since then he'd lain awake, going over every moment, every fleeting expression on her face, the way the candles had made her hair glisten like gold, the way her movements had revealed her limbs through the delicate fabric of her gown, the way her scent had ebbed and flowed as she'd come near, then moved away...

That probably explained why he thought he could smell her scent. Gem had only to mention her name and Ben was picturing her, remembering her scent and the feel of her hand clasped in his, albeit briefly, whenever the dance had called for him to take it. The library just smelled of books. Which was another trigger for his memory, to be honest. The first time he'd met her, she'd had a book in her hand. And he'd soon learned that they were the love of her life. So much so that he couldn't walk into a library, or a bookshop, without thinking of her. That must be why he was imagining he could smell her scent. It was a...a nose memory, if there was such a thing.

'I'm worried about her,' said Gem, heavily.

Horace and Walter made non-committal noises whilst striving, almost convincingly, to look interested. But all Ben's senses went on the alert.

'I don't need to tell you what a disaster her Season was,' Gem continued, walking over to a large desk and leaning back against it. 'I never noticed before, but in society, well, she's...' He ran his fingers through his hair. 'Turns out she's rather shy.' He folded his arms across his chest and stared round the three of them, as though daring any of them to disagree. 'We all know her as a...well, in many ways she's full of pluck. But you wouldn't know it to see the way she freezes up when in company. That's why no man worthy of her saw what a gem she truly is.'

Walter sniggered. Gem glared at him. 'Sorry, Gem,' said Walter. 'Just…you know, gem, and Gem, and all that…'

The grim cast of Gem's mouth relaxed a bit. Someone had given him the nickname of Gem at Eton, because the name of Jasper was a kind of a jewel. He hadn't liked it at one time, but he'd mellowed once his younger brothers had come up to school, one by one. The next in line, Jeremy, who might more properly have been nicknamed Jem, had acquired the even less flattering name of Germ, since Jem was already taken.

Daisy's younger brothers had fared even worse. Joshua had gained the nickname of Trumpet, after both the biblical character's famous battle at Jericho, and his tendency to produce wind at great volume. And the youngest of all, Julius, was known to one and all as the Fit, from the likeness of the name Julius Caesar to the word seizure. In the light of all that, Gem had not fared so badly in the nicknaming stakes. At least a gem was hard, which was a manly characteristic, rather than being compared to either a seed of disease or a debilitating illness. Or just a rasher of wind.

'Anyway,' said Gem sternly, in an attempt to restore some sort of order to the proceedings, 'the thing is, for a girl it's a bit of a disaster to come home from a season without a fiancé in tow. And, from watching how she behaved in London, I can't see that she'd do any better in a second season, or, well, ever really. Which brings me to the point.' He looked at each of them in turn. 'I am asking that one of you, I don't mind which, since you're all good chaps, well, that one of you propose to her while you're staying here this summer.'

The silence that followed this outrageous statement was almost deafening.

Gem gave a short laugh. 'I can see I've shocked you. But, look, when you think about it, who better to marry her than a chap I've known practically all my life? A chap she's known about as long as I have, what's more, since you've spent so much time here in the school vacations. Chaps I have been glad to keep as friends even after we've gone our separate ways in life, which is more than I can say for some of the school chums I brought here, when they seemed like decent fellows but who turned out to be...' he shook his head in disgust '...loose fish. But you fellows...' he held his arms wide, as though embracing them all '...well, you're the best of good chaps. I don't mind which of you wins her. Know I can trust any of you to, er, cherish her, and whatnot.'

The response was, once again, stunned silence.

'I'll leave it up to you to decide which of you will propose first,' said Gem, pushing himself off the desk and making for the door.

Nobody made a move to stop him, though all three swivelled on the spot, like clockwork toys, to watch him leave.

He might be unable to move, or speak, but Ben's heart was pounding. Pounding as hard as it had the night he'd danced with her.

If only he *could* marry her. It would be like a dream come true.

But he couldn't. He had nothing to offer any woman, let alone a beauty like Daisy. She was so…perfect. With her golden hair, and her blue eyes, and her perfect little nose, and her luscious, petal-soft lips that made his mouth water…

His hand half rose to his own mouth, which had never been his best feature, even before Salamanca. Now, with the scarring on his cheek, it stretched even further, giving him an almost permanent sneer.

But even if he wasn't so dashed ugly to look at, he wasn't the sort of man her parents hoped she'd marry. Because she wasn't just beautiful, she was titled and wealthy, too. They'd expect her to make a brilliant match. And he had nothing of substance to offer, except his heart, which she already possessed without having the slightest suspicion. Because he didn't want her to feel sorry for him. Which she would, the tender-hearted creature, if she ever got wind of how he felt about her.

But now Gem was…giving him permission…nay, encouraging him to…

He shook his head. It would never work. Apart from his unsuitability, his unworthiness, there was the far more practical matter of the likelihood that he'd never be able to get the words out. He only had to think how tongue-tied he'd been the night he'd asked her to dance. Hah! He hadn't even managed that.

He'd asked Gem if he would permit him to dance with his sister, and Gem had been the one to lead him over to where she'd been standing and pretty much ordered her to take pity on him. Which she had done. At least, she hadn't looked at him with any more exaspera-

tion than she'd looked at any other dance partner she'd
had that night. In fact, she'd smiled at him when he'd
led her into the set. A smile that had felt like a blessing,
since she hadn't bestowed them on many of her part-
ners. He'd felt favoured, and honoured, and so damned
aroused every time he'd taken her little hand in his that
he'd been worried she would notice the effect she was
having, or that everyone else in the ballroom would.

He'd had to think of cold baths, then sleeping outside in a snowstorm, and then marching across the Pyr-
enees in the dead of winter in order to regain control.
By which time her smile had faded. And he'd been left
with the sinking sensation that, once more, she'd slipped
through his fingers...

'Is there anything to drink in here?' said Walter,
looking around wildly before going to the far end of
the library, where a few armchairs clustered round a
small table, on which stood a decanter and a selection
of glasses.

Horace followed him.

And Ben knew that he'd have to walk over there too.
Or they might guess, from the way he was shaking, and
gulping and, yes, sweating, that he felt as if he'd just
been struck by a thunderbolt.

Chapter Two

Marguerite couldn't believe her ears. Gem thought he could set his friends on her, did he? And she'd be so grateful she'd tamely accept whichever of them deigned to propose? Well, she'd see about that. Just as soon as they left and she could climb down from the top shelf, she'd…

There was the noise of the stopper being removed from a bottle and the clink of a glass. And then the scrape of a chair leg and the creak of leather as somebody sat down.

Bother. They could settle in here for the lord knew how long, once they'd started on the brandy, which, of course, they'd found. Father made sure refreshments were available in any room his guests might wish to use.

Even the library.

'Does he expect us to draw straws for her, do you suppose?'

That was the voice of Walter.

'I don't care what he expects.' That was Horace.

Hairy Horace. 'I ain't going to marry Daisy. Would rather take an icicle to bed.'

What? Well, if he thought she'd ever get into bed with him, he was very much mistaken! She'd rather kiss a…an ape! Which was what he looked like. And acted like, most of the time.

'She isn't cold,' said Ben, 'she's shy. That's what Gem said, remember?'

'Shy?' Walter again. 'She ain't shy, she's just damned unfriendly. Never has two words to say to me.'

And why would she bother, when he was such a… slow top?

'Even if I did screw myself up to the sticking point, she wouldn't have me.'

Well, that was the first remotely intelligent thing she'd ever heard Walter say.

'Ah, but only consider the advantages,' drawled Ben. 'You'd know any child she did have would be of your own get, which is saying something these days.'

Somehow that didn't sound like a compliment. It didn't sound as though he believed she'd be faithful to her vows, but as if no other man would look twice at her. But that was Ben for you. Cynical. Morose. Which was ironic, with that mouth of his that always looked as if it was on the point of smiling. But never did.

'She'd never wear your ears out with all the infernal chatter some girls would,' Ben continued, as though he was ticking the points off on his fingers, which he probably was, since it was an irritating habit of his. 'She's wealthy, and,' he concluded, 'you'd be part of the Patterdale family. Good connection, you can't deny. And

Gem would be your brother. Couldn't ask for a better chap as a brother-in-law. No surprises, either. We've known them all for ever.'

There was a grudging murmur of agreement.

'Sounds as though you'd like to take a pop at her yourself,' said Walter.

'No!'

Well, that was certainly heartfelt.

'I think *you* should,' Ben continued. 'You're the... well, the best of us, Walter.'

'Dammit, Ben, that's not true. You're the highest ranking of us now that you've become an earl.'

'Got to stop thinking of yourself as merely a younger son,' said Horace, in that annoyingly knowing voice he often used when trying to make a point.

'Rank doesn't weigh with her,' said Ben, 'does it, though? Or she'd have had Lord Martlesham.'

'I heard,' said Horace, 'that she couldn't bring him up to scratch.'

Ooh! How dared he? Though it was probably what everyone thought. Lord Martlesham wouldn't want anyone to know she'd turned him down flat. He was too proud. And, coupled with the way her father had decided to remove her from London before she could embarrass him by *humiliating any other decent, honourable men*, he'd have a clear run at telling his side of the story.

'And you're a captain in the army,' added Walter. 'Girls love a man in a scarlet coat. Get your uniform on, Ben, old chap, and dazzle her!'

'Leave him alone, Walter,' said Horace. 'He clearly

don't relish the challenge Gem has set us any more than we do.'

Which shouldn't hurt. After all, she didn't care what either of the others thought. But Ben... Ben, surely, couldn't dislike her this much? When she thought of all the hours she'd spent with him that summer when he'd broken his collar bone defending the ruined priory against, well, Roundheads, she rather thought it was that year. She lost track. If her brothers weren't being Cavaliers and Roundheads, then it was Saracens and Crusaders, or Pirates and Customs men, with each brother's friends choosing a tribe to which they'd belong, and waging warfare all over the estate for the duration of their summer break from school. She'd been so shocked when her brothers had just continued their campaign and abandoned Ben to his sick bed without a backward glance. Even more concerned when neither of his parents had shown any inclination to come and take him home. He'd lain, day after day, on a sofa, gazing morosely out of the window, so she'd heard, while the rest of them had carried on whooping and braying up and down the corridors when it was wet, or fighting pitched battles through the woods and laying siege to the ruins when it was fine.

Until the day she'd got permission from Mother to go and read to him, as long as she had a maid in attendance.

Ben hadn't thought much of the book she'd brought. And had appeared downright suspicious of her motives for visiting him every day. It had taken days to persuade him that, no, she hadn't come to torment him while he was unable to defend himself by *reading at him*. That, on the contrary, she'd been attempting to help him get through a painful and lonely ordeal. *What else*, she'd asked in exasperation, *could you do while stuck inside with only one working arm*? He'd scowled at her for a few moments, shifting a bit as though trying to decide whether to take her words at face value. Eventually, he'd admitted he wouldn't mind playing cards, in an offhand way that hadn't deceived her. He would clearly *enjoy* playing cards. The trouble was, she had no idea how to play any of the games he suggested. He'd been astounded when she'd explained that her brothers never wanted to let her join in, and that even if they had, not one of her governesses had considered learning card games should form part of her curriculum.

They'd both glanced stealthily at the maid, who'd been busy darning socks. And then Marguerite had leaned in, murmuring that she knew where she could lay her hands on a pack of cards, which she'd bring with her the next day.

The maid hadn't cared when Ben had started teaching her the rules of whist, and piquet, and vingt-et-un. And it had been interesting, more interesting than Marguerite had thought it would be, to learn the intricacies of those games. So that once she'd grasped the basic principles, she'd actually wanted to have a go at playing properly.

He'd been at a distinct disadvantage, having only one hand he could use. Until she'd come up with the notion of using all the books he hadn't wanted to listen to her reading to build a kind of screen behind which he could still lay all the cards out flat on the tabletop.

She'd spent hours making allowances for his scowls and grumbles, because she'd known he was in pain and felt so wretched at being left out by his friends and abandoned by his parents. She'd started to think they'd become friends, and had gone out to wave him off at the end of summer when the boys had all gone back to their various homes and he to school. She'd actually looked forward to seeing him again when she'd heard he'd be coming to stay at Christmas, thinking they'd be able to resume their friendship. But instead of showing any inclination to spend time with her again, he'd avoided her like the plague. Flushed bright red and looked at the ground at her feet rather than her when he absolutely couldn't get away with ignoring her altogether. Stuck closely to the pack surrounding Jasper and generally behaved as though he was thoroughly ashamed of having had to spend so much time the summer before in the presence of a mere girl.

And it *still* smarted. But that was boys for you. Males. Selfish beasts, the lot of them!

'I tell you what,' said Horace, 'why don't we go and play at billiards while we try to come up with a way out of this?'

'Why don't we just draw straws,' complained Walter, 'and whoever gets the shortest…'

'No. I ain't leaving this to fate,' said Horace firmly. 'Let this game of billiards be the first of a few challenges between us. So that at least we stand a chance of working our way out of the obligation.'

She heard the sound of glasses slamming down on the table and booted feet marching across the floor, and then the door opening and closing. She raised herself on one elbow and peeped over the parapet warily before making any attempt to emerge from her hiding place. And only when she could see that they'd definitely all gone did she clamber down the bookshelves, leave what should have been the safety of the library, and storm back up to her own room.

She flung open the door, stepped inside and slammed it shut. Then opened it and slammed it once more to relieve her feelings.

Marcie, her maid, who had been scrubbing the back of the armoire, looked up, her jaw dropping open.

'Lor, my lady, never say those young varmints got you in the end? Not with you being so careful, and all?'

Marcie was referring to her two younger brothers, Joshua and Julius, who had arranged a welcome home gift by filling her armoire with pigeons, no doubt hoping they'd all fly out when she opened the door and send her screaming around the room with them fluttering after her. Their trick had failed, for two reasons. Firstly, she had expected them to have laid some kind of trap, so she'd done a thorough inspection, using her parasol to sweep under the bed, in case they'd filled her chamber pot with frogs, and over the canopy in case they'd spread worms all over it, which would drop on her while she lay sleeping, later. She'd also yanked back the bedcovers in case they'd put snails in there, and all that only after pushing the door to her room open with the tip of her parasol in case they'd balanced a bucket

of water on the lintel. The second reason their trick
hadn't worked the way they'd probably hoped it would
was because they'd had to shut the door to the armoire
to keep the pigeons cooped up. And, since it was dark
inside, they'd all gone to sleep. It hadn't been very hard
to pick the sleepily cooing birds up, carry them to the
window, and throw them outside. Unfortunately, in the
meantime, the pigeons had done what pigeons do all
over the clothing in the armoire, which was why poor
Marcie had spent the last little while removing soiled
clothing and then scrubbing down the shelves.

'It wasn't my younger brothers,' said Marguerite.
'It was Jasper.'

'The oldest one? I thought you said he was too top-
lofty to indulge in such pranks any longer.'

Toplofty was exactly the way she'd described James
when talking about him to Marcie when she'd first
come to work for them. Once she'd started to see her
as an ally. 'No, Jasper isn't the oldest one. That is James.
Jasper is the next in line. But how did you know I'd had
an encounter with one of my brothers?'

'You look as if you've been sweeping a chimney,
my lady,' said Marcie. 'Begging your pardon, but you
might just as well have stayed here and helped me scrub
out the cupboard.'

Marguerite went over to the young woman, who'd
been hired to help do housework in the Town house
during her season, and had ended up becoming her
personal maid, for a variety of reasons, and plucked a
feather from her hair. 'At least I haven't ended up looking as though I have been fighting pigeons. This...' she

swept her hand down the length of her skirts, which she noticed for the first time bore the evidence of her scramble up the shelves, and her time lying in the dirt '...is merely dust, not soot.'

'If you say so, my lady,' said Marcie with the cheeky grin and irreverent attitude that had so endeared her to Marguerite.

'And I am glad I did go down to the library,' added Marguerite vehemently, 'or I would never have discovered what Jasper is planning.'

Did he really think she would tamely agree to marry whichever one of those...buffoons asked her to marry him? Who were even now playing billiards to see which one of them would end up with the onerous task of having to propose? Who'd rather take an icicle to bed?

Icicle, was she? She'd show them icicle!

'Marcie, have I anything white to wear for dinner this evening?'

'Why, yes my lady. The things in your trunks are all clean still, and only want pressing.'

'Then press me out the whitest gown you can find. Which I shall wear with the silver gauze overdress.' And finish off with pearls, and crystal adornments, as many as she could cram into her hair and round her neck and up her arms. She'd positively glitter when she went down to dinner. And have frost running through her veins and steel in her backbone, to boot.

Chapter Three

Marguerite wasn't surprised to find the long saloon where everyone gathered before dinner awash with her brothers and their friends. She'd seen the jumble of curricles and phaetons in the stable yard, the mounds of luggage piled in the hall, when she'd arrived earlier in the day.

Neither was she surprised to find that the atmosphere was one of celebration. Everyone was jolly glad Father had cut her Season short so that they could get back to doing all the things they really enjoyed.

James, who had recently become very conscious of his worth as heir to the Wattlesham estates, had invited only the two friends of his who were already lords to stay this summer. Marguerite was not the slightest bit impressed with either of them, even though they were both handsome, and so beautifully clothed that they could have walked out of a fashion plate. For she knew that not so long ago those arrogant, self-satisfied faces had been covered in pimples.

During her time in London she'd witnessed several girls sighing over one of them, Lord Bowes, and comparing his features to those of a Greek god. It had made her want to roll her eyes, although of course she'd never succumbed to the temptation, since that would have been most unladylike behaviour. And not just because she could not sigh and simper over *any* male in that hen-witted fashion. No, it was because she had such vivid memories of the year he'd developed a spot on the very end of his nose, which had grown so big her younger brothers had started calling him Cherry.

Jeremy's friends, most of whom were now at university with him, were all going through the pimply phase right now. They hung together, as close as they could get to James and his friends, trying not to look as though they were listening to the conversation avidly, in the hope they could later emulate the self-assured phrases and mannerisms of the slightly older males.

As for the youths who gathered round Joshua and Julius, they were all sniggering and nudging each other, clearly thinking up pranks they could play on the older brothers. Pranks that would involve ink, or pond water, or a variety of other materials that would spoil the elegant clothing and carefully styled hair of anyone they thought needed bringing down a peg or two.

As for Jasper's friends...

She wasn't going to look at them. Even though she couldn't help noticing that they were all standing together, their heads close, as though discussing strategy.

Mother shot her just the one, rather disappointed glance before continuing to circulate, as she always did, from group to group, making sure all the boys felt warmly welcome. Yes, the boys were all welcome. Mother would do anything for her boys. But would she ever really listen to her daughter? Would she enter into her feelings, or offer her any sympathy, or tell her that it didn't matter if she never married anyone, as long as she was happy?

No. Because as far as Mother was concerned, Marguerite's sole function in life was to become the wife of a man that Father would be proud to call son-in-law.

Tonight, Mother was making it clear that she was still not only puzzled but also extremely disappointed in her only daughter, by bustling around as though she was far too busy with her duties as hostess to waste time on her.

Marguerite lifted her chin and studiously kept her gaze on whichever part of the room nobody happened to be occupying. And concentrated on looking like an icicle.

Finally, Barnes, the butler, flung open the door at the end of the saloon, and everyone began to drift in the direction of the dining room. Because she was aware of what was afoot, she noticed Jasper frowning meaningfully at his friends, who dutifully drifted at a pace that meant they all arrived at the dining table at the same time as her. Walter held out her chair for her, and sat on her left, while Horace took his place on her right. Ben, who had clearly become a master tactician during his years in the army, had managed to veer off at the last moment, and ended up sitting opposite her, with a massive epergne acting as a further bulwark.

If she hadn't known that Jasper had put them up to it, she would have been rather amused by Horace and Walter's clumsy attempts to draw her into conversation. But she did know. And so the harder they tried to overcome their natural aversion for her, the angrier she grew. She had to keep reminding herself that she was a lady. That it was not polite to stick a fork into the back of somebody's hand at dinner, even if it would make most of the males present hoot with laughter at the sight of either Walter or Horace yelping in pain, and wrapping their bloodied hands in their napkin.

Anyway, she'd never, once, descended to the same level of behaviour her brothers thought amusing, and she wasn't about to start now. Besides, she was already in enough trouble with her parents, without creating that sort of scene at the dinner table. On the very first night of their summer house party, too.

It would have been easier if Ben wasn't sitting across from her, smirking at his friends, though...

Unless he wasn't smirking at all. It was difficult to tell these days. He'd suffered a facial wound at some stage in his career in the army, which made the left side of his mouth kick up a bit, so that he looked as if he was sneering all the time. The first time she'd seen it, she'd gasped, wanting to ask him if it hurt, and how he'd got the wound, and where.

But had then felt ashamed of not knowing. It wasn't as if she couldn't have followed his progress across the Peninsula, since the papers always reported news of major battles, and even smaller skirmishes if any officer from one of the noble houses was involved. But she'd been so angry with him, for so long, that it would have felt as if she was…not pining perhaps but showing more interest than he deserved, if she'd done that.

Eventually, the evening reached the point where all the males had consumed so much wine that the conversation began to grow a bit boisterous. And Mother finally looked at her as she rose to her feet, signalling it was time for them to withdraw.

Mother sailed along the corridor in front of her, without once looking over her shoulder, let alone waiting so they could walk arm in arm. Marguerite scowled at her mother's back. Well, if she was expecting her daughter to follow tamely to the music room and show penance for remaining obstinately single by playing the piano for the entertainment of their male guests for hour after hour, with the youngsters sneakily flicking wine or cake crumbs at her while Jasper's friends hovered around her trying to look as though they were doing what he'd asked, she had another think coming.

The moment she reached the alcove that led to the back stairs, Marguerite flung back the curtain and dashed down. Since Mother still had her back resolutely turned, it would be several minutes before she noticed, and by then Marguerite would be down both flights and into the servants' quarters. What was more, Mother took her duties as hostess so seriously that she wouldn't come looking for her when she did notice she'd gone missing. She'd send a maid.

But where to hide? Not in the house. The maids had discovered most of her hiding places over the years. And while they mostly sympathised with her need to hide from her brothers and their vile teasing, and had often pretended they hadn't seen her, they weren't likely to show the same laxity if Mother expressly ordered them to find her.

She'd have to go into the grounds. At night... Oh, bother her decision to wear so much white. She wouldn't merely glisten like the icicle she'd been trying to be but would shine like a veritable beacon with the moon being at the full. Still, she stood more chance of having some respite from...*them* outside than she would indoors.

She went to the kitchen door, pausing only to grab an umbrella and a black shawl from the jumble of coats that were hanging from hooks nearby. The shawl would shield her while she was in the shadows of the house, she hoped. And she always felt safer if she had a parasol or umbrella with her. They were so useful for searching for traps laid by her brothers. And defending herself from the same if she didn't discover them in time.

In her haste to get away from the house she didn't consciously decide which direction to take. But after only a short while she realised that her feet seemed to be conveying her in the direction of the lake. Deep down, she must have known that it was the perfect place for her to hide, even though she was wearing such conspicuous clothing. For in the middle of the lake was an island on which stood one of those follies that had been so fashionable for gentlemen to construct in her grandfather's day. A folly that resembled the ruins of a Greek temple. Built from the purest, whitest marble his money had been able to buy.

Father considered it a folly in more than one sense of

the word, since the cost of transporting so much marble had been almost ruinous. Especially since there was already a genuine ruin in the grounds, all that was left of what had once been a priory before Henry VIII had got his hands on it. The Patterdale family had made it their home until Cromwell's troops had laid siege to it and rendered it completely uninhabitable. After the Restoration, the returning Patterdales had not wanted to restore the old Priory, preferring instead to build a grand new house. That generation had been so keen to spend their money in an ostentatious manner that the shore of the island was now littered with sections of fake columns and huge chunks of marble representing fallen masonry, in the midst of which her white, glistening outfit would blend in perfectly.

Father kept several rowing boats moored at various locations along the shoreline, for use by anyone who wanted to row on the lake, so it didn't take her long to find one and launch it. Rowing across could be a tricky business, because of the strong current that ran through the lake. The boys, who'd staged mock battles on the lake, with the Greek temple representing either a pirate's lair or a smuggler's hideout, had learned that, depending on how much rainfall there had been, the current could run on either side of the island.

But once she got across, it would be well worth the effort it took. Because if any of the maids sent to look for her did suspect she'd rowed across, they weren't likely to follow. Instead they'd probably stand on the shore and shout for her to *Come back, do, before you catch it!* And then they might go off to find a strong footman to row them across, and spend the entire trip flirting and giggling, which would give her plenty of warning, and she could slip off and find somewhere else to hide.

Tonight, she pretty soon discovered, the current was running between the shore and the island. It took her a good while, and a great deal of effort, to manoeuvre the boat round to the far side of the island, where she could beach it out of sight. And just in case anyone took it into their fat heads to take a moonlit row on the lake later on, she took the additional precaution of pulling the boat well up the slope and tucking it under a bank of shrubbery.

Then she went up to the one bit of temple where there was a section of wall into which the builders had set a narrow bench. During the day it was a lovely spot in which to sit. Because the view across the lake to the house was utterly charming. Tonight, as she glanced at the many lights shining from the windows and from the torches placed at strategic locations along various paths, all the view managed to produce in her breast was a pang of rejection as she thought of all the people who were making merry inside, several of them at her expense. And not one of them would be missing her, except perhaps her younger brothers, and that would only be as a target for their crumb-flicking practice.

Still, what did she care? Under the bench there was a chest, in which she'd stowed provisions for just such a night. There were cushions, and a lantern, and books. Providing none of her brothers had discovered them and torn them up or hidden them to torment her.

Although…it wouldn't be sensible to light a lantern, would it? Not when she was supposed to be hiding. Bother! That meant she couldn't sit and read.

She sat down on the bench and drew her knees up to her chin, glaring at the house. Why couldn't she have had sisters? Although would they have been any better? If all they'd liked was fashion or horses or something, then they might have been just as puzzled by her love of reading as her brothers They might even, in spite of growing up alongside her brothers, have turned out like most of the girls she'd met during her Season— so determined to bag a husband that they'd overlook a multitude of faults and go to any lengths to attract the notice of any male with a title, especially if he had a reasonable income. It might, actually, have been worse if none of them had seen anything wrong with being treated as though their only value lay in their potential for marrying well.

She sighed and drew the shawl round her shoulders against a chill breeze that sent ripples ruffling the water and raising whitecaps where the current was running swiftly. It would be just her luck for that wind to presage a shower of rain. Already she could see a dark patch among the many stars, like a giant fist stretching out to clutch a handful of diamonds. She wouldn't be able to stay out here for long, not dressed in all her finery, not if she didn't want it all ruined.

But at least for now she could draw some solace from sitting and watching nature at play, and bask in the absence of pestilential males and disapproving, disappointed parents alike. And imagine an invisible zephyr, drifting her fingertips across the water as she hovered over the lake, leaving a trail of ripples behind her. Although, strictly speaking, Zephyr was a male deity, not a female one. So…

Oh, bother, again. As if she'd conjured them up, by just thinking of a male deity, she heard the sound of coarse male laughter drifting across the water from the direction of the far shore. The echoing notes of a distant church clock striking eleven told her that she'd been out here far longer than she'd thought. Long enough for one set of her brothers' friends to have become drunk enough to feel the need to quit the music room and come stumbling outside for some fresh air.

Even worse, moments later she heard the crunch of a boat being shoved across the gravel bank, followed shortly after by the plash of oars in the water. It was just her luck for a bunch of them to take it into their heads to take a moonlit row round the lake. But at least it wasn't servants, deliberately looking for her. And there were plenty of places to take cover so that even if whoever was rowing about on the lake did chance to look in her direction, they wouldn't see her. She knew every shrub, every boulder on this little island. All she needed to do was crouch down and pull the black shawl over her head, and they would never know she was here.

Not even if they… Oh, and wouldn't you know it, they *were* making for the island, not just rowing randomly round the lake. Just as if they were pursuing her.

Were they pursuing her? For one awful moment she thought it might be the case when she began to make out the very distinct voices of Jasper's three friends.

Not that they'd have a chance of catching anyone if they were on the hunt, not considering the racket they were making. They'd reached that raucous stage of inebriation where they felt the need to communicate with each other at the tops of their voices, even though they were all sitting not two feet apart in the same boat.

'Is it me, or is it hot tonight?' That was Hairy Horace.

'It's hot,' said Walter. 'Deuced hot.' From her vantage point, she saw one of them, probably Walter to judge from what he'd just said, tugging off his cravat, whirling it round his head, and flinging it into the thwarts.

'Don't start trying to take your coat off in the boat,' shouted Ben, as Walter appeared to be trying to do exactly that. 'You'll have us all in the water.'

'Wha's wrong,' slurred Walter, 'with that? Let's have a swim. Cool us off.'

'That,' said Ben, 'is a capital notion. Pull for the island, lads, so we can undress and leave our clothes to keep dry on one of the boulders.'

What? Cursing Ben, Marguerite slid from the bench, hitched up her dress and crawled on her hands and knees to find a better hiding place. By the time she heard the boat crunch into the gravel along the shoreline, Marguerite was safely crouched behind a chunk of marble a bit further from the shore. She peered over the top of it just in time to see Ben jump out of the boat, the mooring rope in one hand. His two friends seemed to be too busy passing a bottle back and forth to make any attempt to help.

'Larss one in,' said Walter, raising the bottle aloft, 'should be the first one to have a crack at the icicle.'

Ben promptly let go of the mooring rope, sat down and began tugging off his boots, making it clear how he felt.

She hated him. She really did. He'd got his coat and waistcoat off before the other two had even managed to stash their bottle and start fumbling at their sleeves.

'Hey, hey, don't do that,' said Walter, pointing at the mooring rope, which Ben had dropped in his haste to get undressed, and which had fallen into the water, 'or we'll drift away.'

'Grab an oar,' said Horace.

'Grab one yourself,' replied Walter pugnaciously.

While what looked like a bit of a scuffle broke out in the boat, causing it to drift away, Ben continued doggedly removing his clothes.

She ought to avert her eyes, she supposed. But, it was just…the contrast was so fascinating. Last time she'd seen so much of him he'd been a boy, with a boy's skinny chest and thin shoulders. He'd filled out since then. A lot. Everywhere. His shoulders were broad now, and his arms were all bulgy with muscle. As he drew his shirt off over his head, her fascinated gaze ran from his broad shoulders, noting the way his body tapered down until it reached a frankly very neat little bottom. She clapped her hand to her mouth to stifle a giggle. She ought not to be looking at his bottom. But somehow she couldn't look anywhere else. Especially not when he was lowering his breeches and stepping out of them.

She gasped. She'd seen her brothers, and their

friends, without clothing several times when they'd been boys. They could never keep their clothes on during hot weather if there was a stretch of open water nearby in which to swim. And she'd seen statues, too, of unclothed males, during her Season, because visits to various museums and galleries had formed part of the entertainment during wet weather. But none of them had…well…that much, down there.

She didn't have long to take stock of all the differences between Ben the boy and Ben the man, let alone compare either state of him with marble representations of the naked male form, because all of a sudden he was running, stark naked, down the beach, his pale limbs gleaming in the moonlight. She kept on watching as he dived in, ducking his head beneath the waves, before striking out, parallel to the shore, as though intending to swim all the way round the island. The way he'd done so many times when he'd been a boy.

It wasn't until he'd reached the southern tip of the island, and rounded the point that she turned to see what the other two were up to. Horace was leaning out of the boat, his arm outstretched, his hand reaching for the heap of clothing Ben had left strewn across a marble slab set half in the water.

Walter began giggling as Horace scooped up Ben's clothing and dropped it into the boat.

'That'll teach him to try and get one over on us,' said Horace, taking an oar. 'Come on, pull for the shore.'

'I *am* pulling for the shore,' Walter protested.

Marguerite watched in disbelief as the pair of them began steering the little rowing boat in a zigzag course away from the island. But only for a moment or two. Because wasn't it just typical of a pack of males to forget all about her, and their initial wager involving her, when they would derive far more fun from playing a prank on their friend?

Chapter Four

Ben waded ashore and ran his fingers through his hair to stop water dripping into his face. Then he ran his hand over his face to wipe it as dry as he could.

God, but it was a beautiful night. He hadn't enjoyed a moonlight swim like this for…well, not since he'd last been here, truth be told. There was something about Wattlesham Priory. An atmosphere of…well, he wasn't eloquent enough to put it into words. He just knew that Gem's father had deliberately set about making this place into a kind of haven for boys.

He'd always felt that he was free to be…*himself* here. That he wouldn't be judged for being whatever he was. Gem's father had never questioned his background or given any sign that he wished his son had invited someone else to stay for the holidays. Ben was Gem's friend, and that was all Gem's father seemed to need to know. It had been here, where all the boys had been allowed to do pretty much whatever they'd wanted, that he'd first begun to believe that he was good at some pursuits. And to start to hope that he might be able to make something of himself, in spite of what his own parents had always said.

He felt that air of…acceptance, of…haven, he supposed, particularly strongly tonight. He lifted his head to look up at the stars. Felt the breeze cooling his damp skin. Listened to the hoot of an owl, hunting, the sharp cry of a vixen. And revelled in the peace. No enemies lurking in the undergrowth. No regimental paperwork waiting for him in some billet, somewhere. No butcher's bill to fill out. Just peace. The blessed peace of the countryside far, far away from any battlefield.

Although when he approached the rock upon which he'd left his clothes he noted that even in England a man needed to think twice before letting down his guard. Because while he'd been swimming round the island, Walter and Horace had thought it would be fun to hide his clothes. He shook his head ruefully, even as a smile began to tug at his lips. The years hadn't changed them. In fact, he should have known they were up to something when they'd let him get out of the boat and get a head start on the latest challenge.

So, the only question was, where *had* they hidden his clothes?

'Walter,' he yelled. 'Horace, come out! I know you're hiding somewhere…'

Instead of hearing sniggering coming from behind the broken wall of the temple or the thick shrubbery, he heard a hoot of drunken laughter come floating from somewhere out on the water.

He whirled round and waded back into the lake. He

was just about to yell at them to come back when he
heard a sharp cry from behind him.

'Ben, no, the current!'

He whirled round, to see Lady Daisy pop up from
behind another of the marble boulders strewn across
this part of the shore.

He rather thought he might have let out a sound that
resembled the yelp of a dog who'd just had his paw trod-
den on, as he instinctively lowered his hands as swiftly
as he could to cover as much of himself as he could.

'What the hell,' he said, 'are you doing out here?'
And how much had she seen? Well, she must have seen
him taking off his clothes...all of them...

But, no, no, not Daisy. She was too ladylike to have
watched. Too disinterested, not to say repulsed by all
things masculine. She would have screwed her eyes up
with repugnance the moment he'd flung his jacket aside.

'Hiding, obviously,' she replied tartly.

'Not very well,' he pointed out, since he could see
her, and she'd spoken to him. And, now he came to
think of it, she must have been watching, to have known
he was going back into the water, and to have shouted
the warning.

And all at once he felt twice as naked. If a man could
be more naked than, well, completely naked...

'Excuse me,' she said witheringly, 'but none of
you had any idea I was here until I forgot myself and
shouted a warning.'

'True,' he conceded. 'Though you had no need to do
so.' And he would *not* take her warning shout as a sign
of deep concern, no matter how much panic he'd heard

in her voice. It was more likely a sign of contempt for what she thought was his lack of intelligence. 'I would not have tried to swim back,' he said resentfully, 'not with the way the current is running tonight. I am not a complete idiot.'

'No, but you are foxed.'

'Not as foxed as the others.'

She snorted. 'You have all been drinking steadily since about four this afternoon.'

'That may be true, but for every glass I finished, they must have downed three or four.'

She didn't look convinced. 'You didn't try to stop them from taking a swim, though, did you? In fact, you were the first one into the water.'

'I thought it might help sober them up.'

She snorted again. 'Well, that worked well.'

He looked over his shoulder, to where he could still hear faint echoes of laughter, drawing further and further away.

'I just hope that when they sober up—' which would probably be at some stage tomorrow '—they remember they stranded me out here.'

She sighed. Shook her head. 'I won't leave you stranded, Ben, without any clothes. No matter what I...' She broke off, shaking her head again. 'I can row you back in my boat.'

Of course, she must have a boat to have reached the island. But...

'No. No, I don't think so, my lady. I—'

'Since when have you ever called me *your lady*?' she said crossly. 'It's Daisy to you lot, isn't it?'

'Well, I—'

'I'm not an idiot either, Ben. I know very well what you call me between yourselves. And to my face when you... Oh, never mind.' She folded her arms across her chest. 'The point is you cannot possibly stay out here all night. You will freeze without clothing or shelter.'

'I think you forget that I have been a soldier for the past six years. I have had to spend nights out of doors in far worse conditions than this—'

'Not, I would warrant, without clothing.'

'Well, no, but I've had to sleep on the ground, in the snow...'

'Oh, stop arguing, Ben. I am sure you have had to do all sorts of unpleasant things when you were in the thick of a campaign. But the point is you are not on campaign now. You are staying at your friend's house, where you ought to be able to have a bed with blankets and sheets and a hot breakfast in the morning. And no matter what you have done, I could not possibly sleep myself, knowing you were out here, shivering and naked in the rain all night.'

'That's very good of you, my... Daisy.' And so typical of her. Others might think she was cold, but beneath her outer reserve beat a heart that was good, and kind, and compassionate. 'But, look, you really don't need to row me back across the lake yourself. Couldn't you just go across and then...send a message to my manservant to row over with some dry clothes?'

She glanced up at the sky. 'I could, I suppose, but it would be quicker to just row you across myself. And then you could shelter in the boathouse while I go and fetch your manservant. Because it is going to rain soon. Can't you feel it in the air?'

'I can, yes, but a little rain won't do me any harm. Not English rain. Summer rain.'

She stuck her fists on her hips. 'I see. You would rather do anything than get into a boat with me, wouldn't you? Would it damage your masculine pride so much to allow a mere female to help you out? Yes, it would. Hah! I didn't think it of you, Ben. I thought at least you were...' She pulled herself up to her full height. 'But I see I was wrong. You despise me just as much as—'

'No!' He couldn't let her think that of him. 'Daisy, that isn't true! I don't despise you! I...'

Instinctively he darted forward. The breeze, which felt so balmy on the rest of his body, felt like icy teeth grazing over his thighs as he came out of the water, and made him shiver.

'You would, in fact, rather freeze out here than be forced to sit within one foot of me for the short duration of the boat ride back to the mainland.'

'No, Daisy...' He strode across the gravel to where she was standing, reaching her just as a flicker of lightning brought the entire scene into bright relief. 'You haven't considered... If anyone were to see you, and me, like this in a boat, in the dead of night...'

'Yes. You would risk being compromised into marrying me, wouldn't you? Well, we can't have that, can we? Freeze to death, Ben, and see if I care,' she said, before turning round and marching away, the sequins on her gown glistening in the faint flicker of another, somewhat closer flash of lightning.

He did freeze, just for a moment, as a dozen scenarios flitted through his mind. But out of all of them the worst, the very worst, was having Daisy believe that he was so averse to marrying her that he'd rather freeze to death. When he would give anything…anything to be the kind of man she might…

'Hold up, Daisy,' he said, trotting after her. Which wasn't as easy as one might think when hanging on tightly to one's dignity with both hands. 'It isn't that I…' Lord, how to explain what he felt for her? Even the tithe of it? 'You should be able to have the choice to marry whoever you want. Or not marry, that's all. I wouldn't want to do anything that might rob you of that choice…'

He just about heard her give another of her disbelieving snorts above the thunder rumbling from one of the banks of clouds that were filling the sky with menace.

He hadn't convinced her that he was speaking the truth. But at least he'd told her. Part of it, at any rate.

She glanced at him over her shoulder as she started pushing her boat across the shore and into the water. 'Are you coming with me, then?'

She shot the words at him like a challenge. Just as the first drops of rain started to fall.

'Yes.' Dammit! He couldn't let her think he'd rather stay out in the… A flash of lightning changed what he'd been about to call rain into one of those English thunderstorms that could send hail the size of lead shot pelting down from skies that had been balmy not five minutes before.

'Only…' He eyed the boat, as it slid into the water. 'I…er…may have a little difficulty getting aboard.'

She glanced down to where he was covering himself with both hands. If he let go with one to steady himself, she was going to see something a virtuous young lady should not see until her wedding night. He couldn't help it. Just being naked, in Daisy's company, had got him reacting in a completely inappropriate manner, in spite of the rapidly chilling conditions.

'If you could just…shut your eyes while I…'

She pursed her lips. 'I can do better than that.' She reached for the shawl she had round her shoulders. 'Here,' she said, holding it out to him. And then, when she realised he'd have to let go of himself in order to take the shawl, threw it to him. 'I will shut my eyes while you…er…cover up a bit. I mean, not *any specific* bit, obviously. I meant… Oh, you know what I mean!'

So she *had* looked. A grin tugged at his mouth as she gripped the oars tightly, steadying the boat in place, shut her eyes, and turned her face away for good measure.

He made short work of knotting the shawl round his waist like a kilt. Thankfully it was of thick woollen material, rather than the flimsy kind of thing she would normally wear in the evening, so it made for adequate covering.

She opened just one eye after he'd got into the boat, as if to assure herself he was as decent as he could be in the circumstances. Although it was growing so dark as the thunderclouds blotted out more and more of the sky that before long, he reckoned, it wouldn't matter if he was completely naked.

'Give me the oars now, Daisy,' he said.

'I am perfectly capable of rowing us both back to the boathouse!'

'Yes, I am sure you are,' he said patiently. 'But in case you had forgotten, I am wet, and naked, and once those clouds unleash their burden, I am going to get a whole lot wetter. And rowing will at least keep me warm.'

'Oh,' she said on a huff. And then pushed the shafts of the oars in his direction. He was glad that she'd seen sense when, not one minute later, the whole surface of the lake hissed and boiled as a heavy shower came pelting down.

'The one good thing about this weather,' she said, nonchalantly unfurling the umbrella that she must have stowed in the boat against the prospect of rain, 'is that nobody else will be outside. We should be able to go straight to the boathouse without having to worry about anyone seeing us.'

'Walter and Horace might be in there,' he pointed out. 'Sheltering from the storm.'

'Would they have the sense to notice the thunderstorm approaching and seek shelter? Wouldn't they be more likely to have gone straight back to the house to find more brandy? Because it looked to me as though they'd finished the bottle they'd had in the boat with them.'

Which sounded as though she'd been paying far

more attention to what they'd all been up to than he'd hoped.

'Nevertheless,' he said, keeping to the facts, rather than allowing the conversation to drift into realms of speculation, 'I think we should take some precautionary measures.'

'Very well. When we get near the shore, I will keep a sharp lookout for any signs of anyone lurking about anywhere.' She sat up straighter and began peering past him over his shoulders. Just as the squall ceased, and a shaft of moonlight speared down from the clouds. Which meant that he could clearly see where the rain had made her dress cling, in spite of the umbrella keeping the majority of her dry. There was a patch just above her knee, for example...

'Ben,' she complained as he fumbled the oar, making a loud splash, 'I thought we were trying to approach the shore stealthily.'

'Sorry, sorry,' he mumbled. 'Cold hands...'

'Well, it doesn't matter. Because there is nobody in sight. You can beach the boat anywhere.'

He pulled hard, until he heard the keel crunch into gravel. 'You, ah, you will have to climb over me to get out, unless I...' He glanced over his shoulder. 'No, let me get out first, and I'll steady the craft. Hold onto the oars for a minute, will you?'

She took them and held the craft still while he jumped out. And then she tossed him the mooring rope, so that he could tie the boat to the nearest bollard, several of which were jutting out from the bank on this part of the shoreline. She stood up, and he'd just held out his hand to help her alight when a rustling noise came from the nearest bank of shrubbery, swiftly followed by some extremely unsavoury cursing.

'He hasn't just got no shirt, dammit,' came the voice of Daisy's oldest brother, James. 'His legs are bare, too. And that's my sister holding his hand. Hi, you, what the devil are you about, holding my sister's hand in the state you're in?'

Not only James, but also his two friends came staggering out of the bushes, clearly the worse for wear.

'Never mind me,' said Daisy, as she leaped to the shore. 'What are you all doing, lurking about in the shrubbery?'

Lord Cherry swept her a short, and rather inebriated-looking bow. 'Setting a trap for the Fit and his friends,' he said, holding up a ball of twine. 'Overheard them plotting, d'you see? Couldn't let them get away with—'

'Never mind what *we* were doing,' said James, pushing his friend aside as he stepped forward. 'What were you doing, at midnight, rowing about on the lake with my sister, *with no clothes on*?'

Ben was just about to try and explain when, with a crunching of booted feet, Jasper and Walter and Horace appeared from the direction of the boathouse, Walter and Horace still giggling like schoolgirls.

'What's all the shouting? What the…?' Jasper came to a dead halt, his brows drawing down into a scowl. 'I know I said I wanted you to try and get Daisy to marry one of you, but I never expected you to sink to these depths.'

'No, you don't understand,' said Daisy.

But Jasper didn't appear to have heard her. Or didn't want to listen. Because instead of waiting to hear what had led them to be in the boat, with him dressed only in a rather itchy woollen shawl, Jasper drew back his arm, and punched Ben in the face.

Chapter Five

'No!' Marguerite couldn't help screaming as Ben went down like a felled ox. Jasper had no right to punch Ben. Ben hadn't done anything.

'Stay out of this, Daisy,' said Jasper, standing over Ben, who was struggling to push himself up to a sitting position with one hand, whilst keeping the shawl from revealing too much of himself with the other.

'Just a minute,' said James, stepping closer and pushing his face into Jasper's. 'What did you mean about them trying to get Daisy to marry one of them? And sinking to depths? Did you put him up to this?'

'Just stay out of this, James,' snarled Jasper.

'I will not,' snarled James right back. 'If you have been responsible for getting your idiot friends to tamper with Daisy's virtue…'

'Oh, take a damper,' said Jasper unwisely. Causing James to punch *him* in the face.

Ben, who really did appear to be a master tactician, took advantage of the fact that her two brothers had turned on each other, to try to get to his feet.

Instantly they both forgot their own quarrel and turned on him instead. James hit Ben in the stomach, and when he doubled over, Jasper hit him in the face again. And down he went.

'Stop it, stop it,' she shrieked as Ben rolled to his side with a groan. Normally, whenever her brothers and their friends got into one of their brawls, she beat a hasty retreat. But then they'd never started a fight over her before. And it didn't feel right to just walk off and leave Ben to fight both of them. Even though she was pretty certain he could give a good account of himself. He was, after all, taller than any of her brothers, and a good deal more heavily muscled. And he had used to be something of a scrapper. It was how he'd broken his collar bone all those years ago, after all. He'd been defending his section of the ruins with such determination it had taken five of them to overwhelm him. And even then he claimed they'd only been able to do so because he'd missed his footing and fallen off the turret altogether. He'd defended his position, then, with the ferocity of a tiger. Where was that ferocity now?

'You cowards,' she yelled. 'Let him fight fairly.'

But he wouldn't let go of the shawl he'd knotted round his waist. Which was ridiculous. He hadn't shown any hint of modesty when he'd stripped off at the lake.

But he hadn't known she was watching, then, had he?

Oh… *Ben*. He was trying to spare her blushes, that was what he was doing. Oh, but what a stupid moment to go all chivalrous, in a misguided attempt to protect her from either seeing, or letting others know she'd seen, him naked.

Men! Idiots, the lot of them.

'Keep out of this, Daisy,' said Jasper. Most unfairly, since he'd been the one to set the whole train of events in motion.

And it felt as if something inside her, something that had been stretched tighter and tighter throughout the frustrating weeks of her Season, only to be given another tug when she'd arrived home to find not only her wardrobe full of pigeons but to overhear this particular brother begging his friends, *any* of his friends, to take her off the shelf, on which at the time she had literally been lying, finally snapped.

She ran at her brothers, her umbrella held like a cricket bat, and took a swipe at their big, fat heads. Both ducked, but there was a satisfying crump as the steel struts connected with the top of Jasper's shoulder. And an even more satisfying moment when both took a step back, with almost identical looks of shock on their faces.

'I have had enough of you two,' she yelled, taking another swipe at them. 'Bullies…' swish '…and cowards…' Swish, swish.

Over the years, Marguerite had seen lots of brawls erupt between various factions of the males staying at the Priory. And the one thing she'd always noticed, but had failed to take into consideration this time, was that the moment one set of males started fighting, all the other males on the premises would start gathering, just as if they had a preternatural ability to smell blood in the air.

So she shouldn't have been surprised that just as Ben, who'd risen to his knees and had just been raising one hand as if to beg for a chance to explain, went down for the third time, after both brothers sidestepped her and her umbrella, people came running from all directions. Including, for some inexplicable reason, her mother.

'Daisy,' she panted, for she had been running. 'What are you doing? Where have you been?'

For the first time since she'd returned to the Priory, Marguerite was glad to see her mother. Because, surely, she'd be able to calm things down? Once she explained that it was all just the result of one of those stupid pranks the stupid males were always playing on each other.

But Mother never gave her a chance to say a word in Ben's defence. She'd glanced around swiftly, taking in Ben's abject, almost naked form, and the angry way two of her brothers were standing over him, fists clenched.

'Daisy,' said Mother sternly, 'stop this at once! This is not the sort of behaviour I expect from you.'

'But, Mother,' she began, waving her umbrella at Jasper and James, 'these two are—'

'I don't care what they may be doing. You should not be mixed up in it. Come away. Right this minute.' Just to make sure Marguerite complied, Mother grabbed her by one elbow, whilst snatching the umbrella from her at the same time.

Which was so unfair. Yet so typical. Once again,

the boys were going to get away with behaving as they pleased. She was the only one getting scolded.

As if to set the seal on her sense of injustice, she saw Ben making yet another attempt to get to his feet. This time, as he went down in a sprawl of limbs, the shawl he had tied round his waist came adrift.

'Don't look,' Mother cried, letting go of her elbow to lay her hand over Marguerite's eyes.

Which was a total waste of time.

Marguerite had already seen it.

Ben knocked on Lord Darwen's study door the next morning, and waited until he received permission to enter before opening it, even though he had been escorted here by a footman who'd told him in no uncertain terms that he was expected.

The tall, slender man, whose golden looks and build Daisy had inherited, was not sitting behind his desk but standing by the fireplace, one elegant hand braced against the mantel. He appeared to have been staring into the empty grate because when Ben entered, he lifted his head and gave him a long, cool, considering look.

From long habit of facing superior officers, Ben stood to attention while Daisy's father just looked at him. Ben knew what he would see. Both eyes were blackened, and his already twisted lip was split and crusted with dried blood. His ribs were bruised as well. In short, he looked, and felt, like a ruffian who'd taken part in a tavern brawl. And felt that he fully deserved to be raked over the coals.

Lord Darwen shook his head. 'Y'know, Ben, during the years you used to visit us regularly, as Jasper's schoolfriend, I grew…fond of you.' Ben almost winced. 'I followed your career in the army with great interest, not to say a feeling of pride as you grew to manhood in the theatre of war.'

That gentle note of disappointment was worse, far worse than if he'd shouted at him. Called him names. For this was the only adult male who had ever treated him as though he had as much right to be alive as any other boy. Who'd ever stopped, upon meeting him in a corridor, to speak to him and listen to his inarticulate responses with patience. And even, on occasion, appearing interested.

'Had you proposed to Daisy in form,' Lord Darwen continued, 'and had she accepted your offer, I would have been only too pleased to welcome you officially to the family. Would have been proud to have called you my son-in-law.'

Ben squirmed. Because he'd always wished Lord Darwen could have been his father. And not just because he'd made this house, and the estate, feel like a haven for boys and young men. He was a man any boy could respect, and admire, and, yes, feel a deal of affection for. Because he was just so…welcoming. Understanding. Tolerant. And, yes, he had his eccentricities, but…

'I swear, on my honour,' said Ben, 'that nothing untoward occurred…'

'You call rowing about on the lake, in the dead of night, naked, with my daughter, nothing untoward?'

Ben heard the first note of anger in the man's voice. And saw it flash from the blue eyes that were normally so lazily tolerant but now looked cold as steel.

'I mean, sir, that it was not as bad as it looked. We...'

Lord Darwen waved an impatient hand to silence him. 'No, knowing you as I do, I don't suppose it was,' he sighed. 'A prank, was it, that got out of hand?'

'Yes, sir, that's exactly what it was,' he said on a rush of relief. He hadn't totally forfeited the man's regard. Lord Darwen hadn't automatically assumed the worst, or refused to listen to his side of things. 'And Daisy, I mean Lady Marguerite, was just trying to help. When the thunder started...'

'It makes little difference, Ben,' said Lord Darwen wearily. 'You are still going to have to marry her. Which, I take it, was the object of the exercise.'

'No, sir,' he said firmly. 'There *had* been talk, it is true, but...'

'Yes, Jasper confessed that he put you up to it. And that you were perhaps more determined than most, since you stand in greater need of her fortune.'

'That is *not* how it was! I would willingly marry her if she was penniless! I would never stoop to—'

'Calm down, boy. I did not really believe his accusations, based on what I know of you. And neither does he, I shouldn't think. Or at least he will probably revise his opinion once he has cooled down and had time to reflect.'

That was good to know. Ben would hate to think that Gem, one of his oldest and closest friends, could really think he'd behave in such a dastardly fashion.

'However,' said Lord Darwen heavily, 'it is what others will think if word of last night's escapade gets abroad. And you can be sure it will. These things always do.'

Ben tried not to shift from one foot to the other as Lord Darwen heaved a sigh. 'I have thought about how we should handle it, and,' he said, giving Ben a rather challenging look, 'my solution is that we put it about that you have had a tendre for her for a long time, but were reluctant to declare yourself until she had her first Season, in case she found someone more worthy than you consider yourself to be.'

That statement was so close to the truth, and delivered with such a penetrating stare, that it winded Ben almost as effectively as any of the punches her brothers had landed in his gut the night before. But then he'd probably given himself away just now by declaring he would marry her even if she were penniless.

'My lord,' he put in, 'you know I'm unworthy. Or at least you must have heard rumours...' The gossip had started while his mother was still alive. Once she'd died, it had grown far worse, he suspected.

Lord Darwen held up one slender hand to silence him. '*That*, my boy, is immaterial. Now, as I was saying, when no such suitor appeared, you finally plucked up courage to, er, make your feelings known. She, er, reciprocated, there was moonlight, the romance of rowing her on the lake, your passion overcame you...what have you,' he concluded, waving his hand in one of those elegant flourishes that could denote so many things.

Ben was too stunned to speak. Lord Darwen regarded the shameful circumstances surrounding his birth as *immaterial*? Didn't he think that Daisy deserved a man who wasn't living a lie?

'We shall hold the ceremony in our chapel,' Lord Darwen continued, 'as soon as you have procured the necessary licence. And since I happen to know you are unlikely to have the funds to do so...'

Only then did he walk to the desk, on which lay a purse and a sealed letter, both of which he picked up and tossed to Ben, who managed to catch them even though his fingers didn't feel as if they really belonged to him. Probably because the whole scenario felt unreal, like something he might dream when suffering from a fever. 'I have written a letter to a cousin of mine,' Lord Darwen said casually, 'a bishop, who can expedite the matter for you. It contains my blessing on the union, while glossing over the reasons why I am insisting on a swift and private ceremony, rather than a grand society wedding.'

'Th-thank you, sir,' said Ben, cradling the purse and letter to his bruised, aching chest. And feeling like a worm. As if he was taking advantage of a man, nay, a whole family, who had never been anything but generous to him. 'I don't know how I can ever repay you.'

Lord Darwen gave him a long look. 'By being a good husband to my daughter, of course. We shall hold the ceremony as soon as you return. By that time, I will have made her see the merits of accepting this match.'

What? She was still trying to resist the pressure to marry him?

'Sir, if she is the least bit unwilling, I will not—'

'Don't you be as much of a fool as she is being,' Lord Darwen snapped. 'I thought you, at least, would see sense. I can understand her having some damn fool-ish notions in her head since she spends so much time with it buried in books, rather than living in the real world. I indulged her mother's whims to give her a glit-tering Season, and what did she do with it? Wasted it! She could have had her pick of the Ton's most eligible bachelors but, no, she turned her nose up at the very best of them. So she has nobody to blame but herself if I put my foot down over this little affair.' He leaned back against the desk, folding his hands over his chest. And Ben understood. Lord Darwen was punishing Daisy by making her marry him. *He* was to be her penance for…disappointing her father.

Now he felt lower than a worm.

'You appear to be genuinely fond of her,' said Lord Darwen, 'which is a start.'

Ben felt slightly less dreadful. For *that* statement sounded as though her father was glad he was handing his only daughter over to someone who would love her.

'And from her behaviour last night,' Lord Darwen continued, 'I suspect she is not indifferent to you either.'

The moment she'd stood over him, using her um-brella to keep her brothers at bay, flashed into Ben's mind. Her actions had stunned them all, for she usu-ally flounced off with her nose in the air if ever a brawl broke out in her vicinity. Did her father think…could it really mean…that she cared? About him? The man was usually very astute. But in this particular instance

Ben didn't think her behaviour signified what he'd implied at all.

For she'd been calling her brothers bullies and cowards, so the chances were that it was more about the unfairness of the fight she'd objected to.

'In fact,' Lord Darwen was saying, as Ben argued away the possibility that Daisy's actions might have indicated she cared for him, 'my only regret about her having to marry you, Ben, is that it is probably too late to give you the advice I have given my own sons as soon as they reached the age of beginning to take notice of women. You have been in the army, too, where there is so much more opportunity for young men to succumb to the temptations of the flesh. So you are unlikely to be able to come to her pure of body.'

Ben's cheeks flamed. He was all too aware of Lord Darwen's views on what he termed *loose women*. Gem had related enough of the talk Lord Darwen had given him to have made Ben far more wary of women of easy virtue than many of his fellow officers. Besides not having the funds to purchase the dubious pleasures those women offered. Or at least that was what he told himself when he wasn't able to raise much enthusiasm for the blowsy, smiling women who bore so little resemblance to Daisy that they might have been another species altogether. And recoiled from the few who did, superficially at least, because to have bedded any other blonde, slender girl would have seemed almost profane. As though he would have been defiling her memory.

'I am aware of your views on…er…that sort of behaviour, sir. Gem—' Ben began.

'I dare not hope that it caused you to abstain completely,' said Lord Darwen gloomily. 'Because even though my son may have repeated some of what I told him, you will not have had the benefit of going to the hospital to see one of the wretches in the last stages of syphilis.' He shook his head, with apparent regret, while Ben remembered Gem's account of that visit, and his complaint that most fathers took their sons to a brothel when they reached the age of needing some form of release from the urges that made a boy so restless, not a lunatic asylum.

'The women who sell their bodies for gain are frequently diseased,' Lord Darwen said, with a kind of passion that revealed a loathing bordering on obsession. 'They pass on such diseases to their customers, who then pass on the taint to their poor innocent wives. And any children born to such a couple are never as healthy as they ought to be. It is not what I want for my family,' he concluded sternly.

'I did take note of your warnings, sir,' he admitted. 'And while I am not completely innocent—' because he was only human, after all '—I believe I am healthy.'

'That's something, I suppose.' He frowned. 'As for the rest of the advice I have given my sons, it is too late for you now that you are betrothed to Daisy.' He heaved a sigh. 'I am sorry she does not take after her mother. With her willowy build and obstinate nature, I cannot hope that she will make you a very good wife, let alone provide you with many healthy sons.'

Ben gritted his teeth. And almost clenched his fists as well. Lord Darwen had no need to tell him what advice he'd given his sons about choosing a wife because Gem had told him all about that as well. Lord Darwen had stressed that when Gem started thinking about taking a wife he should beware of women with pretty faces and forward manners. He'd advised him, and no doubt James and Germ as well, to choose a woman who was plain and homely looking, one who would be loyal, with a strong constitution and broad hips so that she could bear him children without going off into a decline immediately after.

A rather smug look crossed Lord Darwen's face. 'Her mother, now, she's so plain that I've never had to worry about other men trying to poach her from my side. And she has borne me five strapping sons, as well as a daughter. And look at her now. Does she lie about on a sofa all day, quacking herself, like so many of those society wives who were once renowned beauties? No. Healthy as a horse! Still,' he continued, almost apologetically, 'Daisy's dowry will be some consolation to you.'

If this were any other man but Daisy's father talking about her as though she was the runt of the litter, and only marriageable because she came with a sizeable dowry, Ben would have no hesitation about knocking his teeth down his throat. But it *was* Daisy's father. And he really believed what he was saying. That Daisy was somehow unlikely to be a good wife, because she was beautiful, and slender, and had a mind of her own.

'I don't care about her money, sir,' Ben reminded him through teeth that he had gritted in lieu of damaging anyone else's.

'Very commendable, given your circumstances, I grant you, but in years to come you will sing a different tune,' Lord Darwen replied cynically.

Ben didn't think so. He didn't think he'd be able to touch a penny of her money, given the way their marriage had come about.

He'd have to see if there was some way he could make it all over to her, so that she could spend it as she wished. Besides, if there was anyone needing consolation it was Daisy. He did, at least, *want* to marry her.

'But there is some advice I can give you,' said Lord Darwen. 'Advice I intend to give all my sons upon the occasion of their marriage. And it is this...'

When Ben emerged from Lord Darwen's study, what felt like several hours later, he found Gem lounging in a chair in the corridor outside, an enigmatic expression on his face.

The scowl faded when Ben took a handkerchief from his pocket and mopped his brow.

'I see the old man gave you a good jobation. Only what you deserve,' he said almost cheerfully.

If only the man *had* given him a jobation. He could have withstood that. Because it *was* what he deserved. But to have been given instead an extremely detailed lecture about how to give a woman pleasure in the marital bed, along with an exhortation to keep the woman in question so occupied, so frequently that she would never have cause, let alone the energy, to stray... And that woman was Daisy! The man's daughter! It had been the most excruciatingly uncomfortable hour he'd ever endured.

'Well, I certainly feel like a worm,' said Ben gloomily.

'You are a worm,' Gem growled. And then surged to his feet and rushed at Ben, who didn't even have time to mount a defence.

Although, as it turned out, he didn't need it. Far from attempting to hit him again, Gem flung his arms round Ben, hugging him and slapping him on the back at the same time.

'Daisy told me what happened,' he said. 'That it wasn't deliberate. Sort of thing that could happen to any chap after dipping a bit too deep.'

How like Daisy, to be so generous. To step in and explain how they'd come to be in such an awkward situation. To prevent Gem from thinking the worst of him. When she had nothing to gain from it.

Gem drew back, grinning. 'Welcome to the family.'

Chapter Six

Marguerite had watched Ben riding down the main drive not long after breakfast, his ramrod straight back set resolutely against Wattlesham Priory and all its inhabitants.

It was rotten of Father to have thrown him out. Even though *she* hated the place when it was swarming with her brothers and all their friends, she knew that Ben had always loved it here. And he'd only just reconnected with Jasper after all his years away abroad with the army. It had been his first visit since…she cast her mind back…that year after the summer of the broken collar bone.

Although, perhaps exile from the Priory was not such a dreadful penance for him, if it meant escaping a whole lifetime leg shackled to *her*.

She sighed and turned from the window as he dwindled into a faint, dark smudge that merged in with the ironwork of the front gate. Ben may well have escaped that dire fate, but she still had Horace and Walter to fend off. Unless, after last night, Jasper had come to his senses and would call them off? She could but hope.

A soft knock at her door interrupted her before she could really start planning any defensive strategies. When she opened it, she saw Vale, one of their junior footmen, standing there.

'His Lordship requests your presence in his study, my lady,' he said. Then gave her a sympathetic look before adding, 'At once.' He shifted his weight from one foot to the other. 'I am to escort you there myself.'

In other words, Father was not going to give her the chance to run off and hide somewhere and avoid the dressing down he clearly meant to give her.

'Very well,' she said. Because it would be Vale who got into trouble if she didn't comply. And, while she wouldn't have willingly answered such a summons, neither did she want to bring down Father's wrath on anyone else today. It was bad enough that Ben had suffered for the episode last night.

Perhaps once Father had vented the worst of his displeasure she might be able to get him to listen to the truth about what had happened last night. That might not only solve the problem of Horace and Walter but it might also result in him forgiving Ben for the part he'd played. For it really didn't seem fair that Ben should pay such a heavy price for the escapade.

Only...when had Father ever listened to anything she had to say?

He would listen to Mother, though. Except...oh, dear, it really was too bad that she was in Mother's black books too.

She gave up all hope of taking that course when she reached the study and found not only Father but also Mother waiting for her. She had absolutely no chance of pleading her case to Mother in the hope she might soften Father's heart, not now. The fact that they were both here meant they'd already discussed the matter and had reached a unanimous decision.

She bowed her head and clasped her hands at her waist, waiting for the onslaught to begin. There was no point in making any excuses. Ben had warned her that they ought not to have got in the boat, and she hadn't listened, and her brothers, and then her father, had punished him for what had been, essentially, her misdemeanour. She deserved whatever punishment her parents decreed.

'Captain Lord Flinders,' said Father, 'has agreed to all my terms. You will marry him when he returns with the special licence.'

Marguerite looked up in shock. Ben had gone to get a special licence? He was coming back? 'M-marry him? B-but…'

'He agreed with me that there is no other way to salvage your reputation.'

Mother fumbled for a handkerchief. 'When I think of the brilliant matches you could have made, if only you hadn't behaved so…with such…coldness…' she said, on a sob.

'Yes,' said Father bitterly, 'it is a great pity, if you had to end up marrying one of your brothers' school friends, that you couldn't have organised it so that I hadn't had to waste so much money on your come-out.'

'Oh, no,' said Mother plaintively. 'It wasn't a waste. For once I had the pleasure of showing off one of the most beautiful women in the room. It was my proudest moment to think I had produced something so lovely,' she said, waving her damp handkerchief in Marguerite's direction, 'when I am so plain and ordinary. And I so enjoyed dressing her up in all that finery, and seeing her look so marvellous in everything I bought her when I never managed to look like anything more than a bag pudding with frills, no matter how expensive the silk.'

That had been the one thing about her Season that Marguerite had enjoyed—bringing her mother so much untrammelled pleasure. And having not only her undivided attention for once but also being her first priority. Oh, she'd always known that Mother loved her. It was just that she never seemed to have much time for her, when one of the boys was always falling off something and breaking a limb or catching some nasty disease. Mother had always *liked* the fact that Marguerite was happy to sit quietly with a book somewhere, and not add to her worries. But it meant that they'd never spent much time together.

'She's a beauty, I grant you,' said Father repressively.

'Yes, I have always been so glad she took after you in looks, rather than me,' said Mother, gazing up at the husband she still adored, after so many years of marriage and bearing him so many children. 'And it doesn't matter, does it, that the boys take after my side of the family?'

Marguerite waited, as she always did, for Father to say something kind about Mother's appearance. Mother was no beauty, it was true, but she had kind eyes, set in that square face, and a loving expression. Instead, he said, as he always did, 'Not at all. Your features, set in a masculine frame, make them all look rugged and strong. Which is a good trait for a man.'

Which made Marguerite want to slap him. And yet Mother smiled at him, with gratitude. Gratitude!

'So,' said Mother, 'you won't berate her any more about her Season, will you?'

'It wasn't just the expense,' he retorted. 'I wouldn't have minded it if it had come to something. But when I consider how much of my time I wasted, going to balls and parties, for which you know I have absolutely no taste. And picnics!' He shut his eyes as though he'd suffered a sharp pain. Which was a bit *de trop*. Everyone knew Father's views on what he considered *women's pastimes*. He never even allowed Mother to stay in London during the Season for much more than a fortnight, and then only if he happened to have some business of his own to transact.

'If you had taken a firmer hand with her,' said Father to Mother, with more than a touch of irritation, 'she might at least have done her duty by the family. And then there would have been no need for any of this!' He waved his arm in a broad sweep, denoting, Marguerite supposed, the present situation.

'But Daisy has always been such a good, quiet girl,' Mother protested. 'I never needed to do more than just drop her a hint...'

'Well that was clearly your mistake. You should have used the birch occasionally.'

Mother gasped. And then something happened that Marguerite had never witnessed before. Mother got a militant look in her eye. 'You never used the birch on the boys,' she pointed out. 'And sometimes—'

'They never did more than indulge in youthful high spirits. I have never needed to do more than give them a stern talking-to if I ever thought they were getting close to crossing the line. *They* listen to *me*. *They* know *their* duty. The only thing I ever expected of *her*,' he said, jabbing a finger in Marguerite's direction, without taking his eyes off Mother, 'was to marry well. And look what she's done instead!'

Marguerite tried not to wince. She was used to hearing Father's opinion of her worth within the family. Which was well below that of his sons. He had never valued her for herself but only for how she might benefit his much-loved sons one day, by *marrying well*. He'd even once explained to her that although he might tell her brothers to beware of falling for a pretty face, he did not hold her looks against her, as long as she put them to good use. It was not her fault that she'd taken after his side of the family, which tended to be tall and slender, with very fair hair and attractive features, after all, was it? '*In the eyes of the world*,' he'd even gone so far as to say just before they'd gone to London, '*you will do me credit.*'

In the eyes of the world? Yes, which implied that he didn't think she was, or could ever be, a credit to the family. Not in any way. And now she'd lived down to all his worst assumptions about her, hadn't she, by not *marrying well*?

'I am sure she couldn't help it,' said Mother. 'Attracting so much attention from so many eligible gentlemen when she is used to living such a quiet life must have been dreadfully confusing.'

Confusing? Revolting, more like. She'd started to feel like a cow who'd been fattened up for market, with all the drunken lords eyeing her up the way she'd seen fat farmers do at auction before making their bids. With Father standing in the place of the auctioneer.

'No wonder she couldn't make up her mind,' Mother was persisting, screwing her handkerchief up into a ball between her agitated fingers.

'She had,' Father snapped, 'a perfectly respectable offer. From a man I wouldn't have been ashamed to call son-in-law...'

'But Ben isn't so bad, dearest,' said Mother, holding out her hands to Father in entreaty. 'He has always been a good boy. We know him well, don't we? Far better than we could have hoped to know Lord Martlesham. Who went to *Harrow*,' she said, lowering her voice as though speaking of some great crime, 'don't forget.'

'Yes, there is that. It is what I told him, myself.'

'So, then...' Mother turned to Marguerite with a hopeful smile. 'You aren't going to be silly any more, are you? About marrying Ben, I mean. I know you said last night that it was all the result of one of their silly pranks, and I believe you, but still...' She spread her hands wide.

'I still don't see why I have to marry him,' Marguerite began.

'How about,' said Father, icily, 'because I have said

so?' He turned on Mother. 'You have spoiled her, that's what you have done. Cosseting and pampering her, instead of teaching her the value of obedience.'

'B-but choosing a husband, dearest, that is such a big decision for a girl. Perhaps it isn't a question of being disobedient, but just—'

'It is rank disobedience!' He strode over to where Mother was sitting and glared down at her. 'You should have taught her to behave the way all the other girls in London seemed to behave. Not once did she make any attempt to flatter or please a man. Instead she turned up her nose at them when she thought nobody was looking. And did you reprimand her? Even once, for her hoity-toity manners?'

Marguerite had always been extremely grateful that Mother hadn't done any such thing. Or at least, although she'd given Marguerite lots of hints about how she could use her charms to fascinate a man, she had never taken her to task for not doing so. On the contrary, once or twice she'd said she was pleased by her modest, refined, ladylike behaviour, because Father would hate to think she might be a flirt.

Marguerite almost groaned. She just couldn't win. She would have earned Father's wrath in London if she had flirted the way other girls did, she was sure of it. But now he was saying that he didn't like her displaying the modesty he kept on saying he prized so much in her own mother.

Nothing she did, or said, was ever good enough.

Mother's shoulders drooped. 'I confess,' she said penitently, 'I was too busy enjoying myself, seeing her attract so many admiring looks. It was like reliving my own disappointing season all over again, only this time being *noticed…*'

Father's mouth pulled into a grim line. 'Disappointing? How can you possibly have found your own season disappointing when *I* sought you out? Made you an offer?'

Marguerite watched, in horror, as Mother's eyes darted all over the room as though searching for an answer that would deflect his anger. But there wasn't one. Poor Mother had tried to defend her, and all that had achieved was to bring Father's wrath down upon her. Which wasn't fair. Marguerite was the one at fault. The one to cause her parents to come to the brink of an argument when they *never* fought with each other. About anything.

It looked as though the only way to stop them, before they really got going, was to create a distraction.

'Mother, Father, please, don't…'

They both turned on her with identical expressions of surprise, almost as though they'd forgotten she was there.

'If…if you really think I ought to marry Ben, then I suppose…' Now it was her turn to twist her hands together at her waist. 'I mean, it isn't as if I met anyone I like better.' And she had liked him rather a lot, at one point in her life. 'And,' she added glumly, 'I'm not likely to, am I?' Her brothers had brought dozens of friends to stay, over the years, and they were all the same.

Males, from her observation, were basically pack animals, who enjoyed nothing better than bounding around the place, wreaking as much havoc as they could. When you got them into a ballroom, they could pretend to be civilised, for an hour or so, but the moment they'd dropped their female relatives at home off they went to some mill, or tavern, or some other revolting, low place where they could revert to type. At least with Ben she knew exactly what she would be getting.

'It just seems a shame,' she continued, 'to push him into it, when I'm sure it isn't what he wants…'

'You see?' Mother beamed up at Father. 'She isn't being rebellious for the sake of it. She is just thinking of poor Ben's feelings.'

Yes, poor Ben, having to take *her* off her family's hands.

Father's expression softened a touch. He no longer looked furious. Just irritated. 'Well, if that is all that it is, then it's all settled. And, look, Daisy,' he said to Marguerite, 'Captain Lord Flinders doesn't mind marrying you at all, not now I've told him how much wealth you will bring to the union.'

He might as well have thrashed her. Nothing could have hurt her more than hearing him tell her how he'd managed to get Ben to comply with his edict to marry her by reminding him how rich that would make him.

Why couldn't Ben have just wanted to marry her, to save her reputation? Not that it needed saving. Not over a stupid incident that nobody outside the family would ever hear about.

This felt as if Father was seizing on the whole episode to force Ben to get Marguerite out of his hair for good. Dangled a big, fat dowry in his face as a sweetener. Because he'd never known what to do with her, had he? She just…wasn't a boy.

And every time he'd warned her brothers to beware of pretty women, she'd felt it like a slap to the face… the face that he so often said was pretty. Even though he said he didn't hold that prettiness against her…

Mother leapt to her feet. 'We will have so much to do in so little time. I had so hoped we could have a big society wedding, but there.' She blew her nose. 'A private ceremony, in our own chapel, will be…well, far more romantic,' she said hopefully. 'Now,' she said, going over to Father's desk, and picking up his pen, 'I need to make a list…'

Romantic? What was romantic about being pushed into marrying a man who didn't want to marry her?

Although… Father was smiling down at Mother, with his usual air of complacency. And Mother was enjoying herself. They were both pleased with her for once. Which was…a strange feeling. And one that she may as well make the most of because it wouldn't last long. She had only two, or perhaps three days before the ceremony. And then…

Her stomach swooped. She would leave Wattlesham Priory with Ben, to go to his estate, about which, she suddenly realised, she knew nothing, and start on a whole new life.

She wasn't ready.

Chapter Seven

Three days later, and she still wasn't ready.

Oh, her trunks had all been packed and loaded onto wagons, and she was wearing a beautiful carriage dress, so that they could set off immediately after the ceremony. The chapel was decked out with the most glorious flowers that the gardeners had gleaned from the hothouses as well as greenery from the furthest corners of the estate. Yes, everything *looked* perfect.

But her heart knew better.

She hadn't seen Ben since her brothers had flattened him into the gravel at the side of the lake, well, except through the window when he'd ridden away the next morning. She'd heard that he'd come back with the licence. She'd also heard the celebrations that had gone on until the early hours of the morning as all her brothers had banded together to toast the groom.

Not that she'd have been able to sleep anyway, not after what Mother had told her would happen on her wedding night. Oh, she'd couched it in glowing terms, saying that it was the most marvellous thing, and would lead to her having babies. But it had not sounded at all marvellous. It had sounded undignified, and uncomfortable, and, well, frankly a bit humiliating.

But she would have to endure it. Because she'd given her word now, that she was going to marry Ben, and if she backed out…

She shuddered. It didn't bear thinking about. Seeing Father wounding Mother with his criticism of the way she'd brought up her daughter had been too awful. She couldn't do anything that might set him off again and cause Mother to…possibly even *cry*. Not when Mother had been the only one to take her part, even if it had been in a rather timid way.

So she lifted her chin when Father arrived to escort her down to the chapel. Accepted his lukewarm compliments on her appearance stoically. And kept her shoulders well back all the way along the corridors, to the entrance that led into the chapel from the house.

She was a bit surprised to see Joshua and Julius waiting for her, one on either side of the chapel door.

'We wanted to be the ones to present you with your wedding bouquet,' said Joshua, holding out a beautiful arrangement of white roses and sweetly scented pinks.

Having thrust it into her hands, they darted into the chapel and clattered up the stairs to the seats in the gallery reserved for the family.

'That was good of them,' Father observed, with a smile. 'Good lads, the pair of them.'

'Yes,' said Marguerite, feeling rather…touched by

their gesture. Perhaps they weren't such monsters after all. Perhaps they did have some decent qualities.

As she entered the chapel on the arm of her father, the guests, all friends of her brothers, turned to look at her, mostly looking rather the worse for wear. She lowered her head, reluctant to meet with the grins and elbow-nudging she was sure they would indulge in. And saw a snail emerge from her bouquet and begin crawling across her gloved hand.

She shook it off, only to disturb a couple of slugs, which had been curled up between the flowers.

She sucked in a short, sharp breath. The little beasts! Oh, not the slugs, they couldn't help it. She meant Julius and Joshua. She should have known they couldn't show her even the tiniest bit of respect, not even on her wedding day! She gripped the bouquet tightly, fighting back the urge to fling it as far from her as she could. It would only make everyone laugh at her. She'd have to do what she always did when any of her pestilential brothers played one of their horrid pranks on her. Pretend she hadn't noticed. Or that she didn't care. And so, grim-faced and quivering with fury, she stalked slowly to the front of the chapel, dripping slugs and snails all the way.

And there stood Ben. The very epitome of a reluctant groom with those bruises standing out in vivid contrast to the paleness of his face. He did not smile when she reached his side but kept facing forward, his back rigid, his expression miserable.

She turned from him to thrust her bouquet into Mother's outstretched hands, to the sound of muffled giggling from her two younger brothers. And from then on kept her gaze fixed on their chaplain, making her responses through gritted teeth whenever it was her turn.

And then Ben was sliding off her snail-slime-streaked glove to place a ring on her finger, and the chaplain was pronouncing them man and wife, and all she could think about was getting her hands on her horrid little brothers and making them pay for ruining what might have been...well, no, it probably wouldn't have been the kind of wedding most girls dreamed of but at least she might have gone through it all with some dignity. Instead of which, Mother was handing her back her bouquet with a perplexed expression on her dear face, and then Marguerite was laying her hand on Ben's arm and walking the length of the chapel to the outside door, where the servants, who hadn't been able to fit inside, were all lining the path to the waiting carriage, with smiling faces, to see her come out.

They all clapped and cheered as she walked, still with one hand clamped to Ben's arm, to the carriage, and, because none of this was their fault and she was going to miss them, she tried to smile back.

Vale, the footman, who was standing by the steps of the carriage Father had lent the pair for their bridal trip, since Ben didn't possess one, was beaming at her, too. But it was the unsmiling Ben who handed her in and, once Marcie had scramble in after her, shut the door. Ben, and his manservant, Sergeant Wilmot, she noted as they mounted up, were going to ride their own horses.

The inside of the carriage was decked out with yet

more flowers, which filled the interior with a lovely scent. Marguerite glowered at them. Had her younger brothers been busy in here, too?

'Do you know,' she said to Marcie, the moment the carriage lurched into motion, 'what my dear little brothers gave me as I went into the chapel?' She held up her bouquet.

Marcie began to smile. The smile froze when yet another slug fell out and plopped onto the floor. She drew her feet back swiftly. 'Oh, my lady,' she said, shaking her head. 'The little…'

'Beasts, yes,' she said, lowering the window and, pausing only to make sure nobody was in her firing line, throwing it as hard and as far as she could. When she sat back, she eyed the flowers festooning every available surface of the interior of the coach. 'I won't feel safe until we've checked every last petal,' she said, 'for creepy crawlies.'

Marcie shuddered.

'In fact,' said Marguerite, coming to a decision based partly on how good it had felt to fling her bouquet away and see it go splashing into a pond, thus returning the slugs to their natural abode, 'it would probably be best if we just chuck the whole lot out of the window to make sure we won't have who knows what falling into our hair all the way to Shropshire.' Which was where, she now knew, Ben's estates lay.

Marcie set to with a will, untying the bunches of flowers from the window straps, the lamp holders and the luggage nets for Marguerite to fling out of the window, until the carriage was blessedly free of floral insults. They didn't encounter any more slugs, but they did get showered with earwigs once or twice, and there was also one rather fat toad nestling in the luggage net beneath a posy of the brightly white marguerites, after which she was named.

By the time they'd cleared the carriage, Marguerite was trembling. She wasn't sure if it was with anger or some other kind of nervous reaction to the final fare-well her brothers had seen fit to give her. All she knew was that she felt like crying. Or screaming. Or kicking something. None of which was at all ladylike.

She had to content herself with drawing a clean handkerchief from her reticule and blowing her nose. It didn't help all that much. She was going to have to think of something…positive about today, and the situation in which she found herself, or she might end up giving way to a fit of the vapours. Or giving way to the almost overwhelming temptation to abandon all her years of schooling in how to behave like a perfect lady.

But she wasn't just Lord Darwen's only daughter now, was she? She was Ben's wife. Which meant now he would expect a certain standard of behaviour from her, too. Oh, how she wished she had something left she could throw out of the window to relieve her feelings. But she didn't. So she was just going to have to follow her own advice and try to find the silver lining. It didn't take her all that long to come up with the comforting notion that at least it would be the last time Joshua and Julius would be able to play any pranks on her. Not until such time as Ben invited her family for a visit.

That was one aspect of getting married she hadn't

considered before. But it stood to reason that Ben was not going to indulge in any such behaviour, didn't it? A man wasn't likely to put slugs in his wife's…bed, for example, not if he wanted to enjoy the activity Mother had warned her he'd expect there, and on a frequent basis, too.

She blew her nose one last time and smiled at Marcie, who'd so staunchly helped her rid the carriage of every last vestige of her brothers' handiwork without a single protest. Apart from the one yelp when a shower of earwigs had caught her by surprise. 'Thank you for coming with me, Marcie, and at such short notice, too. When you only agreed to come to the countryside with me from London to see how it would suit you.'

Marcie gave a huff. 'Well, I liked what I seen of your father's estate, right enough. But it was a bit too…' she screwed up her face '…rigid below stairs, if you know what I mean. Not that anyone tried to put me in my place, like, not with me being your personal maid.' She giggled.

'Me, a lady's maid! You could have knocked me down with a feather when you asked me to help do your hair that time your brothers…' Had been up to their usual mischief, resulting in the total destruction of a style that had taken Briggs, the top-lofty dresser hired at great expense for the Season, to create. And since neither Marguerite nor her mother had been willing to face her displeasure, they'd seized on Marcie and begged her to repair the damage if she could.

'Your skill made it made it easier for me to insist on getting rid of that awful Briggs,' said Marguerite with feeling, 'when she tried to get some poor footman turned from his own post when he couldn't find my cloak.' Briggs may have always made sure that Marguerite was the best-dressed debutante in any ballroom. But she had also intimidated Mother and been unkind. And been furious when Marguerite had returned from the masquerade ball at the Lambournes' without her cloak, when the footman in charge of fetching it hadn't been able to locate it.

Everyone had been relieved when she'd left their employ, even Mother, who'd then been able to start making her own decisions about what to buy Marguerite, and what she should wear on any given occasion without running the risk of having her opinion sneered at.

'Any road,' said Marcie, 'I never thought I'd ever travel outside London. And now not only have I seen Wiltshire but I'm also going to see Shropshire. And all this lovely countryside in between,' she sighed, leaning to look out of the window. The countryside was pretty, Marguerite conceded, after following Marcie's example. And it wasn't as if she'd seen all that much more of England than Marcie. She'd been brought up at Wattlesham Priory, spent a month or so in London, and was now travelling to Ben's estate.

They stopped at several coaching inns to change the horses that were pulling Father's carriage, where Ben and his man spent their time seeing to their own mounts. And they stopped for the night well before it started growing dark. Because, Ben explained, he didn't want to push their riding horses to the point of exhaustion.

Ben came to the coach door as Vale let down the steps. As he had done at every other stop en route, to ask after her welfare and to tell her where they were and how long he planned to stop, before striding off to rejoin his man and help look after his own horses. They clearly meant a lot to him. He wouldn't let ostlers touch them and fed them from supplies he'd brought himself.

'Your father has arranged rooms for us here, overnight,' he said, offering her his arm. And then something flickered across his face as they set off in the direction of the inn door. 'I hope…' He shook his head. 'I should like to set out early in the morning, if…' He frowned. 'We have several days' travel ahead of us. Your father has arranged the overnight stops on the way, but we will still need to keep up a reasonable pace…'

She glanced up at him in some surprise. He sounded so uncertain. Ben never sounded uncertain. Morose, yes. Sarcastic, yes. Pedantic, even, sometimes. But never uncertain. He was an officer in the army, for heaven's sake. Used to bawling orders at men and having them obeyed without question.

Well, that was clearly what getting married did for a man who'd fought his way halfway across Europe. No wonder he spent so much time with the horses at each stop they'd made. It must give him a valid reason to appear to be too busy to speak to his new bride.

She didn't know if it was just that she was tired after the journey or still on edge from the morning's assault by slugs and earwigs, or because she'd just had that startling idea that Ben had been trying to avoid her all day, but, anyway, she found it very hard to speak to him when at last they sat down to dinner.

They were eating that dinner in a private parlour that was part of the suite of rooms they had, attended by inn servants. And every time she looked at his poor battered face, she couldn't help thinking about what he'd expect from her later tonight. He'd want to kiss her with that rather sulky, lopsided mouth. And he'd probably remove most of his clothes, as well as her own. Mother had said so. And once she thought about removing clothes, her mind went straight back to the way he'd looked, naked, in the moonlight.

Every time he lifted his fork to his mouth, she recalled the way the muscles in his upper arms had bunched and flexed as he'd rowed her across the lake. And every so often, when a hank of his thick dark hair flopped across his forehead, she got a strange yearning to tidy it up. As an excuse, she rather thought, to run her fingers through it so she could find out if it was as soft as it looked.

When she finally gave up the pretence of eating anything and rose from the table to go to the bedchamber in which her travelling luggage had been placed, he got to his feet, too. Which made her glance down at his thighs, which she'd also seen tantalising peeks of through the knots in the shawl.

He cleared his throat.

She made herself look at his face.

'I, er, ought to warn you,' he said, 'that is… I hope you aren't expecting too much. We haven't had much opportunity to…er…discuss things, and you ought to know...' He faltered to a halt, looking as uncomfortable as she felt. Which made her feel even more uncomfortable. She'd assumed he would just come to her room and...and *do* it. Not stand about talking about it!

'My mother told me all about it,' she said hastily.

'She did?' He raised his brows. 'Well, then, so you know—'

'Yes, yes, all that I need to, in the circumstances,' she said. And then found herself completely unable to meet his gaze. Because she suddenly was not only very aware of how very masculine he was but also that she was female. And that her particularly female parts felt as if they were pulsing and swelling. And that before very much longer he might be looking at them. Well, he had the right now she was his wife. Especially as she'd already seen every last inch of him. Her face flaming, she dashed from the room and shut the door firmly behind her. And then tottered to the nearest chair.

Why on earth had he wanted to *talk* about it? Had he no consideration for her feelings? Or faith in her character? Surely he hadn't been worried she might... shriek with alarm when he came to her room or put up some sort of opposition?

Although...perhaps some women did that. Which would explain why Mother had been so insistent that she should permit her husband to do exactly as he wished, however strange it may seem, because even though it might seem intrusive, she would enjoy it. Once she got over the initial discomfort.

She tossed her head then beckoned to Marcie to help her prepare for bed. She may not have arrived at her wedding night by a conventional route, but she was a bride now, and would not shirk one iota of her duty to her husband. To that end, she instructed Marcie to help her into the nightgown that Mother had suggested would be perfect for this occasion. It was a scandalously revealing confection of pale blue silk, trimmed with lace. Mother had said she couldn't resist buying it.

'I wanted you to be prepared,' she'd said, 'just in case we had to leave London before you had time to indulge in the purchase of your own trousseau. And just as well I did,' she'd concluded triumphantly, as her own maid had folded the garment into silver paper and put it in Marguerite's set of travelling luggage.

'Leave my hair loose, once you have brushed it,' Marguerite told Marcie, who usually braided it up neatly at night. Mother had said that a man liked to see his bride's hair loose, across the pillow, and warned her that if she bound it up he would only undo it.

Marcie giggled as she began to remove the pins from Marguerite's hair. 'Oh, it does look lovely, my lady,' she sighed, when she'd brushed it out so that it flowed over her almost bare shoulders. 'Like silk, it is. Like sunshine,' she added, sifting a portion through her fingers. 'His Lordship will think he's died and gone to heaven when he sees you,' she predicted, with a wistful sigh.

Marguerite hoped that was true. That he'd find her…attractive enough to do all the things Mother had vaguely hinted at. Because she was beginning to rather look forward to doing them. Ben was…well, he had an amazing body. All muscle and hair. And she'd noted the way his hands had tended to his horses today, with a

deft assurance that had provoked a feeling rather like…
well, no, it wasn't jealousy, precisely. More a sort of
wistful curiosity about what it would feel like to have
those hands tending to *her* body.

She shifted as a burst of masculine laughter drifted
up from one of the rooms downstairs.

Was he down there, fortifying himself with Dutch
courage?

No. Ridiculous to let thoughts like that prey on her
mind. *Nothing* made Ben nervous. He was a soldier.
Father said he'd become renowned in military circles
for his bravery.

So why wasn't he marching in through that door
and…conquering her virgin territory?

She was still wondering that by the time her candle
started guttering. By which time she'd started to mull
over his cryptic utterance after dinner, about her not
expecting too much. Had that been a warning?

But even if that was so, even if he didn't want to…do
what Mother had said husbands wanted to do, couldn't
he at least have come in to bid her goodnight? And perhaps just kiss her cheek? Surely that wasn't too much
to expect, was it? He must know she was nervous…

She glanced at the windows, where Marcie, in her
excitement at preparing a bride for her wedding night,
had forgotten to draw the curtains. She could see nothing but blackness outside. Some wedding night this was
turning out to be! Nobody was stirring now anywhere
else in the inn. She wouldn't be a bit surprised to learn
she was the only person still awake in the entire place.

Sitting up in bed, all decked out for her groom's delec-
tation, while he was…

Her fingers curled into her counterpane like claws.

How typical of a man. To leave her…stewing, in
this welter of unpleasant emotions while he…well, he'd
probably downed a whole bottle of brandy and was now
sleeping it off somewhere.

She should have picked up on the clues. From the
grim expression on his face during the ceremony itself,
to the way he'd chosen to ride his horse, rather than
travelling in the coach with her. The way he'd spent as
little time with her as he possibly could. He hadn't even
tried to see her before the ceremony, and offer her any
kind of reassurance…

And why would he, when he obviously wanted to
marry her as little as she'd, initially, wanted to marry
him?

And yet *she'd* planned to make the best of the match…

Ooh…when she thought of the number of times
she'd remembered what he looked like unclothed, with
a strange kind of…pulsing awareness of her own femi-
ninity… When she thought of how she still reminisced,
with fondness, over the summer of the collar bone, and
had hoped they might rekindle that friendship… When
she thought of how she'd told her parents she wasn't
likely to find another man she preferred…*meaning* it…

She'd even donned this sliver of nothing, and left her
hair flowing loose round her shoulders in the hopes of
pleasing him.

When she would have done better to remember the
things he'd said about her when she'd been lying con-

cealed on the top shelf of the library…how her main
value as a wife was the fact that she was Jasper's sister.
Apart from her money, that was, which she'd already
learned from Father had been the one thing that had,
finally, persuaded him to marry her. The only value she
had, in effect, was her relationship to Jasper, and her
dowry. There was nothing about her as a person that
he found even…palatable!

And now, now she remembered how he'd stayed silent when Horace had said he'd rather take an icicle to
bed. And how she'd assumed that he hadn't agreed with
Horace. Because he'd spoken up in her defence, just a
bit, saying Walter ought to be glad she wouldn't wear
his ears out with a lot of incessant chatter. But perhaps
he *did* feel as if he'd rather take an icicle to bed. He
certainly wasn't here, was he?

Right, well, if the only thing he appreciated about
her as a person was her disinclination to chatter inces-
santly…if he valued a quiet bride, then a quiet bride he
was jolly well going to get.

She huffed, and flung herself down into the pillows,
but she couldn't get to sleep. She was too…too…angry.
Too hurt. Her mind wouldn't stop going over and over
all the stupid assumptions she'd made. And her stomach was actually churning.

It came as a relief when she heard the first stirrings
of grooms in the stables outside, and inn servants bustling about, lighting fires and cranking the handle of
the rather creaky pump in the yard beneath her window.

Grateful that she could at last give relief to all her
pent-up feelings by *doing* something, she flung aside

the bedcovers and yanked on the bell pull to let the servants know she was ready for breakfast. Ready to start letting Ben know how *she* felt about having to marry *him*.

Which she could easily accomplish by not talking to him.

See how much *he* enjoyed getting the cold shoulder!

Chapter Eight

Ben had lingered as long as he could over the indifferent brandy the landlord had insisted was his very best. He could not stay in this sitting room for much longer or someone might come to clear away and catch him there, and think that he was reluctant to bed his beautiful bride. Which might lead them to think there was something wrong with her.

He tossed back the last of the drink, set his glass down on the table, and strode to the door to her room. And paused with his hand in mid-air. He knew exactly what was wrong with her. She'd had to marry *him*, that was what was wrong with her. He let his hand fall to his side. Only a very insensitive man, or a very cruel one, would attempt to enter the room of a bride who'd spent the whole day demonstrating the way she felt about marrying him by flinging every symbol of her nuptials as far from her as she possibly could.

He might have known she hadn't *seen sense*, which was what her father had assured him when he'd returned to Wattlesham Priory with the licence tucked close to his heart. He should have smelled a rat when they'd advised him not to *pester* her before the ceremony because she was too busy with wedding preparations.

It was only too clear, now, that although somehow Daisy's father had compelled her to go through with the wedding, she was very far from happy about having to do so. And why should she be? She was getting a very poor bargain. Even on the surface, he had little to offer any woman. Let alone one as beautiful as Daisy.

But, Daisy being Daisy, she had been gracious and polite, and had smiled for her well-wishers. Because that was what she was always like in public—a pattern card of good manners. Of ladylike behaviour. She never let anyone know what she was thinking, which was why some people said she had ice running through her veins.

He'd seen the heart of her, though. The compassion she'd shown, the very real sympathy for him that summer he'd broken his collar bone, when *his* family had just abandoned him to *her* family's care. The hours she'd spent with him, trying so valiantly to find some common ground, some way she could keep him from being utterly miserable. And even now, years later, she was still so tender-hearted that she hadn't been able to leave him to shiver with a thunderstorm under way, after his so-called friends had stolen his clothes and stranded him on the island.

Though it had cost Daisy her freedom. No wonder she was furious. Not that she had let anyone else see how upset she was. No, Daisy had kept it all bottled up inside until she was out of sight of her family. The way she always did. The number of times he'd watched her stalk away, her nose in the air, after her brothers had played some particularly humiliating trick on her, as if it was all so much water off a duck's back...

He'd guessed she'd stamped her feet, or thrown things, or cried only when in private. Just as it had only been once she'd driven far enough away from her family that they wouldn't see her reaction before she'd vented her true feelings about their wedding. And he didn't blame her. Even though she didn't know the half of it. Lord Darwen had acted as though it didn't matter. But Ben knew different. He was not the kind of man Daisy should have married. And if she ever found out what he really was...

Shoulders slumped, Ben went into the tiny room into which the footman had taken his things. Lord Darwen's footman. He pulled off his jacket, reflecting that even if she'd been...willing, Ben would probably have found it rather awkward to do anything of a romantic nature in a bedroom that had been arranged and paid for by her father, with her father's servants bustling about, and her father's advice about how to pleasure a woman ringing in his ears.

On the whole, it was better to just...wait until she'd calmed down, and they were in their new home.

Oh, yes, Ben, he reflected bitterly as he pulled his shirt over his head and hung it over the back of a chair, that was a *wonderful* idea. Once she'd seen the state of Bramhall Park and realised what her act of impulsive kindness had got her into, he wouldn't be a bit surprised if that was the last straw.

It was all very well her saying that her mother had told her all about what to expect when she got there, but even he had been shocked, when he'd finally gone to claim his inheritance, to see just how much havoc the Fourth Earl had managed to wreak during those last few months of his life. Her mother couldn't possibly know about that, since Ben hadn't told anyone.

He couldn't let her walk into all that without giving her fair warning. She already resented the fact she'd been coerced into taking his name. In the morning, he'd have to explain it all to her. All? No, not all. Just the bit about the dilapidated state of his house. No matter how badly she reacted to that news, it would be far worse for her to find out when they arrived. But as for the rest… He shuddered. Pray God he never had to tell her of his deepest shame. Not for his sake alone, but for hers. She shouldn't have to bear the indignities he'd had to endure all his life.

But Daisy didn't give him the chance to confess to any of it. She took her breakfast in her room, and stalked across the inn yard to the carriage when it was time to set out, without deigning to so much as glance at him, even though he was standing holding open the carriage door for her.

And, no matter what he did, she managed to evade him for the entire day. Her maid and the footman her father had sent to attend her on the journey both aided and abetted her, scurrying about with messages and taking a sort of defensive position between him and

Daisy whenever it looked as though he might get an opportunity to speak to her. To warn her. It was as if she'd flooded her moat with water, lowered the portcullis, and raised the drawbridge to keep him at bay.

His heart sank. Once she saw Bramhall Park there would be no cajoling her out of her mood. But what had he expected? Just as in every other area of his life, his marriage was going to turn into a sham. He had inherited an estate that was teetering on the verge of bankruptcy, a house that was practically derelict, and a title without any of the honour that should go with it. So why wouldn't fate decree that he marry a woman who would ensure that the relationship remained one in name only?

The only place he'd ever felt as if he mattered, as if he belonged, had been in the army. Oh, he'd enjoyed his visits to Wattlesham Priory, and larking about with Daisy's brothers when he'd been a schoolboy. But he'd always been aware that he was just a visitor. That when the holidays came to an end he'd have to go back to his real life. But in his regiment, why, he'd fitted in from the very first day. Because there he'd had...value. Nobody cared who his father was, or what sort of woman his mother had been. Everyone treated him on his merits, on his accomplishments.

He'd been a fool to sell out when he'd inherited the title, just because Boney was all but defeated. What kind of idiot took that, along with him inheriting at the precise moment when Daisy was about to be launched into society, as some kind of divine sign? What kind of fool had he been to hope that, with his lack of experience with women, he'd somehow have been able, during an assembly or a picnic, to tell her…to persuade her…?

A self-deluded, lovelorn fool, he reflected sourly, just as the dark clouds that had been steadily amassing finally blotted out every last ray of sunshine. Which meant that when they drew into the village of Bramley Bythorn, for which he now, as the Fifth Earl of Bramhall, was responsible, she would see it at its gloomiest.

Although perhaps once they'd driven through it, that might work in his favour. Perhaps she might not notice, in the gathering gloom, how overgrown the driveway to the house was, or that the lawns to either side of it had reverted to meadow. Yes, perhaps it was for the best that she was arriving on a gloomy evening. Tomorrow would be soon enough for her to discover what a poor bargain she'd made in marrying him, in regard to the state of his property anyway.

As they'd driven through the last village, Marguerite had wondered what sort of landlord could let so many of the buildings get into such a state. No wonder the few villagers who'd watched them drive by looked surly.

It was only when, almost as soon as they'd left the last dilapidated dwelling behind, they turned through a set of open gates and set off down a drive that was three quarters potholes that it occurred to her that it was Ben. Ben was the landlord who'd allowed his property to fall to rack and ruin.

Marcie, who'd been wriggling about and peering out of the window with increasing frequency, suddenly turned to her, a frown on her brow.

'Are you sure this is the right place, my lady? I mean…'

Marguerite glanced out of her own window. And bit down on her lower lip. 'I think it must be. Vale said John Coachman thought we would arrive this evening. And surely no innkeeper would leave the grounds of his property looking so…untidy if he wanted to attract paying guests, would he?'

'Untidy?' Marcie peered out of her window again. 'That's just like you to say it so politely, my lady. It's a…a rank wilderness, that's what it is. What kind of a man brings a bride to a place that looks like nobody has lived here for fifty years?'

Marguerite pondered for a moment before venturing an answer. 'Well, you know, Ben…er… His Lordship only inherited the title recently. Less than a year ago, in fact. And the village couldn't have fallen into such disrepair in that amount of time. This must be the way it was when he inherited it.' It *must* be.

'You'd have thought he could have got someone to mow the lawns, though, wouldn't you,' said Marcie in disgust.

Well, yes, if he had the money to pay someone to do it. But Walter and Horace had said, hadn't they, in the library, that he was the one who would benefit most from marrying her as he was the one most in need of money. Which she'd thought was just a symptom of greed at the time. But if he couldn't afford to pay gardeners to mow the lawns, let alone repair all those thatched roofs in the village, then he clearly did need money. A lot of money, if he intended to put everything to rights.

She supposed at least she could understand, now, why Father had managed to talk him round so easily. No decent man could allow his tenants to put up with such conditions if, by the mere act of marrying, he could acquire enough money to start making the necessary repairs. And, she grudgingly conceded, even if she was, at present, very angry with Ben, she'd never doubted that he was at heart a decent sort of man. Only what woman could possibly tolerate being simply a means to an end? Not one with any pride, that was certain. Which meant that even though she could understand Ben's motives in jumping at the chance to get his hands on her dowry, she didn't hurt any less.

Why couldn't he have agreed to marry her because he wanted to get his hands on *her*? Instead of demonstrating, on their wedding night, that he most certainly did not. That depressing reflection meant that she was completely unable to muster a smile when the carriage drew to a halt in front of a house that was entirely in darkness and Vale came to open the door and let down the steps. But then, his face, too, was particularly wooden.

Behind him, she could see Ben dismounting stiffly from his horse, and the servant who'd been with him in the army get down and take the reins of both horses. Ben approached her with a grim look on his face. As though he had bad news to break to her. Or wasn't sure what kind of reception he was going to get.

She lifted her chin and squared her shoulders.

'We need to go round to the back of the house to gain entry,' he said, in a tone that she thought sounded rather defiant. 'There are only two servants left, and it isn't fair to expect them to come to the front and answer the door when they will be busy in the kitchen, preparing our meal.'

He turned on his heel and strode off.

Well! He might at least have held out his arm and escorted her to the door he'd spoken of, rather than just walking away and expecting her to trot obediently behind him.

Only she'd rebuffed him every time he'd attempted any such thing during the last two days of their journey here, hadn't she? Or pretended she hadn't seen him. So it probably served her right if she entered her new home, and met her new servants, from two paces behind her new husband, rather than on his arm.

But…only two servants? How on earth did they manage to look after a place this size? As they walked the entire length of the front façade of the Jacobean building, she counted the windows on the second floor. Thirty. Which meant inside there must be probably half as many rooms. And more still on the floor above, and several in the attics. And when they reached the end of the façade and went through a little wooden door into a rear courtyard, she saw that the house had two wings, each of which looked almost as big as the main house.

Two servants wouldn't be able to, she decided. And she mustn't expect them to have done so. She would be gracious, to *them*, she vowed. It wasn't their fault, after all, that their employer hadn't hired anyone else to help out.

Ben finally ducked in through a small, plain wooden door and held it open for her to pass inside.

'Welcome to Bramhall Park,' said Ben, with what sounded like heavy sarcasm.

She stepped into what turned out to be a kitchen, in which two women were standing, nervously twisting their hands in their aprons. One of them was middle-aged and plump. The other was a half-starved-looking slip of a girl.

'This is Mrs Green,' said Ben, indicating the older woman, who bobbed a curtsey, her wide eyes fixed on Marguerite with evident wariness. 'And this is Sally,' he said, as the skinny girl followed suit. 'Ladies, this is my bride. Your new mistress,' he said, giving her a challenging look as he waved for her to step forward.

'It is lovely to meet you,' she said, going over to the older woman and holding out her hand. The woman, slowly realising she was being invited to shake it, finally took it and allowed Marguerite to pump it up and down. 'It is just the two of you, I believe,' said Marguerite, repenting shaking a cook's hand when she'd been in the midst of preparing a meal but determined not to yield to the urge to wipe her now rather sticky hand lest she insult the poor woman.

'My goodness,' she said brightly, 'what a lot of work you must have to do.' She turned to the skinny girl and shook her hand as well. It wasn't as if it was going to get much dirtier, now, was it? 'Sally, is it?' Sally made a startled sound, then looked down at her hand in wonder, as if nobody had ever willingly touched her before.

'You must be wanting your supper,' said the cook.

'We was just about to go and set the table in the dining room, my lord, er, my lady,' she said, her eyes swivelling from one to the other, 'only, well, there ain't no fancy dishes left. Nor eating irons fit for a bride...' She clasped her hands at her waist, her brow creasing in consternation.

'What do you usually do when His Lordship,' said Marguerite, indicating Ben, 'comes to stay? Do you eat in the dining room?' She turned to look at him.

'No,' he said. 'But then I... That is, I have always eaten in the kitchen, with the staff, so I saw no reason to change things when I...' He shifted from one foot to the other.

He had always eaten in the kitchen with the staff? How...peculiar. But there wasn't the time to consider that for long.

'Well, I can see that I will have to see about the lack of china and, er, *eating irons* in due course. But for tonight we may as well all eat together in here. If there are enough dishes and so forth?' She'd already surreptitiously glanced around the kitchen, which did at least look clean and organised, unlike what she suspected lurked in the rest of the house.

'Oh, yes, my lady,' said the cook, bobbing yet another curtsey, just as Vale came in through the kitchen door with the first of her trunks. 'Sally, will you show this chap where to take Her Ladyship's things? If we don't have to try to arrange things in the dining room, I can manage here on my own for a while.'

'You won't have to manage on yer own,' said Marcie. 'I can help out. No, don't argue,' she said, as she began stripping off her gloves and overcoat. 'I'm sure I can do what needs doing to get a dinner on the table.'

'But,' said Ben with a frown, 'you are a lady's maid, not a...cook or a scullery maid.'

Marcie gave one of her scornful snorts. 'Well, you surely don't expect me to swan off upstairs and wait for someone to come and wait on me when it's clear you don't have enough servants to cater for you and my lady, let alone your manservant, and Vale, and the coachman and groom.'

'Goodness, yes,' said Marguerite. 'We had better set out nine places.' The kitchen table was easily big enough to seat three times that number, and she guessed that it was where the staff had taken their meals in the days when there had been a full complement of them.

'Daisy,' said Ben, approaching and speaking to her in an undertone, 'you cannot mean to sit down and eat in the kitchen with the servants.'

'Why not? You do. Apparently.' And why was that? She was on the verge of asking him when she remembered that it wouldn't give the right impression. She was supposed to be giving him the cold shoulder, not indulging in curiosity about his habits. 'And, anyway, what sort of person would I be if I insisted on having my food brought to me in another room, when it will cause so much work for those two poor creatures?'

She was just taking a breath to remind him that her name was Marguerite, not Daisy, and she would thank him to have some consideration for her feelings, when he said, 'Thank you,' with a throbbing sort of intensity. 'You cannot think what this means to me. To...to them.'

It gave her a funny feeling to have him speak to her like that. With that look in his warm brown eyes, as though she was...was doing something that pleased him. As though he thought she was doing it to impress him. As though she cared what he thought of her.

Well, she couldn't have that! So she tossed her head. 'Well, it would be silly to insist on dining in a room that sounds as though there wouldn't even be a fire lit, or any sort of comforts, when it is so lovely and warm and cosy right here, wouldn't it? Besides, it is only for the one time. I am sure I can survive.'

His intense expression turned to one of disappointment. As though he completely believed she was so shallow and selfish as she'd intended that statement to sound. 'Yes. Of course. How stupid of me to think...' He stood up straighter, which had the effect of making him move away from her. Which hurt.

'I shall make the tea, shall I, Mrs Green,' he said, turning to the cook and giving her the benefit of his crooked grin. He then started moving about the kitchen with an ease that spoke of familiarity. Marcie tied an apron round her waist and started stirring something on the stove. While the cook went to a drawer and grabbed a bunch of cutlery.

'Let me set the table,' said Marguerite, crossing to the big, deal table where the cook had dropped the whole lot with a clatter. Apart from wanting to be useful, it would give her something to do other than standing there watching Ben moving about the kitchen as though she couldn't take her eyes off him. 'I am sure

I can do that, which will free you to see to the more… complicated tasks required.'

The cook beamed at her. 'Well, 'tis a pleasure to see that Master Ben has found himself such a…lovely girl to marry. One as who will pitch in and roll up her sleeves, and not turn her nose up at us common folk.'

Ben's shoulders stiffened a bit as though he would have liked to point out that so far he hadn't discovered anything lovely about his bride at all. The cook, meanwhile, was fishing a handkerchief out of her pocket and blowing her nose.

'What with the way things have been the last few years,' she began, breaking off to shake her head at the precise moment Vale appeared in the doorway and let out a rather unfortunate word when he saw Marguerite setting the table.

'You should not be doing that, my lady,' he said, scurrying over, his face red. 'Let me.' He reached for the cutlery.

'Have you finished carrying all the luggage to my room?'

'No, but—'

'Well, then, you would be of much more use if you did that. I can easily wield cutlery but not, I fear, my trunks.'

'But, my lady…'

Marcie chose that moment to shoot him a look of scorn. 'I told you, my lady, didn't I, that things below stairs in your parents' house were rather rigid? A place for everyone and everyone in their place.'

'Well, I daresay it made things run smoothly. But we don't have the luxury of having one particular servant to do only one specific task, do we, Vale? For tonight we are all going to have to pull our weight.'

'Yes, my lady,' he said, and went out of the back door, presumably to fetch the rest of the luggage, his face flaming.

Marguerite couldn't claim that the meal was a great success. Her father's coachman, and groom, and Vale were all extremely uncomfortable sitting at the table with what they kept muttering were *their betters*. Marcie kept shooting Vale scornful looks, which had the effect of making him appear increasingly wretched. The cook and the scullery maid kept apologising for the state of the house, no matter how many times Marguerite assured them she didn't hold them in the least to blame. And as for Ben and the leathery-faced man she was starting to think of as his henchman, they ate in a surly silence, which did nothing to dispel the strained atmosphere.

Ben had never been what you'd call the life and soul of any party, though. She couldn't expect him to suddenly act like a genial host. Particularly not when marrying her, and bringing her here, was something he would have avoided it if it hadn't been for the idiots he called his friends.

Which conclusion made her feel suddenly very weary. Nobody had ever really wanted her. Her parents certainly hadn't rejoiced when they'd produced a girl child. Father had never known quite what to do with her, and Mother had always spent far more time and effort on her boys. So why should a husband…treasure her? She'd had enough for one day. She just wanted to be on her own. The way she so often did.

She cleared her throat. 'If it isn't too much trouble, I should like to go to my room now. It has been a long day.' She gazed round at the detritus of the meal on the table with a sudden feeling of guilt. She'd never before thought of the work that would go into clearing away after a meal. She'd always just got up and left it, knowing there was an army of people whose job it was to do it.

But tonight she could see that it would be down to the people sitting here with her.

'I… I should help with the dishes,' she said aloud, as the notion finally occurred to her.

'Absolutely not,' said Vale, getting to his feet. 'You get off to bed, if that is what you want, my lady. We can clear up down here.'

'Just wait until I've drawn some hot water for your wash,' said Marcie, 'and I'll come up with you. If…if Vale wouldn't mind just showing us where, exactly, we should go.'

'Of course,' he said. And went to the stove to draw water from a little spigot into a jug that he refused to allow Marcie to carry.

It was a relief to leave the kitchen, and her gloomy husband. Although for some reason she couldn't resist turning back to glance at him, just once. He wasn't watching her leave. He was just sitting slumped at the head of the table, staring broodingly into his tankard. As though he'd put her out of his mind already.

Fine. She didn't care. She hadn't wanted to marry him either!

Chapter Nine

But it wasn't as easy for her to put Ben out of her mind as he'd appeared to have done with her, not when the first thing she saw, on entering the room Vale led her to, was his trunk. At least, yes, it must be his trunk. She certainly didn't own one as battered as the one standing under the window. And, anyway, a sword, still attached to its belt and lying across the lid, was a massive clue.

She suspected that if she were to move the sword and lift the lid she'd see all his personal things. His shaving equipment, and clean shirts, and...his uniform. The one he'd worn at the ball the night he'd danced with her.

She swallowed, her hand going to her throat where a lump of...something like regret was making her feel...

'It's not very clean, is it?' Marcie's scathing tones, coming from just behind her, drew Marguerite's attention from Ben's trunk, and the memory of how magnificent he'd looked in uniform. She looked around the room properly for the first time and saw that it was indeed distinctly grubby. The curtains were dusty, the windows grimy, and spider webs festooned every corner and hung thickly from any bit of ornamentation on furniture or fireplace.

'That girl, Sally,' said Vale, apologetically, 'told me this was the best room in the house.'

'From what I've seen so far,' said Marguerite, 'I wouldn't be a bit surprised.' She approached the bed, warily. 'Though it looks as if someone has made an attempt to make the bed, at least, usable.' The bed hangings were not as dusty as the window curtains, as if someone had given them a bit of a shake, and the coverlet was definitely clean. She turned it back and leaned in close. The pillows smelled freshly laundered, as did the sheets.

And as she straightened up, it struck her that though the whole house showed signs of neglect, at least she wasn't going to find frogs, or earwigs, or slugs anywhere that they wouldn't occur naturally. Nobody here was likely to deliberately try to scare her. There were probably no ills here that couldn't be cured by the efforts of an efficient housewife.

'Tomorrow, we're going to have to roll up our sleeves and get cleaning,' she said. 'No, actually, I think I ought to go around the whole house and make a list of what jobs need doing first, just in case it is more than just a case of housework that is required. Thank you, Vale, that will be all,' she said, noticing the footman still standing by the washstand, looking as though he was struggling with some immense internal debate.

Whatever he'd been thinking, he managed to keep it to himself. He resumed the appearance of a well-trained footman and gave her a deferential nod before leaving the room.

Marcie was already pulling a fresh nightgown from Marguerite's own trunk. One of the handful of scandalously brief slivers of silk Mother had somehow purchased without anyone knowing while they'd been in London.

'No, not that one,' she said. Even though Ben had made his intentions clear by leaving his trunk in her room, she was not, not, *not* going to get all worked up like she'd done on their wedding night. Nor was she going to leave her hair loose or put on a nightgown expressly designed to please and excite a man.

And she was not going to lie awake all night, wondering why he wasn't interested in anything about her apart from her money. If he came up here…no, *when* he came up here…she'd…she'd…

'The muslin with the square neck,' she said to Marcie, who was looking more bewildered the longer her mistress stayed silent, clenching and unclenching her fists.

As the girl laid the simple and modest nightgown across the foot of the bed, she muttered, 'Not fitting to expect a fine lady like you to put up with such conditions. No wonder you want to let him know you aren't very pleased with him. I'd give him what for if I wasn't so aware that it ain't my place.'

Marguerite said nothing. What Marcie was thinking wasn't strictly true, but she had no intention of admitting that it wasn't the state of the house that had offended her but Ben's reluctance to visit her room and behave like a bridegroom at any of the stops they'd made en route. She didn't want anyone knowing that three days into her marriage she was still a virgin.

'Thank goodness I come with you, my lady,' said Marcie as Marguerite was climbing into bed. 'You are going to need me, like nobody has ever needed me before.'

That simple, yet heartfelt declaration struck a chord. For Marguerite had always wished somebody might need her. Or at least that they might find her presence in their life of importance. But more than that, it was good to learn that somehow she'd inspired Marcie to feel such devotion that she wanted to stay and help her, rather than saying that the conditions weren't what she was used to and she'd be seeking employment elsewhere. For the first time in her life Marguerite realised she had a…well, an ally.

She watched Marcie leaving the room, a bundle of laundry clutched to her chest, and almost smiled. But then the odour of dust and neglect made her wrinkle her nose instead. She wished she'd thought of asking Marcie to open a window before she left. Then, since she felt too tired to get out of bed and see to it herself, she pulled the coverlet up to her chin so she could at least breathe in the smell of laundered sheets.

She scowled up at the canopy overhead, wondering what she should do when he came to her room. She could probably express her feelings very succinctly by throwing something at him. Unfortunately, there was little to hand that she *could* throw, not without regretting it instantly. There simply wasn't enough china to spare to go throwing it about and smashing it recklessly.

Although there was bound to be a local market, where she could pick up some simple wares to tide them over until she could send to a decent supplier for proper china and crystal so she wouldn't have to eat off chipped plates and drink from pewter tankards. Mrs Green would know where to buy such stuff. She'd also be able to tell her where to get hold of more linen, and if there was someone they could employ, right away, to do the household laundry. From the feel of Sally's hands, she'd been doing it, as well as other menial chores around the kitchen. Which was too much to expect the poor girl to do, now that there were more than a handful of people living here.

She wished she had a pen and some paper to hand. Or that it wasn't too dark to see to write. There was so much that needed doing, and she didn't want to forget anything. Although, rather than feeling daunted by the prospect of all the hard work she could foresee taking up her immediate future, she was beginning to feel a strange kind of…excitement.

Because, for the first time in her life, she would actually have a purpose. A reason to get up in the morning. She wasn't going to have to rack her brains to find some way to fritter away the gaps between meals. She was going to be busy, and useful. This house *needed* her to put all the deficiencies to rights.

And, thanks to her mother's insistence that her most important function in life would, one day, be the oversight of an establishment such as this one, and had made sure she'd had formal lessons in household management, as well as sharing hints and tips, she was fairly confident that she was up to the challenge.

Her heart gave a funny little lurch. She'd come to bed angry with Ben, and resentful that he saw her as a means to an end, but to be honest she was… Well, she was itching to get started. Not that she had any intention of telling *him* that. No, he didn't deserve to know that she was looking forward to exploring the house, and making lists of what needed doing, and seeing his wreck of a home brought back to its former glory… Because he should have warned her what she was going to face here. So she could have brought a little band of workers from her mother's house, to give the place a thorough cleansing before she took up residence.

Although, on second thoughts, she wouldn't have derived half as much satisfaction if she had been able to do that, would she? In fact, by organising the work herself, it would be like putting her own stamp on the place. She could do it exactly the way she wished. She would be in charge. Her! Who had never been trusted with anything of a practical nature. Father had always looked down his nose at her, saying she was too pretty to ever amount to anything more than an ornament on some man's arm. But she would not be a mere ornament in this setting. She would be *useful*.

With a little smile playing about her lips, Marguerite pulled the sheets right up over her head and went to sleep.

Downstairs, in the study, which was the one room in the house the Fourth Earl seemed to have used frequently, and was therefore relatively habitable, Ben pulled his army greatcoat round himself and huddled up in the least draughty corner of the room. He'd been too proud to go with the other men to the stables, where Wilmot had made a bivouac for Vale, and the coachman, and groom, out of straw and all the blankets he'd been able to find. Because to sleep outside, in the stables, would be to admit to everyone that he still wasn't welcome in his wife's bed.

He could put his theory to the test, he supposed...

No, what was the point? He knew how she felt about marrying him. She'd made it plain over the last couple of days, by refusing to speak to him. And tonight, by being pleasant to everyone else at the table whilst contriving to act as though he wasn't even there.

Where had she gone, that girl whose eyes had roved over his naked body with frank curiosity and what had looked like admiration when he'd waded out of the lake? What had happened to the tender heart that wouldn't let him sleep out of doors when rain was on the way?

It had all vanished during that fight when they'd reached shore. When she'd watched her brothers beat him to the ground, over and over again. Or perhaps it had been later, when her father had insisted she marry him.

He pulled his greatcoat up to his ears. If he could sleep on his study floor, he could easily have slept on the ground at the back of the folly, where he knew there were mounds of soft grass. He could have *insisted* she go back to the mainland and send a servant back for him but, no...he'd succumbed to the chance to spend time alone with her. To carry on showing off his physique by rowing her to shore, because his damned pride had been puffed up by the way her eyes had roved over his naked torso. He'd wanted her to carry on looking at his muscles and admiring them.

So all this…disdain that she was sending his way was entirely his own fault. No more than he deserved.

He tugged his boots, which he was using as a make-shift pillow, into a slightly less uncomfortable position under his ears. If only he had more experience with women. It was all very well her father saying that it was better to come to marriage with a clean slate, but if he had taken up even a few of the opportunities that had come his way over the years, he might have some idea how to begin…well, wooing his wife. Breaking through to her.

Because of his years soldiering he kept on thinking in terms of laying siege to a citadel, especially after he'd pictured her raising her drawbridge. But he couldn't just throw up earthworks and place guns on the heights to batter down her defences, could he? Not even in a met-aphorical sense. When an army attempted to conquer a castle, or a city, nobody cared all that much about the casualties. At least, it never stopped them from doing what was necessary.

But he didn't want to do anything that would hurt Daisy. And barging in and battering down her defences by brute force would most certainly hurt her.

The other alternative, of crawling to her and begging for her attention was equally repellent to him. He didn't have the stomach for that sort of grovelling. *Only mon-*

grels grovelled. He shivered at the echo of the voice he'd heard speak those very words, in this very room. And his gaze snagged for a moment or two on the riding crop lying on a side table, before swivelling to the shotgun propped against the wall by the double doors that led out to the rear terrace. The shotgun that had belonged to the Fourth Earl and now, he supposed, belonged to him. In spite of everything.

He rolled onto his side and stared resolutely at the wall. He knew, only too well, that if someone didn't like you, they just didn't like you, and it made no difference what you did. After the age of about eight or so he'd stopped bothering trying to get either of his parents to approve of him, let alone show any affection for him. And as for people outside the family circle, well, if they didn't accept him as he was, he walked away from them.

Just walked away…

Chapter Ten

Marguerite slept soundly for the first time since she'd learned she had to marry Ben, and bounced out of bed the next morning, eager to get started on the transformation of Bramhall Park.

They all ate in the kitchen again, just as they'd done the night before, with about the same amount of awkwardness. She did her best to put the servants at ease, but with Ben and his henchman glowering at everyone, it was an uphill struggle. After a while she began to wish she was sitting next to him, rather than at the far end of the table, so she could have kicked him. Although, looking back on the times he'd stayed at Wattlesham Priory, he'd never been particularly talkative first thing in the morning. Or at any other time of day.

'Will you have time,' she said to Mrs Green, 'to show me around the house today?'

'Well, once the breakfast things are done...' she said, with a frown. 'I suppose I could take an hour before starting on the midday meal...'

'You won't get through the half of it in that time,' said Ben. 'I don't mind doing it.'

He *didn't mind*. Not, he *would be delighted* to spend time with her on their own. No, and if she took him up on his grudging offer, she'd have to put up with him glowering at her, just like he was doing now, the whole time. Well, she *wasn't* going to put up with that. Besides, she still wasn't speaking to him, was she? He hadn't come to her room *again* last night. And she hadn't expected him to, just because his trunk had been there. Not that she'd been disappointed. She *hadn't*. But if she had, *if* she was feeling…insulted and disappointed this morning, it would be rather difficult to convey that frame of mind to him when, if he were the one to show her around the house, she'd have to be continually asking him questions.

'Mrs Green,' she said, ignoring Ben's suggestion, 'I would prefer it if you could spare me the time, since you will have much more idea of what wants doing than His Lordship.' Or the place would not be in the state it was in.

Everyone around the table must have heard the rebuke she left unspoken, since all of a sudden everyone except Ben was staring very hard at their plates. Ben leaned back in his chair, his mouth pulling up into one of those cynical smiles he was so good at, as if to say, *So that's the way it is, is it? How childish of you.* Which made her itch to throw what was left of her toast at him. She satisfied herself by lifting it to her mouth and devouring it in one bite instead.

'If Mrs Green can spare the time to show you over

the place, it will leave me free to see to some pressing business I have,' said Ben as though her refusal to accept his invitation was of supreme indifference to him. 'Go and saddle up the horses, Sergeant Wilmot,' he said curtly to his henchman.

And as for having pressing business...hah! He was just going to go out for a ride. Probably to the nearest hostelry.

Well, she didn't care. Let him go galloping off all over the place. It would have the benefit of getting him out from under her feet. But, goodness, wasn't she glad she'd eaten that last bit of toast. Or she might well have yielded to the temptation to throw it at the back of his head as he got up and strolled away.

Once they'd cleared the table, Mrs Green led Marguerite and Marcie up several dusty staircases, so they could begin the tour of the house up in the attics. Marguerite was pleased to discover minimal damage in any of the little rooms that had once probably housed servants, most of which looked as though it was due to birds getting down the chimneys and not being able to get out.

'Do any of the roofs leak?' If they did, surely the attics would be in a far worse state.

'No, the roof is sound.'

Well, that was something. 'So the work that needs doing will be mostly in the form of cleaning,' said Marguerite, 'and redecorating, then.'

Mrs Green gave her a strange look. 'I had better show you the family rooms before you make any decisions about that,' she said cryptically, before leading her down one of the flights of stairs they'd just climbed up.

Every room into which Marguerite ventured on that floor looked as if burglars had ransacked the place. There were bare patches on walls where paintings had once hung, bare boards where there ought to have been carpets, and what furniture was left was of the meaner sort. Ben's family must have been selling off everything that had any value for years, by the looks of it.

'Now, this,' said Mrs Green, pausing outside the only door they'd come to so far, which was locked, 'was Her Ladyship's room. Where, by rights, you ought to be sleeping, but...well, when you see it you will understand why we didn't make any attempt to...' She petered out, fumbling at her belt for the set of keys that, so far, she hadn't had to use.

When she finally got the door open, Marguerite gasped. Far from being devoid of furniture, like all the other rooms she'd been in, this one was cluttered with all kinds of stuff. But all of it was slashed, or smashed, or tossed to the floor.

'Lor lumme,' cried Marcie, who'd kept a respectful silence so far. 'It looks as if a madman ran amok with an axe in here!'

Marguerite couldn't have described it better herself. The bed curtains hung in tatters from their moorings, at least the ones that hadn't been wrenched down and left lying on the floor. The coverlet was slashed, the pillows ripped open so that the feathers had drifted all over the place. All the bottles that had once stood on the dressing table had been toppled over, some of them now lying splintered across the floor. The mirror was smashed, and clothes had been wrenched from the armoire, the door of which still stood open. And someone had ripped off sleeves and collars and so forth from many of the gowns before strewing them all over the room.

'His late Lordship did all that,' said Mrs Green, 'after Her Ladyship died. Then locked the door and forbade any of us to go in.'

'My…my word,' said Marguerite, who was standing stock still in the doorway. It was the only room she'd seen so far that she didn't want to enter and have a good look around. It was too…terrible. So much emotion had been vented in here that to walk into it would have felt like an intrusion on someone's grief. 'He must have loved her very much.'

'Loved her?' Mrs Green looked at her with raised brows. 'Not by the end he didn't. And once she'd gone, he spent the rest of his life…' She pulled in a sharp breath. 'Well, it's not my place to say.'

No, it was for Ben to tell her. Only that would mean going to him and asking him to open up to her. Which he wasn't likely to do. He'd always been a closed off sort of person, and…besides, she still wasn't speaking to him, was she? And she wasn't going to relax her attitude until he'd shown some signs that he thought of her as more than a means to an end. So far, they'd found nowhere in the house that had a bed, apart from the room she'd slept in, which meant that he must have gone out to the stables last night with the male staff, rather than force himself to act like a real husband. Which meant that they all *knew* that he hadn't made any attempt to bed her yet. And of course they were all too concerned about keeping their jobs to openly mock her for being still a virgin with a very uninterested husband, but she would know that they knew, and that they probably discussed her when she wasn't there to hear it.

And if he didn't want her that way, then she was blowed if she was going to go…crawling round him, asking him questions about his family, and what had happened in this house, as though she was fascinated by him. Even if she *was* burning with curiosity. She had too much pride. She wasn't going to let anyone suspect she cared one jot about his reluctance, she vowed as they went down another flight of stairs to another floor, which Mrs Green said contained the public rooms, and which was in pretty much the same condition as the rest of the house. She'd thought that nothing else could shock her after the mess they'd found in what should have been her bedroom. That was until Mrs Green opened the door to what she called the library.

Marguerite froze at the sight of all the bare shelves. Then gasped in horror when she caught sight of a pile of books, many with the spines ripped off, in a heap by the fireplace.

A cold sensation gripped her stomach. He couldn't have…

'Did Ben's father…burn books in that fireplace?'

Mrs Green nodded. 'As many as he could. He spent many a winter evening in here, drinking his way through what was left of the cellar, ripping up the books and warming his hands by the flames.'

How could anyone commit such an atrocity? 'He…

he must have been mad!' No wonder Ben had always been a bit glum, even as a boy. Only imagine having such a father as this. One who went around smashing things and burning books. No wonder he never talked about his home and his family. Who would want to talk about this sort of thing? And no wonder he'd spent so much time at Wattlesham Priory. It must have seemed like heaven to stay with a family who behaved fairly rationally.

'Well, I don't know about that,' said Mrs Green. 'There's no getting round the fact that he behaved a bit odd in his last years. But he knew what he was doing all right,' she finished darkly. 'But if you can spare me now, I should like to get back to my kitchen. I can show you round the servants' hall and the downstairs rooms another time. Dinner won't make itself.'

'Yes, yes, of course, you get on,' said Marguerite, still shaken by the desecration of what looked as if it might have once been a very fine library.

'Lor lumme. No wonder His Lordship is a bit Friday-faced,' said Marcie, echoing her own thoughts precisely. 'Being brought up with a lunatic for a father couldn't have been exactly a lark.'

No. And the signs of violence, of malice even in the utter destruction of his wife's room, as well as a per-fectly innocent library, made her wonder if he'd ever suffered at the man's hands. She recalled the way his parents had ignored the letter Mother had sent, inform-ing them when he'd broken his collar bone. The way he'd said he ate his meals in the kitchen...

Oh, Ben. No wonder he hadn't made much effort to

put his estates to rights. No wonder he'd stayed in London, living the carefree life of a bachelor…since he'd left his regiment, anyway. If she'd had all this…she looked around the library with a shudder of revulsion… at home, she would have stayed in London, drinking and going to balls, and all the rest of it as well.

It made her want to go to him, and…and comfort him.

But what would happen if she did? She'd learned her lesson after the summer of the broken collar bone. He might tolerate her efforts, while he had no other company, but the moment he was up and on his feet again he'd taken great pains to stay well away from her. He wouldn't want her to show him any sympathy. Any more than she would want someone to commiserate with her over her continued virginal state. It was too intrusive to anyone with an ounce of pride. And Ben, she suddenly perceived, had far more than an ounce. He fairly bristled with it sometimes.

Well, that made two of them. And she had no intention of letting him rebuff any overtures of sympathy she might make. It was up to him to make the first move.

Given Vale's attitude the night before, Ben would have thought he'd take to his heels at the first opportunity. So he was very surprised, after the coach Lord Darwen had lent them to make their trip here departed, to discover the footman with his shirt sleeves rolled up, a bucket of water at his feet, energetically cleaning the kitchen windows.

'Not leaving us, then, Vale?'

The footman turned. 'Not while Her Ladyship needs me,' he said, wringing water from the rag dripping in his hands.

'You think she needs you?'

'A lady like her needs a manservant to protect her at all times,' he said a bit mulishly. 'Besides there not being anyone to do the heavy work about the place.'

At his side, Ben felt Sergeant Wilmot bristle.

'Indoor work, I mean,' said the footman with a disarming grin. 'But just until she's decided what she wants doing, I thought I might as well make a start on the windows.'

Ben nodded. 'I am sure she'll be pleased you chose to stay.'

'Her maid, too, I shouldn't wonder,' said Wilmot, making the footman's face turn an interesting shade of pink. Ah. Ben had noticed that Vale and Marcie seemed to alternate between looking at each other more than was entirely necessary and trying to avoid each other. When they did have to converse, they did so in extremely formal tones and with very flushed faces.

He hoped the footman had more success with his courtship of the maid than he was having with her mistress. He probably would. Vale was tall, and good looking, and had that disarming grin. And smooth manners. He probably had women sighing after him wherever he went. He… No, it wasn't fair to resent the footman for his success with women. It wasn't visions of his ultimate success with Marcie that was making him jealous, anyway. It was the fact that he was certain that Daisy would be pleased to have the footman around. When she'd made it so clear that she didn't want her own husband anywhere near her.

He trudged through the rest of his duties that day. Though his mood grew increasingly black over the next few. The Fourth Earl had created even more of a mess than Ben had suspected. The damage extended not only to the village of Bramley Bythorn but out to the surrounding areas. He'd come here thinking that with Daisy's dowry, and a lot of hard work, he might be able to restore prosperity to the area. But the more locals he spoke to, the more certain he became that it was going to take something in the nature of a miracle.

It took him three days spent discovering the extent of the damage the last Lord Bramhall had wrought before he gave up hope. He woke up on the hard floor of his study with a crick in his neck and the cold certainty that today was not going to be any better. Because he just didn't belong here. He never had. And he never would. The locals looked on him with distrust, not to say suspicion when he tried to talk to them. The servants here all looked to Daisy for their orders. She charmed them. Well, she charmed everyone.

He was starting to envy Vale and Wilmot their bivouac in the hayloft. While they spent their evenings drinking the ale that Sergeant Wilmot sourced from the one local hostelry remaining, he lay alone in here on a cold, hard floor.

He didn't belong with the staff. He wasn't welcome in his wife's bed. His wife, who was all sweetness and light with everyone else but who could barely bring herself to speak to him.

He got up and rolled up his improvised bedding, the way he'd done so many times on campaign, before hiding it in the trunk he'd removed from his wife's room before she'd had the chance to order him to do so. He might just as well be on campaign, he reflected as he slammed the lid shut, considering the discomfort he was enduring. In fact, if he were on campaign, he would at least have a defined place in his regiment. He'd have duties that nobody else could do. And he'd have companionship. The companionship of his brother officers. And the respect of his men.

The depressing thought made him wish, not for the first time, that he hadn't sold out. Especially since Boney had escaped from Elba and gone on the offensive again. But who could have foreseen that he'd have gained so much support as he advanced through France? And without having to fire a single shot? Or that Europe would be teetering once more on the brink of all-out war?

He glanced around the study with loathing. He'd never been happy in this place. And he'd been a fool to think it might be different now that the Fourth Earl, and his older brothers were dead. None of them had wanted him to inherit. They'd even taken steps to ensure he wouldn't. Which meant he had no training whatsoever that might have prepared him to manage estates that had come to him in such a poor state.

He could almost feel the disdain the three of them had always shown him oozing from the walls. Urging him to go back to where he belonged. With the rest of the men Wellington had recently referred to as the scum of the earth.

He bowed his head and took a deep breath. One of the things that every soldier learned was that sometimes the only sensible thing to do was to retreat in good order.

And that time, he decided, had come.

After breakfast, he was going to get hold of Daisy and make her listen to him, whether she wanted to or not.

Just once.

Before he left.

Chapter Eleven

Ben was looking particularly morose this morning, Marguerite noticed when he slouched into the kitchen for breakfast. He really must hate being married to her.

Well, she was not going to let anyone know that she cared. In fact, she made more effort than ever to appear to be perfectly happy and looking forward to another day spent exploring the rooms, and the stores, and making lists of what needed doing and where she could start.

As soon as she finished breakfast, she rose to her feet and made for the door, Marcie at her side.

'One moment, my lady,' said Ben darkly, getting to his feet as well. 'I need to speak with you.'

'Oh, can it not wait? I was planning to start work on the dining room this morning.' She'd put on an old dress that she didn't mind ruining, and she was going to tie a scarf over her hair, the way she'd seen housemaids do when tackling particularly dirty jobs. It was going to be rather fun. 'I have found enough pieces to furnish it again, and with a bit of cleaning...'

'No, it cannot wait,' he said, stalking over to her and taking her by the arm. 'Let us take a walk outside,' he went on, gesturing to the kitchen door.

How dared he grab her like that, in front of...everyone? And how dared he make her...walk so close to him, so that she could feel the heat coming off his body? A body that called to hers in a way that was so unladylike. So inappropriate. So...*humiliating*, since he was so completely immune to her?

'Really,' she said, shaking him off the moment they were outside, and far enough from the kitchen window that nobody could see. 'Must you manhandle me in this...brutish fashion?'

'Just this once, yes,' he growled, opening the door to the walled garden, where the cook and little Sally had managed to keep an astonishing amount of vegetables growing, between them. 'And then you will never have to suffer my odious presence again.'

What? A cold hand seemed to clutch at her insides. It sounded as if he was leaving her. No, that couldn't be true! It would be too humiliating to be left behind like some...well, not even like a worn-out shoe, since he hadn't even bothered trying her on for size, as it were.

'What do you mean?'

'I mean that I am going to put this farce behind me.'

Farce? He thought marriage to her was a farce? How dared he?

'I mean,' he continued, 'that I am going to write to my commanding officer, asking to return to my regiment. Since you clearly dislike being my wife so much that you cannot even bring yourself to speak to me, I have decided that it would be best for both of us if I remove my odious presence from Bramhall Park and go back to doing what I do best. You will, I am sure, enjoy your position as Countess far more if you don't have to endure the company of the Earl. I thought it only fair to warn you of my movements, even though you so clearly do not care about them.'

She took a breath to object. But he didn't give her the chance to say one single word.

'Oh, you need not worry about how you will manage for funds once I've gone. I will write to my man of business before I go, instructing him to give you full access to your own wealth. Because I would rather walk naked into a snowstorm than touch one penny of it. Do you hear me?'

Oh, yes, she'd heard him. He'd rather walk naked into a snowstorm than touch a penny of her dowry.

'And should I get posted somewhere dangerous, which is very likely considering the state of affairs in France, I can also assure you that the settlements ensure you will become a very wealthy widow.' He gave a bitter laugh. 'That will no doubt suit you very well.'

Marguerite stood still, watching him storm away, through a haze of tears. How could he think she would enjoy being a widow? How could he think so poorly of her? He must…really hate her to say such a thing. She hadn't thought he disliked her that much. He'd given her no indication that he felt strongly at all. He was reserved, it was true, but then he always had been reserved. But to hear him accuse her of wishing him dead...

He might as well have slapped her.

In fact, she didn't think it would have hurt as much. Oh, dear, and now she really was crying...

She stumbled to the far end of the walled garden, where there was another gate that led, so she'd been told, to the gardens. She hadn't explored the grounds before, thinking that it would be better to concentrate on the house itself to start with. But she had no intention of letting anyone, not even Marcie, catch her crying over Ben!

The door was stiff and needed some persuasion before it would open. But that just suited her mood. She needed to kick at something. Shove at something that would yield, eventually. Because Ben himself was...

Ah! The door gave way, and she half fell into what might once have been an orchard but which now resembled the kind of forest that ought to be in a fairy story. A fairy story with an evil witch at the centre, who'd put a curse on the fruit so that nobody dared eat it, otherwise why would it be lying, ankle deep and rotting in mounds beneath every gnarled tree? And why else would there be chairs, and little tables, and other odd bits of furniture strewn all over the place and resting at odd angles, as though there had been a battle between various factions that had ended in a Pyrrhic victory for the chairs?

The moment the word *battle* popped into her head, she thought of what Ben might have to face if he went back to the army. He'd already been injured once. And must clearly expect something of that sort could happen again, or why would he have mentioned her widow's jointure?

She came to a halt next to an apple tree, thick with green fruit that nobody had bothered to thin out, and leaned against the trunk.

How could Ben say such things? How could he? She'd been offended, yes, when he'd said he planned to leave. That had struck a blow to her pride. But to hear him say he'd rather risk dying than live with her any longer...ooh, that struck at something far deeper than pride. And it had *hurt* when he'd said, in that sarcastic way he had, that he hoped she'd enjoy being a widow.

Of course she wouldn't enjoy being a widow! What kind of person would experience a moment's happiness, knowing she'd driven a man to his death? And not just any man but *Ben*?

She reached into her pocket for a handkerchief, but the first thing that came to her hand was the scarf she'd been going to tie over her head. Still, it was cotton, so it would do. So she pressed it to her face. To her eyes.

She didn't want Ben to die.

She just wanted him to...to like her. To find her attractive. To...want her...just a tiny bit. Enough to make her a real wife.

Instead, she'd...she'd driven him away. Completely. Had turned what had started out as indifference to active dislike.

And the worst of it was that she had nobody to blame but herself. She could have...*tried* to...

But she'd never dreamed that…well, snubbing him would have had such a dramatic effect on him.

But, then, nothing she'd ever done had ever had any effect on anyone else. She hadn't thought anything she did *could* affect anyone else. Other people, that was to say, her brothers and their friends, always seemed so… certain of themselves. So invulnerable. It had never occurred to her that not speaking to one of them, of showing her anger with him, might have made him feel… well, *any*thing!

But it had.

Oh, but she was wicked to drive a man from his own home. Especially a man who hadn't done a thing to deserve it. Why, when she compared his behaviour to hers these last few days…

He'd behaved like a perfect gentleman, that's what he'd done. He'd given her no indication he hated being married to her. He'd been polite, if taciturn…but, then, Ben *was* taciturn, wasn't he? And she'd felt free for the first time in her life to do whatever she wanted. There was no governess breathing down her neck, reminding her how she ought to behave. No anxiety about what she would find waiting for her in any room of the house, or at least nothing that had been put there deliberately to upset her, so that her brothers could laugh at her reaction. And no overbearing husband, telling her what he expected of her, the way she'd dreaded for so many years. He'd just let her do whatever she wanted.

And in return for his forbearance she'd behaved like a spoiled child. She'd ignored him, refused to speak to him, whilst deliberately being as friendly as she could with everyone else. In front of him, too, so that he couldn't escape her...spite. And it was no use making the excuse that she'd never expected him to feel anything much. She wouldn't have behaved as badly as she had if she hadn't wanted to provoke some sort of reaction, would she? And she'd succeeded.

Oh, she groaned, bending over at the waist and pressing the scarf to her mouth to stifle the sound, so that nobody would overhear. She'd never been so ashamed of herself in her life.

She was going to have to apologise. Tell him that the last thing she wanted was to be a widow. Not if it meant Ben would die. Which it would, since he was her husband.

Surely he would listen? There was still hope, wasn't there? Hope that he might stay and try again, if she promised to try harder. Or even at all. Because so far she hadn't made a single attempt to behave like a wife, had she?

She blew her nose. She didn't relish the prospect of apologising. Explaining herself. It would be dreadful... but not as dreadful as letting him march off to war and then waiting for the letter to arrive, informing her she was a widow. Which would make her feel as if she'd murdered him.

She'd have to go and find him. Right away. Before he did anything irrevocable. He'd said he was going to write to his commanding officer, hadn't he? Not that he'd already done so.

Right, then, she'd have to swallow her pride and go looking for him while there was still time.

Surreptitiously, though. She didn't want the staff to know that she was about to climb down off her high horse. But what to tell them?

As she racked her brains for an excuse to cover her sudden interest in her husband's whereabouts, her eyes snagged on a chair with its legs in the air like a dog waiting to have its tummy tickled. That was it! The furniture! She could tell them she'd found all this furniture in the orchard, and wanted to ask Ben about it in case he thought any of it might be worth salvaging, or whether she could just use it for firewood. That ought to do it. Or at least it was as good an excuse as she could conjure up on the spur of the moment, for why she was suddenly so determined to go and speak to Ben in the middle of the day.

Blowing her nose one last time, she made her way back to the house.

Ben shut the door to his study firmly behind him, went to the desk, sat down, and buried his head in his hands.

What had he done? He groaned. Burned his bridges, that was what. Said all the wrong things, rather than the things he'd meant to say. Because the moment she'd accused him of being a brute, all the feelings he'd kept dammed up for so many years had come bursting out on a wave of bitter anguish.

He lifted his head and pushed his hair back off his face. All those years when he hadn't been able to string two words together when he was within touching distance of her, and now, when he had finally made a speech he had said such wounding, despicable things that he'd alienated her for certain.

It was over. His marriage. Before it had even got started. But wasn't that just the story of his life? He'd always had the appearance of good things, but the reality of them always dangled just out of reach. The only place where his aspirations and his ability to make them happen had coincided was in the army.

And the sooner he got back to his regiment, the sooner he could start recovering from marrying the only woman he'd ever loved, the only woman who could tie him up in knots and make a total fool of him. The woman he'd managed, once she'd been within his grasp, to alienate completely.

He was just pulling a sheet of paper from the top drawer to write to his man of business about Daisy's financial security when he heard someone tapping at the window. He whirled round, his heart pounding… hoping that it was Daisy, that she had come to…

It plummeted to see Miss Fairfax, the daughter of the local squire, standing by the large double doors that gave onto a terrace that led to what had once been a fine lawn. It was the habitation of rabbits now. The Fourth Earl had, by all accounts, sat by the open doors on fine evenings taking pot shots at them, to judge from the craters in what was now a meadow, and the fact that his gun still stood propped by the window.

Not now she'd seen him it looked as if nothing was going to get rid of her. For she was tapping on the doors again with increasing impatience, even though he'd turned his back on her in a clear indication he was in no mood for visitors.

'You shouldn't be here, Miss Fairfax,' he snarled as he unlocked the doors and opened them. And not just because he was in no mood for visitors. It wasn't decent behaviour to come calling on him without her mother, or at the very least a maid, in tow.

She pouted at him prettily as she brushed past him to step inside.

'Now, Ben,' she said, untying the ribbons of her bonnet, then tossing it aside. 'Is that any way to greet me? When I have come to welcome you home?' She stepped right up to him and smiled up into his face. 'Have you missed me as much as I have missed you?'

'I haven't missed you at all,' he said in some surprise.

'Oh, how cruel of you to say so,' she said, with a shake of her head.

And then, to his utter shock, she flung her arms round his neck and kissed him full on the mouth.

He was in the process of reaching up to yank her arms from his neck so he could push her away when there came the sound of a gasp from the vicinity of the door. He whipped his head round. And saw Daisy standing there, her eyes wide with shock in a face that was turning paper white.

'I…' She swallowed. 'I beg your pardon,' she said, stepping back into the corridor and shutting the door behind her.

Hell! If his marriage hadn't been pretty much ruined before, it was certainly over now. For her to find him in the arms of another woman, only a few minutes after he'd spoken to her that way…

'Who was that?' Miss Fairfax was still hanging off his neck.

'My wife,' he said bitterly, pushing her away.

'Your wife?' Now it was Miss Fairfax who looked shocked. 'You cannot be married! There has been no notice in any of the papers.'

'It was a private ceremony. On her family estate. Only last week.'

'Oh,' she said. 'So there was never any chance you would marry me, no matter what I did, was there?' She sighed. 'She's not going to be very pleased with you now, is she?'

That was putting it mildly. He had already shocked and disgusted her with his outburst earlier. And now that she'd seen him kissing, or at least appearing to kiss, another woman in the house she considered her own…

'You couldn't have done more damage if you'd been *trying* to wreck my marriage,' he snarled at her. 'Get out!' He pointed at the open door.

She drew herself up to her full height, which wasn't all that much.

'My bonnet, if you please,' she said haughtily, holding out her hand.

He fetched it, thrust it at her then, the moment she'd stepped out onto the terrace, slammed and locked the terrace doors in her face.

And then went to find Daisy, so he could explain…

Chapter Twelve

Marguerite reeled from the nauseating sight of Ben, her husband, in the arms of another woman and ran to the nearest door that would take her outside. She had to get out of the house into which her husband had brought another woman. A house where he was busy kissing another woman. When he'd never even looked as if he might ever consider kissing her.

She ran blindly along weed-choked paths and through tangled shrubbery and then across an overgrown meadow, until she couldn't run any further. And doubled over, gasping, pressing her hand to the sharp pain of the stitch in her side. Although she'd already felt as if someone had punched her, right in the gut, before she'd started running.

That was what she got for swallowing her pride and deciding to climb down off her high horse. That was what she got for thinking all she needed to do was talk to Ben and everything would be fine. That was what she got for walking into her husband's study, unannounced, believing that the worst he would be doing was writing a letter she didn't want him to write.

She'd caught him, red-handed, kissing someone else. A very pretty, dark-haired, well-dressed someone else.

A lady.

Not some village maiden that he might have explained away as being a... Well, she believed men referred to them as their 'convenients'.

No, that dark-haired lady was someone who mattered.

She let out a rather hysterical little laugh.

No wonder he wasn't interested in her. No wonder he had been so reluctant to marry her.

Oh, why hadn't he just told her father that his heart was already engaged? That he was in love with someone else?

And then she pictured the scene if he had. Father coldly furious, showing him the door and forbidding him to return. Her brothers probably all thrashing him again on his way out. Him losing, in one fell swoop, his closest friends and his right to visit a house where he'd run tame for so many years.

He really must have felt as if he'd been caught between the devil and the deep blue sea. But...how on earth had he supposed he could make any of this, their marriage, work?

Although at least now she could see why he hadn't made a single attempt to come to the marriage bed. If his heart already belonged to that dark-haired beauty, then he would have felt as if he was betraying her by sleeping with his own wife. So not visiting her bed wasn't as much of an insult as she'd first thought. Not if his reluctance was not, primarily, about her at all. But about trying to stay as faithful as he could, in the circumstances, to his true love.

She straightened up as her breathing slowed and the pain in her side abated. Oh, Ben. How awful it must have been for him, juggling his obligations to two women at once. When she considered how torn he must be, having to marry a woman he didn't love to save her reputation and get his hands on her money, it was a wonder he'd been so polite to her. Especially when she'd been such a…shrew about it. But no matter the provocation, he'd been like a rock, impervious to her tantrums, behaving at all times like a perfect gentleman. He'd never reproved her when she'd been rude. He'd never made any demands of her.

Instead, he'd encouraged her to behave as if she was the mistress of the house, which she'd explored to her heart's content. And he'd given her free rein to make whatever improvements or changes she wanted.

She kicked at the bole of the tree she happened to be leaning against. It was all very well seeing now why he'd acted the way he had, and admiring his forbearance, but if he'd wanted a paper marriage, because of that black-haired damsel, why hadn't he just said so? Why let her assume that…?

Because she hadn't given him the chance, had she? He'd started warning her not to expect too much that first night, and she'd interrupted. And then she'd been so busy throwing a tantrum over an imagined slight that she'd made it impossible for him to broach any subject at all, let alone such a sensitive one as a former love. Current love, by the looks of things.

Well, he might love another woman but he'd married *her*. He was *her* husband. And she was…blowed if she was going to stand meekly aside and let the pair of them carry on under her roof! She would jolly well tell him so, and then…

Well, there was no point in demanding that he have the decency to stop carrying on in the marital home, was there? Because he was already planning to leave. His excuse had been that he wanted to re-join his regiment. But if that pretty, dark-haired girl loved him back she might well go with him. Hah. Of course she'd go with him. She wasn't going to stay here and watch Marguerite take the place in local society she no doubt coveted for herself.

Oh, what a mess.

A wave of weariness washed over her. She needed to sit down. Preferably somewhere dark, where nobody could see her and she would not have to see anyone else.

She lifted her head to see if there was, perhaps, some cave or dungeon nearby into which she could crawl. And saw that she was not very far from a cottage with sagging, green thatch that looked exactly the sort of place that would be dank and dismal enough inside to match her mood.

On the doorstep, sitting on an upright chair with a dish of peas in her lap, was a wizened, white-haired woman, regarding her with her head tilted to one side.

Marguerite realised with shock that she must have run all the way across the Park's land and reached the outskirts of the village. And that this woman had, like as not, watched her running from the estate, staggering to a halt and pulling all sorts of faces as she'd relived the moment in the study and her subsequent revelations about her disastrous marriage. Which made her want to turn and run again.

'Would you like some water,' said the woman, 'dearie?'

It would be rude to just run away after the woman had expressed concern. And pointless to pretend nothing was wrong. So Marguerite pulled her manners around her like a shield and attempted a wobbly smile.

'No, thank you. I am fine. Really. Or I shall be when I've got my breath back.'

The woman nodded. 'You're welcome to come and sit for a bit in the shade here. Lovely and cool it is, with the breeze blowing through the house.'

She had wanted to sit somewhere cool. And it occurred to her that this was one of Ben's tenants. She ought not to make things worse by offending a woman who could be one of the most influential of them. Which she well could be, in spite of the dilapidated state of her house, merely by dint of being so old. The oldest tenants who lived round the fringes of Wattlesham Priory were related to nearly all of the families in the surrounding area, and it wasn't likely to be so very different here.

'Thank you,' she said, and stepped through the remains of what had once been the woman's front gate. 'What a lovely garden you have,' she said, admiring the profusion of marigolds and strawberries flanking the path, and the peas winding their way over everything they could climb.

'My Sam helps me keep it up,' she said, pulling a dish of peas still in their pods from a chair next to her so that Marguerite could sit on it. 'My grandson,' she added. 'Not that he'll be doing it for much longer, I don't 'spect. Soon as he's old enough he'll be off to the factories, like the rest of 'em.' She sighed.

'I don't really understand,' said Marguerite, as she sat down, 'why people leave the countryside to go and work in factories. I have seen one or two, and they always look so noisy and dirty.'

The woman snorted. ''Cos there ain't no choice. Poor folks have to work or starve. And it's no use thinking a growing lad can survive on what I can grow in this little patch. Or that he'll want to stay with an old woman when there's girls, some of 'em pretty, in the towns.'

'Yes, but...' She frowned. 'Surely there is work here for a lad that can keep a garden as beautifully as this?' She waved her hands at the profusion of plants, neatly and vigorously filling the small square of ground. And compared it to the wilderness of every patch of earth she'd seen at Bramhall Park.

'Ah, but he's male, ain't he?'

'What does that have to do with anything?'

'Well, the old Earl wouldn't employ men, not after the way that wife of his carried on, would he? Not in the house, to start with, and then later not in the grounds neither.'

His wife...that would be Ben's mother...had...*carried on*? Good grief. Well, that certainly accounted for the appalling destruction of the former Countess's rooms, she supposed. But...to drive all the men from the area? Wasn't that going a bit too far? Had there been no limit to the...foolishness and eccentricity of Ben's father?

'But,' Marguerite mused, 'the old Earl has gone now, hasn't he? Surely your Sam could ask for work from the new Earl? I mean, there's plenty of it up at the house, and in the grounds, from what I've seen.'

The woman gave her a long look. ''Twon't be easy for the new Earl to employ locals either, though, will it? Given the way the old Earl behaved.'

She didn't see why. Besides, he wasn't going to be here much longer, was he, if he planned to run off with that...that...*minx*! And minx she must be, Marguerite decided, to sneak into a married man's house and carry on like that when the wife was in residence.

'Well,' she declared, 'there is a new Countess, too. And *she* is certainly willing to hire as many staff as are willing to apply. And so you may tell everyone. In fact, I hope you will.'

The old woman grinned at her. 'Sally said you was a good sort. Said as how you'd be just the one to start righting the wrongs as have gone on here for nigh on a generation.'

'Sally?' The scullery maid?

'Aye. My granddaughter. One of the last ones to hang onto her job up at the big house, just so's she could send what money she could to me and Sam. Not that it were much, but with that...and this here patch of earth... we've scraped by. Mother Porter,' she said, holding out

her gnarled, and rather green hand from where she'd
been shelling peas, for Marguerite to shake. 'And I'm
guessing you are the new Countess? Lady Daisy? Am
I right? Only there's no other beautiful golden-haired
lady round these parts, as I don't already know.'

Lady Marguerite, she wanted to say, almost as badly
as she wanted to wipe her hand down her apron after
shaking the older lady's rather dirty one. But to do either would feel not only rude but also rather...pompous,
considering she was wearing an apron. The one she'd
put on when she'd planned to spend the day cleaning
the dining room. And that this woman had seen her
running, in tears, and then doubling over with a stitch.
And then laughing a bit hysterically. And been so kind.

'Yes. I am the new Countess,' she therefore said.
'And, yes, I do intend to start righting the wrongs that
have been taking place here.' She did. She really did.
For what was the use of sitting about in a cave or a dungeon, bemoaning her fate? What had she got to complain about, really? So, she'd married a man who was
in love with someone else? So, he was about to run off
with his true love and leave her here, less than a week
after their marriage? So, she would never feel as if she
could show her face in society again?

But...she hadn't exactly enjoyed her one foray into
London society anyway, had she? She'd never felt as
if she fitted in. She could already hazard a guess as
to which of the shallow, ambitious females she'd met
would delight in gossiping about her spectacular hu-
miliation. So...what did she care what they said? She
was not, she was starting to learn, Lady Marguerite,

that useless, showy creature whose only value was ornamental. She really was a Daisy. A plant that could thrive in humbler surroundings.

She lifted her chin. She might end up alone, and too embarrassed to face Town gossip. But she would never go hungry. She would never have to put up with a leaking roof, the way this woman must be doing, to judge from the colour and shape of the thatch, or live in fear that her relatives would leave her penniless and unable to fend for herself. One thing she did have, and Ben had promised that she would keep even when he left, was money. Pots of it.

Oh, she wasn't going to fool herself into thinking it would be easy. Actually, she mused, pursing her lips, she would rather it wasn't. She would face all sorts of challenges, she was sure, hiring what locals were left and luring back the ones who'd gone to the factories with promises of more jobs. But it would give her a purpose. And she wouldn't have time to dwell on Ben and what might have been.

She stood up and brushed down her skirts. 'It was lovely to meet you, Mother Porter. Thank you for the chance to…er…rest, and…'

The old woman nodded. 'I'll be seeing you again, then? At church, mebbe?'

'Of course.' Daisy looked up the road to the village church, which was barely bigger than the private chapel in which she and Ben had married.

The old woman nodded again. 'Then I shall put word round that you'll be there. And that you're hiring on.

And mebbe…' She spread her hands wide. 'Well, it will be a start, won't it?'

'I hope so,' said Daisy. Because it would give her something to look forward to. Somewhere to be, and something to do, rather than sit about moping about Ben for the rest of her life.

She laughed bitterly as she recalled the many, many times she'd wished that people would leave her alone. Well, she'd got her wish. Ben was going to do just that. He was going to leave her in this run-down house, in the practically deserted village. And nobody of worth in the area would call on her, except to gloat.

Well, she'd show him. She'd show everyone! She'd enjoy cleaning up the mess that Ben's father had made, and Ben had not seen fit to put right. And she'd stock the library with books. Books that she had chosen. Books that…

Books were expensive, though, weren't they? Would she have enough money to fill that library? And if she did, would she have enough money to repair Mother Porter's roof, and all the roofs of the other houses in the village that needed re-thatching? She had no idea how much it cost to re-thatch a house. She had little idea about anything to do with land management.

Well, she'd just have to find out. Father's steward would be able to tell her anything she needed to know. Or even James. What was the point in having so many brothers if she couldn't put them to good use? And, come to think of it, wasn't James always complaining that Father didn't let him have enough to do, that he wouldn't loosen his grip on the reins? Right, then. She would challenge James to come here and see if he had what it took to turn the place around. With any luck he'd enjoy finding some purpose to his life, just as she was about to do.

Funny, she'd never thought of her oldest brother as someone lacking in purpose. But today she was looking on all sorts of things through different eyes. Through the eyes of a daisy rather than a marguerite. Someone who'd been brought low rather than always being shielded in a hot house or staked up by careful gardeners in a well-tended border. She wouldn't be surprised to learn that it was because James had so little responsibility that he ended up playing pranks and spending so much money on clothing and horses and other fripperies.

Perhaps nobody was what they appeared on the surface.

Perhaps, she mused as she reached the furniture-strewn orchard, she could reward herself with one book for every cottage she repaired. After all, she could only read one book at a time, couldn't she? And then each book would be extra special. Because she would have earned it.

Which was something else she'd never done, wasn't it? Earned anything she possessed. Everything she had, she had because she was daughter of the Earl of Darwen. She hadn't even acquired her husband through anything she'd done, or because of anything special about her. It had all been down to some stupid lark. And keeping up appearances. And keeping the peace.

She sighed.

Perhaps Ben was right. Perhaps she would be happier as…not as a widow but as a woman living alone, making her own decisions and taking responsibility for the welfare of other people. She'd always suspected she'd be a failure as a wife. She could never lower herself to fawn over some stupid man, the way her mother fawned over Father, simply because in his youth he'd been so very handsome. Likewise, she would have thought a man stupid if he'd married her because of the way she looked. And venal if he'd married her for her money. Which reflections had only made it harder to see any of the males she'd met as husband material. The man she might have *truly* wanted to marry didn't exist. Not in the real world. He could only exist, and that in fleeting snatches, in the realms of her imagination.

But anyway it was too late to wonder what might have been now, wasn't it? She'd married Ben. Alienated Ben. He was leaving her, she had nobody to blame but herself, and she was just going to have to get used to it.

Chapter Thirteen

As soon as Ben managed to get rid of Miss Fairfax he went off in search of Daisy. God knew what she must be thinking after catching him with that…insufferable woman hanging off his neck!

But he couldn't find her. He supposed he shouldn't be surprised. Daisy was exceptionally good at hiding. She'd had so many years' practice during the school holidays when her brothers brought their friends home, and they'd regarded teasing Daisy as the highest form of sport. He'd discovered one or two of her hiding places at the Priory, but she hadn't been here long enough for him to know about the ones she'd found here.

After going through every floor of the house, and finding nothing but empty rooms, he came to a halt on the threshold of the dining room. The dining room she'd said she was going to tackle today. He should probably have looked here first. He opened the door, his heart pounding. There was Vale with a duster, and Marcie with a mop and bucket, but of Daisy there was no sign.

His heart felt as though it was shrivelling up in his chest as he saw what this meant. There hadn't ever been much of a chance for him and Daisy to make a go of it, but after this morning's episode…he shut his eyes…*two* episodes, there was no longer the slightest shred of hope.

He might just as well go straight out and shoot himself right now.

Only what would become of her then? Where would she live? He had a suspicion that whatever heir the lawyers ferreted out of his tangled family tree would send her packing.

He ran his fingers through his hair with a feeling of impatience. Only cowards shot themselves and left their dependants to clean up their mess. And he was no coward. He turned away from the dining room and strode down to the stables. He may not know where her hiding places were, but as a boy he'd found many of his own about this estate. Whenever he'd been threatened with the birch, or his mother had pushed him aside impatiently and irritably, or his brothers had forbidden him from joining in with whatever they'd been doing, he'd walked away. And come to one of the places around the estate that other people rarely visited. He'd never been in more need of the thicket of hazel bushes down by the lake than now. With his horse cropping the turf behind him, and the wind shimmering over the water, maybe he'd find…if not peace then at least a frame of mind where he could make rational decisions, instead of haring off at the behest of his deepest, darkest fears like a startled, well, hare.

And, as so often happened when he was down there by the water, under the shelter of bushes that should have been pruned back instead of being left to run rampant, he achieved a measure of calm. At least, by the time he thought dinner would be ready he felt composed enough to face her across the table. Because by now he'd worked out that whatever went on in their marriage, she was the kind of person who would not want anyone else to know about it. She'd put on a brave face for the staff.

He marched into the kitchen, his jaw clamped so hard that he wasn't sure if he'd be able to open it far enough to get a forkful of food into his mouth. But, as he'd predicted, she was there. So he could at least see her. Watch her. And note all the changes that one day's work had wrought. At previous meals she'd smiled frequently, though never at him. Tonight she hardly smiled at all, and the few smiles she did bestow on the others had a brittle quality that indicated, to him at least, how much they were costing her. And instead of shooting him the occasional disdainful glance, she was hardly able to look at him at all. As though she couldn't bear to look at him again after what she'd seen him doing the last time.

Well, she was going to have to look at him eventually. And speak to him. Or at least listen to what he had to say. Because he couldn't let her think that he'd willingly taken Miss Fairfax in his arms. That he'd prefer to have *any* other woman in his arms.

He managed to maintain an appearance of calm all the way through the meal. But then, he'd had years of

practice of keeping up a front whenever he was anywhere near her. Of concealing any signs of his interest
in her lest she or anyone else noticed and mocked him
for aiming too high. Or took steps to prevent him getting anywhere near her, ever again.

But as soon as Mrs Green began clearing away the
dishes from their last course, he got to his feet.

'It is a fine evening,' he said to Daisy. 'Why don't
we go for a walk?'

She looked up at him with a haunted expression on
her face. He braced himself for the barrage of excuses
she'd no doubt throw up. Excuses that he had every intention of demolishing. They couldn't carry on as they
were. He *had* to speak to her. Explain at least what she'd
seen going on in his study that morning, if nothing else.

'What a good idea,' she said, knocking the wind out
of his sails. She got to her feet and made for the kitchen
door. 'I wanted to consult with you about some things I
saw in the orchard. Perhaps we could go there?'

'A good idea.' The orchard was far enough from
the house that nobody was likely to come along and
overhear whatever they had to say to each other. But
not so far that it would become unbearable to walk the
distance there whilst holding back all the things he
needed to say.

But it turned out to be Daisy who couldn't keep her
feelings to herself. They'd hardly crossed the kitchen
yard before she cleared her throat.

'I want to apologise,' she said, as he put his hand to
the latch that opened the gate of the walled garden. 'For

barging into your study this morning without waiting for you to say I could come in.'

His hand seized up on the latch.

'*You* are apologising?' He'd assumed she'd been so willing to come out here because she couldn't wait for the chance to rake him over the coals. 'For...coming in without waiting for my permission?' Didn't she care about what she'd found him doing? Of course she didn't care. Why should she care? Nobody had ever cared about him, so why should his wife be any different? He took his feelings out on the gate by pushing it far harder than was necessary to open it, before making a sweeping gesture with his arm, indicating that she should go through.

'Yes. It was terribly tactless of me,' she said, sidling past him warily, 'wasn't it? But then, I had no idea you were...' She paused, with her back to him, sucking in a short, rather ragged breath, 'in love with someone else.'

'In love with someone else?' He yanked the door shut and marched up to where she was standing, head bowed, apparently engaged in studying the neat row of cabbages at the side of the path. 'I am not in love with anyone else! Is that what you thought?' Yes, it was. But rather than act the jealous wife, she was apologising for interrupting him.

Because she didn't really care what he did.

He walked a few paces away from her, his gut writhing. She thought so poorly of him that she really believed he'd play her false? In the marital home?

He whirled round, anger finally sweeping aside the reticence he normally felt in her presence. Reticence that kept him from ever speaking his mind, lest she think him a fool or despised him. But she couldn't think any worse of him than this, could she?

'Do you really think I would entertain a lady-love with you in the house? What kind of man do you think I am?'

'Well, a very unhappy one,' she informed the cabbages, since she appeared to be unable to look him in the eye. But not even his subordinates in the regiment could do so when he roared at them the way he'd just roared at her. Perhaps he ought to...

'I knew you didn't want to marry me,' she said, halting him in mid-thought. Not want to marry her? What the hell had given her that idea?

'Well, you made your feelings very clear,' she answered him without him even having to voice his surprise. 'But until this morning, when I saw that it was because your heart was already engaged elsewhere, I didn't understand. I just felt...insulted that you didn't want to consummate our marriage.'

'What? I...' She thought he didn't *want* to consummate their marriage? Where on earth had she got hold of a foolish idea like that?

'No! You've got it all wrong!' He paced away from her. Turned, to find she'd followed him, a perplexed expression on his face.

'What have I got wrong, Ben?'

Where to start?

'You did say you wanted to leave me,' she pointed out, while he stood there, attempting to marshal his thoughts

into some kind of order, 'to go back to your regiment...
and then, when I saw you with that woman...'

'Right. Let's start with her,' he said, taking her arm
and towing her along the path to the end of the walled
garden so that they could have the conversation in the
orchard, as they'd planned. 'Miss Fairfax,' he said with
a shudder of distaste, 'is not my lady-love, and never
has been. She is a neighbour. The daughter of the local
squire. She must have ridden over when she heard I'd
come back, I suppose, because, believe me, I did not
invite her here. I had no communication with her whatsoever. She took me totally by surprise when she burst
into my study and flung herself at me.'

Daisy looked up at him with a slight frown. 'But...
you were kissing her...'

'No. *She* was kissing *me*. I just...froze. As I said,
she took me by surprise. Me, a seasoned soldier,' he
said with a disgusted shake of his head. 'I had no idea
I was being ambushed.'

She tilted her head to one side, as if considering
what he'd said. As if replaying the scene in her mind.

'It...it does sound unlikely. I mean, why on earth
would she have done such a thing? If you gave her no
encouragement?'

But she didn't sound as though she was accusing
him of lying. Rather, the tone of her voice suggested
she was as puzzled by Miss Fairfax's extraordinary
behaviour as he was, and really just wanted to know
what may have caused her to do it. The relief that she
appeared to be willing to believe him was so great that
he felt a bit dizzy.

'I have been thinking about that,' he said grimly. 'And I believe she may have thought I was…susceptible. After all, she is very pretty,' he said, ticking that point off on one finger. 'And…' he held up a second finger '…she knew I thought so when I was much younger. But she always made it plain that she was only interested in my older brother. But…and this is crucial,' he said, holding up a third finger, 'it wasn't William himself that she cared about, I eventually learned, but his title. Because when he died, she promptly switched her efforts onto my next brother, Paul, and now, it seems, she is targeting me.

'She was very annoyed when you walked in. She says she had no idea I was married. Which could be true. Newspapers from London with the announcement of our marriage may not have arrived at her father's house. Or she may not have read it.'

'That makes sense,' said Daisy thoughtfully. 'I mean, no woman in her right mind would fling herself at a married man like that,' she said scornfully. 'She would have nothing to gain and all too much to lose.'

Unless she was fathoms deep in love with said married man. Which had clearly not occurred to Daisy.

They walked on in silence for a moment or two before she glanced up at him sharply. 'So, if you are not in love with someone else, then why…' She pulled herself up. 'No, never mind. I am sure you have your reasons.'

The fiery blush staining her cheeks reminded him of her accusation that he hadn't wanted to consummate the marriage.

'Are you wondering why, so far, I have made no attempt to, as you put it, consummate our union?'

She ducked her head but nodded. 'It doesn't matter, Ben, really it doesn't. I… I have been only thinking of myself, I see that now. I have been abominably selfish…'

'And angry,' he put in. 'You were so angry the day of our wedding. Flinging your bouquet away the moment you could…stripping the carriage of any sign that you were a bride. Refusing to talk to me…avoiding me. What kind of man would attempt to make love to a wife who was making it so abundantly clear that she could not stomach the mere sight of her husband, let alone his touch?'

'Oh, Ben, is that what you thought? I never dreamed…' She shook her head. 'I am so sorry,' she said on a sort of guip. 'It wasn't you at all. It was my brothers. You see, they put slugs in my wedding bouquet. Didn't you see them dripping all over the chapel floor on my walk up the aisle? Didn't you hear them sniggering? They…they thought it was amusing to mock me, on my wedding day. And the worst thing was I fell for it.

'After all the years of dodging all the horrid things they wanted to do to me, I thought that at last, on my wedding day, they were trying to show me that they… cared about me when they brought me that bouquet, but no!' Her pace picked up. Her skirts swished as she marched through the long grass, throwing up clouds of seeds and dust. 'And it was more of the same in the carriage. Earwigs, and…a toad,' she said on a shudder.

'A toad,' he said. Then lengthened his stride so that

he could keep up with her. 'Very well, I can see that it wasn't just because you had been pushed into marrying me that made you behave so...er...angrily on our wedding day. But since then? You have avoided me as much as possible. And when we have had to be in the same room you have managed to avoid exchanging one single word with me. Whilst speaking to everyone else, charmingly. You have frozen me out, Daisy. What was I supposed to think?'

She hung her head. 'Exactly what you did, I suppose. That is...well, I was so cross on my wedding day that when you stayed away all night I had no idea it was because of the way I'd been behaving. I just thought you...well, I felt rejected. And so I thought, Right, if he thinks the only good thing about me as a woman is that I don't chatter all the time, then I'll show him how quiet I can be...'

'You thought... Hang on a minute, where on earth did you get the idea that the only thing I liked about you was that you don't chatter?'

'Oh, that horrid discussion you and Walter and Horace had in the library after Jasper begged one of you to save me from eternal spinsterhood.'

'You overheard it all?' Then she *had* been there. He hadn't imagined her perfume lingering in the air.

His mind flew back to the incident, trying to recall who had said what. He remembered being sickened, angry and furious on Daisy's behalf. He knew he'd defended her from some of the unpleasant things the others had said about her. But...all she'd taken from his defence of her had been the fact that he wanted her not to speak to him?

He'd been trying not to give his feelings for her away. The way he always did. He may have spoken…sarcastically to try to deflect the others from suspecting the truth. Sarcasm was often his first line of defence…

'Dammit, Daisy,' he blurted. 'If I had known you were there…'

She shrugged. 'Oh, well, it is too late now to change things. At least you…if you had known I was there, you may have spoken differently, and perhaps given away the fact that I was there somehow…'

'Never! You know that, surely? I mean, I never did so before, did I?'

She glanced up at him, then away. 'No. You never did. Out of them all, you were the only one I didn't mind…' She trailed into silence, but he knew what she'd been going to say. Because he'd lingered, occasionally, after the others had gone away, and seen her crawl out of whatever nook she'd been hiding in. And they'd share a conspiratorial grin.

'I have to repeat my apology, Ben,' she said earnestly. 'None of what has happened has been your fault. You were just as much a victim of the whole horrid set of circumstances as I was, and yet while I've behaved like a…spoiled child, stamping my feet all over the place, you've behaved like a perfect gentleman.

'You put me to shame. I didn't realise how poorly I'd been behaving until you came and told me you wanted to return to your regiment.' She turned to him then, her hands clasped, and looked up into his face with eyes

that swam with tears. 'Ben, I couldn't bear it if my behaviour drove you to go back, and you sustained some
horrid injury, or even, as you hinted, d…' She gulped
back the word as though even to say it was too awful.
'I don't want to be a widow, Ben. That is…' she shook
her head as though in exasperation '… I don't want
anything bad to happen to you. That is what I came to
your study to tell you.'

'You came to tell me you…don't want to be a widow.'

'No! Well, yes. But I mean I don't want you to go
away. Oh, Ben, I know I've been a beastly sort of wife.
I know you wouldn't have chosen to marry me even if
you'd been looking for a wife, but…now that I know
you aren't in love with anyone else, couldn't we…try…
to make the best of things?'

Make the best of things? Was that the best offer she
could make him?

He paced away from her, running his fingers through
his hair in a kind of anguish. Marrying her should have
been like a dream come true. Though he'd never dared
allow himself to so much as dream of it, had he? She
was so far out of his reach, in every way.

And now, hearing her say she was prepared to *make
the best of things…* Why wasn't he jumping for joy?
Why couldn't he simply gather her in his arms and
laugh, and say, yes, why not? And then take her to bed,
and pretend that it was easy, and casual, and didn't matter to him one way or the other?

Because it would be agony, that was why. Knowing
that while he was fathoms deep in love with her, all she
was doing was *making the best of things*.

He'd feel like a beggar, gratefully accepting the scraps she chose to throw his way. He'd feel like a spaniel, following his master's every move with hopeful eyes. He'd feel like…like he always did. Waiting for approval, for love, from people who would never, ever give him what he wanted.

'Ben?'

He heard the tremulous, hopeful sound of her voice, but he couldn't turn round and face her. Not with his emotions in such turmoil.

So he did what any soldier faced with insurmountable odds would do. He retreated. Deeper into the orchard.

Chapter Fourteen

Daisy watched the slumped set of his shoulders as he walked away, her stomach hollowing out. What if he decided he didn't want to try to make their marriage work? She wouldn't blame him, not after the way she'd behaved so far. He must be thoroughly disgusted with her.

She clasped her hands to her waist, where she felt so hollow, even though they'd only just had their main meal of the day. If only she'd taken more notice of Mother's little homilies as she'd been growing up. Mother had offered all sorts of advice about how to win a man's heart. Advice she'd scorned, since she'd judged all men by the behaviour of her brothers and come to the conclusion that they were all beastly creatures. And she hadn't wanted to marry any of them if they were going to treat her the way Father treated Mother. She hadn't wanted to have some man telling her what to do and expressing disdain when she didn't live up to his standards. Father had been a rather disapproving, rather strict father, but at least he had left her alone if she'd gone and sat quietly somewhere, with a book. But a husband, she'd suspected, would not.

But now...now she didn't *want* Ben to leave her alone. Oh, if only she'd tried to learn some of the attitudes Mother had kept telling her to try during her Season, instead of concentrating on freezing men away. Then she might have some notion of how to get her husband to want her, the way she wanted him.

And, yes, she admitted it to herself now. She wanted him. She'd been intrigued by his body when she'd seen him naked in the moonlight. Fascinated by the way his muscles had rippled when he'd been rowing her across the lake. Become positively heated when Mother had told her what she might expect on her wedding night.

And stricken when she'd seen another woman kissing him. Furious. Jealous. All those things she'd never thought she could feel about a man. And it was no use telling herself that it was merely a proprietorial thing, because Ben was *her* husband and he had no right to break his vows so soon after making them. She rather thought she'd have felt the same if she'd seen him kissing someone else even if they weren't married.

She kept watching Ben until he'd disappeared into the tangle of the gardens. What was she going to do if he decided he didn't want to make their marriage work? What would she do if he decided returning to his regiment was preferable to living under the same roof as an...an icicle?

There was nothing she could do.

And the worst of it all was that if he did leave, she would have nobody to blame but herself.

She made her way back to the house in a sombre mood, finding it hard to reply cheerfully to Marcie's chatter as she helped her prepare for bed. And slept only in exhausted snatches because she started at every noise, imagining it to be the sound of Ben's horse, galloping away. If only he weren't sleeping in the stables but in one of the other bedrooms inside, she might even have plucked up the courage to go to him and…and…

But there her resolve faltered. Even if she did know where he was sleeping, she had little idea of how to make a man see her as a desirable woman. She could simply remove her nightgown, she supposed…

Only, if he still didn't want her, she'd feel humiliated, standing naked before him. It would feel worse than anything that had happened so far.

There had to be a way she could persuade him to stay here long enough to show him that she wasn't just a spoiled, childish creature who thought of nobody but herself. Perhaps if she told him that she had noticed how needy his tenants were, and that she'd hoped to begin helping them, he might see her in a different light?

Or perhaps not. She didn't really know how he felt about his tenants and the derelict state of his holdings. He might want to just wash his hands of them all. After all, he had spoken about returning to his regiment, which suggested he wasn't all that concerned about them. Or didn't think there was anything he could do…

It took her so long to fall properly asleep that she was late down for breakfast. She didn't think she'd have made it at all if it hadn't been for Marcie coming to wake her, reminding her that it was Sunday, and she'd promised Sally's grandmother she'd go to church today and start meeting more of the locals.

Ben looked up at her when she got to the kitchen, his expression impossible to read.

'Good morning,' he said, getting to his feet. 'You look very smart.'

'Thank you,' she said, taking her place and reaching for the cup of tea Mrs Green had already poured her. 'I intend to go to the local church this morning.'

'It is a long walk,' said Ben.

'Yes, and I gather you don't have a carriage I can use.'

'No,' he said stiffly. Defensively?

'I...' He fiddled with his spoon, before glancing up at her warily. 'Would you like me to provide you with a riding horse?'

She wrinkled her nose as she considered his question. At least he was talking to her. She'd wondered if he would after yesterday.

'I am not sure,' she said as she slathered butter onto a thick slice of fresh bread, 'that it would be appropriate for me to trot up to the church door on horseback.'

He scowled. 'There are other days of the week. You will want to get about, surely? And I can lend you Sergeant Wilmot to act as your groom. Or...' He tilted his head to one side and looked at her thoughtfully. 'Don't you enjoy horse riding? Now I think of it, I don't recall ever seeing you hack about the Priory, not in all the time I spent there.'

As she chewed on her bread and butter, she considered the question. Did she enjoy horse riding? The truth was she had no idea. She'd always told everyone she didn't when she'd been growing up, in pure self-defence. Because if she'd spent much time in the stables, her brothers would have assumed she was either trying to impress them or trying to spoil their fun. Which meant she'd taken great pains to demonstrate she had no wish to do either.

But when she'd been in London, she'd wistfully wondered what it would have been like to be one of those ladies who rode in the park in their stunning riding habits and little jaunty hats, rather than sitting sedately in a carriage, surrounded by grooms and footmen. In short, dependent on males.

And now, well, it sounded rather tempting to have her own horse. And never mind what he'd said about having Sergeant Wilmot escorting her. If she had her own horse, she could go with Ben whenever he went off on one of his rides.

'I will consider it,' she told him. 'But this morning, I am going to have to walk, I fear.'

'And if you don't want to be late,' put in Mrs Green, 'you'd best set off sharpish.'

She washed down the last of her bread with a gulp of tea and got to her feet. 'Will you…?' She broke off at Ben's set expression. Perhaps it was expecting a bit too much to hope he would go to church with her just because she'd asked him. 'Do you plan to attend?'

'I had better,' he said, with a distinct lack of enthusiasm. 'Because I don't want you to have to face the reception the locals are likely to give you, without support.'

'Oh?' She flashed Marcie a smile as the girl handed her a clean pair of gloves, a bonnet and a parasol. And bit back the answer that sprang to mind—that she wouldn't be without support, because Marcie would be with her. And, she suspected, because Marcie was going, Vale would go too, no doubt using the excuse that his presence would add to her consequence. But if she said as much she risked making him think she didn't want to spend as much time with him as walking to church and back would take.

On the other hand, she didn't want to push him into doing anything he didn't want to do.

Oh, why was it so hard to know what to say?

While she was dithering and pulling on her gloves, Ben got to his feet.

'The locals have no reason to love this family,' he said, tugging down his jacket sleeves and making for the kitchen door. 'The late Earl was not a good landlord.'

'No. I noticed that the first time we drove through Bramley Bythorn,' she said, as he opened the door and extended his arm for her to take. Very well, then. He'd made up his mind to go to church with her. She could just accept his escort with gratitude. And perhaps, on the way, just explain why she was so determined to go. 'Then the other day,' she began airily, as though she wasn't still shivering inside with the horrid feelings that had driven her to leave the estate, 'I got talking to Sally's grandmother.'

'Mother Porter?'

'You know her?' Of course he did. He must know everybody in the area. 'Of course you do. Anyway, during the course of our...chat... I promised to do what I could to help with getting people jobs. There is so much work that needs doing after all,' she said, waving her hand at the expanse of meadow through which they were making their way. At one time it must have been a lawn. Possibly even with a path across it. 'And she said she would put the word about, so that people who wanted to meet me might come to church to do so.'

'Mrs Knowles is going to love that,' said Ben dryly.

'What do you mean? Who is Mrs Knowles?'

'The vicar's wife. She would have preferred it if you had gone and visited her, rather than Mother Porter, and asked for *her* opinion about what wants doing and who is deserving of your help so that she could have guided you.'

'Would you have preferred me to have gone and consulted her?' The moment the words had left her lips she blinked in some surprise. Because, for the first time in her life, she had asked a man what he would have preferred her to have done. Because she truly wanted to know what his preferences were.

He shrugged, as though it didn't matter to him either way.

'I am only pointing out that she is the kind of woman who needs to feel important.'

'Ah. Well, hmm... I don't want to alienate the vicar's wife, of course.' And it wasn't as if she'd done it on purpose.

'I think it is too late. She will probably have taken against you on principle already.'

'Because I spoke to Mother Porter about the state of the village, rather than her?'

'No. Because you have married me.'

'Oh, dear. Is your name really in such poor odour in these parts? I suppose it must be, since your father was such a terrible landlord. Whatever ailed him to leave his tenants living in such awful conditions? And why would he not employ more of them?' She pulled herself up short. Mother Porter had said it was because Ben's mother had been a bit too free with her favours. Ben was bound to feel unhappy about that. Well, anyone would, wouldn't they? If her own mother had behaved so scandalously…no, she definitely ought not to mention it.

'Mother Porter told me that young people have had to go to the manufacturing towns, rather than staying here,' she rushed on, filling the heavy silence emanating from Ben. 'And it made me think…' She darted him a sideways glance. He was staring ahead, broodingly. If he wasn't thinking bitter thoughts about his mother's behaviour, behaviour he probably wished she knew nothing about, then he could well be wondering how to tell her that the task of undoing all the ills she could see in this part of the world was well beyond her capabilities. After all, what did she know about parish affairs, or employment, or poverty? She'd grown up in the lap of luxury.

And taken it all for granted. She lowered her head, watching her feet ploughing a furrow through the long, thick grasses alongside Ben's heavily booted ones. From behind them came the sound of Marcie's laughter and the low rumble of Vale's voice. They sounded so carefree. So easy in each other's company.

'What,' said Ben, after such a lengthy pause she'd started to think he might not say another word all the way to church, 'What did you think?'

Think? Oh, yes, she'd been about to tell him her plans and then stopped, thinking he'd think they were silly.

'Oh, well, it is probably all very foolish,' she said. 'And there are probably dozens of reasons why none of what I have been thinking will work…'

'Well, then, you had better tell me what you have been thinking before you tell anyone else, so that I can stop you from…'

'Making a fool of myself?'

'No, I didn't mean that…'

'Well, I appreciate it, anyway. And it is a good idea. You see…' she cleared her throat '… I have been thinking…' She felt her cheeks heat. She had never really shared her thoughts with anyone before. She had been the only girl amongst five brothers, whose delight in life was to tease her. Mother had always put them first. Nobody shared confidences with Father, it was unthinkable. And none of the governesses she'd had over the years had been interested in anything she might have to say. Their task had been the reverse—to instruct her in what she ought to think.

But Ben was different. Even if he mocked her, he

would at least prevent her from being mocked by anyone else. He'd just said so.

She took a deep breath. 'I know I have not been much of a wife to you so far. And I know you probably don't like me very much at the moment, which, actually makes it easier for me to speak frankly,' she admitted, suddenly realising it was true.

'But I am certain that there is one way in which I can benefit you. I am rich. And that was one of the things I overheard that day in the library, how much you are in need of my fortune. And since I've been here, I have seen it with my own eyes. Your holdings are in a terrible state, Ben. I know,' she put in hastily when he made as if he was going to protest, 'it is not your fault. And I also know that you said you wouldn't touch a penny of my money, but, honestly, it would help me to think that some good might come from our union. I mean, if we cannot be happy with each other, then at least we can use my money to benefit your people.'

Ben's scowl deepened.

'That is…that is only the broad outline,' he said, after a short pause, during which it looked as though he'd been weighing his words carefully. 'Your intent to make everything all clean and shiny around these parts. You have not laid out yet just how you intend to affect this transformation of the mess,' he said, his lip curling, 'I've inherited.'

Oh, dear. She'd pricked his masculine pride. But that was only to be expected, wasn't it? Men didn't like to hear ideas from females. They liked to be in charge. And if she made suggestions he hadn't thought of, would he be even more cross with her?

She sighed. He'd already threatened to leave. Nor had he made a positive response to her suggestion that they try to start again. So what had she got to lose?

'Well, take this meadow we're walking through,' she said, just as they were coming to the end of it and were about to set foot in the lane that ran through the village. 'Couldn't we give people permission to graze their animals on it? Or even encourage them to do so? Or say that if they come and mow it they can use the hay to feed their stock over winter? It would not only tidy the place up but give them both work and provisions. And then there's all that fruit going to waste in the orchard,' she added, as they turned and began to climb the steep lane that led up to the squat little church. 'I'm sure I heard somewhere that pigs will eat anything. Couldn't we feed them all those windfalls lying there, rotting? And then have a couple of days when we invite locals to come in and help thin the crop, and later harvest it?'

'Do you plan to give away the entire crop?'

Plan. He'd said *plan*, as if it was entirely up to her what she did. Otherwise he would have asked what she *proposed* to do with the crop, so that he could either grant or withhold his permission.

'Oh, well,' she said, her heart kicking up a bit, 'I don't know. I am not sure how many people are living hereabouts, for one thing, but whatever we do have left I mean to use for pies and preserves. I know I have the reputation for being completely useless, but I have been taught all the things a lady in charge of a large property needs to know.'

'Mrs Green used to make pies and preserves from the fruit when I was a boy, I do remember that,' he said. 'If she had the help she needed, I'm sure she would love to do so again.'

He approved! Oh, it was only of one of the things she'd suggested, but it felt as if she'd just cleared an immense hurdle.

'And as for all that furniture... Ben, why on earth,' she said, gleaning the courage from his positive response, to ask him the question that she'd been dying to ask him, 'are there all those tables and chairs and suchlike scattered all over the orchard?'

'Oh, as to that, it was the Fourth Earl's doing. As I expect you will have gathered.'

'He turned all that furniture out into the orchard to rot?'

'Well, no, he ordered the servants to burn it. But there was so much. Apparently they did have a few bonfires, but once he died, they didn't see the sense in carrying on with such a wasteful practice. Besides which it took a lot of hard work to drag it out of the rooms, down the stairs, along the corridors, and out to the field where he decreed it ought to be burned.'

'Yes, I imagine it would,' she mused, as they drew near to the churchyard wall. Especially if he was turning staff off at the same time. But that was where their ability to share confidences had to cease. There were other people straggling up the path to the open church door. People who turned to look at them as they drew near. People who could overhear whatever they said.

Ben seemed to stand up straighter as he went inside and looked neither to the right nor the left as he led her up the aisle to a rather ornate pew at the very front of the church. It was clearly his family pew. Her own family had one similar to it in their own parish church.

She got the impression of murmured comments sweeping through the sparse congregation as she took her place at his side. Naturally she pretended not to notice but went serenely through the routine of kneeling and bowing her head in prayer, and then sitting at Ben's side to wait quietly for the service to begin. Since they were right at the front, she could not see how people reacted to them being there. But she could feel all the eyes boring into the back of her head.

And from Ben's rigid posture and grim expression, so could he.

Chapter Fifteen

It was different, attending church with Daisy on one side and a couple of her servants on the other, from what it had been when he'd sat here with his family. And not only because they were all gone.

As they knelt, and stood, and sang hymns together, their backs resolutely turned to the rest of the congregation, he got a feeling of...not being alone, for once, to face the gossip, and the hostility, and the sniggers.

It stayed with him when the service ended, and they made their way to the porch, where the vicar was standing to bid farewell to the few parishioners he had left.

As Ben and Daisy had been sitting right at the front, they were the last people to leave the dimly lit church. Everyone else who'd attended was already gathering in little groups in the churchyard, gossiping with their particular friends whilst pretending that they weren't waiting to catch sight of him and his wife.

The vicar, to Ben's surprise, held out his hand for him to shake.

'Good to see you in church, my lord,' he said. Ah, so that explained the sudden shift in his attitude. Ben was now the owner of this village, and therefore the church, and had the disposal of the living in his gift. It was in the man's interests to be courteous.

Mrs Knowles, his wife, who'd been in a huddle with the squire and his lady, took a deep breath, then bustled over.

'Indeed, it is good to see you both,' she said, giving them a rather forced smile. It looked as though she would much rather be turning her nose up at them both, and the fact that his newly acquired rank and influence meant she needed to be careful about what she said was leaving a very nasty taste in her mouth. 'And something of a surprise, too. I did not expect you to lower yourself to attend such a poorly attended rustic service as you must find here,' she said, turning her barely suppressed irritation on Daisy.

'Really?' Daisy affected a puzzled frown. 'Whatever gave you the notion that I would take no interest in my husband's people and wish to meet them?'

Mrs Knowles gave an arch little laugh. 'Well, we all know that you are used to much finer things. A much better class of person.'

'My dear,' the vicar began, gravely, 'I did warn you not to take notice of gossip. My wife,' he said apologetically, 'has heard from acquaintances with whom she corresponds that you were a very top-lofty sort of person, my lady. That is why she has not so far plucked up the courage to pay you a courtesy visit. She did not think she would be welcome.'

'Not welcome the wife of the spiritual leader of the parish?' Daisy raised her eyebrows in a gesture of astonishment. 'What nonsense. You must come to tea,' she said to a fiercely blushing and clearly irritated Mrs Knowles. 'I have much to learn about the parish and its inhabitants, and who better to ask about them than you?' She then gave Mrs Knowles the benefit of the kind of smile that probably only Ben could see was rather ironic.

Having thoroughly confounded the vicar's wife, Daisy turned from the porch door to begin making their way down the path.

They were stopped almost at once by the bulky form of Colonel Fairfax, the local squire, with whose wife and daughter Mrs Knowles had been standing.

'Hah. Hmph,' he said. 'Surprised to see you at church, lad. I mean, my lord,' he corrected himself, turning red. 'I…ah…' He glanced at Daisy. 'Felicitations are in order, I see.'

The squire was a blunt sort of fellow so Ben took his words at face value. But his wife was another kettle of fish. While Colonel Fairfax was shaking his hand, Mrs Fairfax was running her eyes over Daisy, pursing her lips in a way that suggested she was totting up how much her hat had cost and guessing that her elegant gown had come from one of the most exclusive London modistes, before lifting her brows at the sight of her shoes, which were still damp from walking through the long grass to get here.

'I heard you had done very well for yourself,' said Mrs Fairfax in a rather scathing tone. If she'd been a

man Ben would have been sorely tempted to plant him
a facer. Even though they were in a churchyard with
the entire population of Bramley Bythorn looking on.
To openly accuse him of marrying Daisy for her money
was such an insult…

'Thank you,' said Daisy sweetly. 'How kind. Mrs…?'

'Colonel and Mrs Fairfax,' said Ben through gritted teeth.

'Fairfax?' Daisy looked around the churchyard
and spotted their daughter, standing nearby, her back
turned, apparently deep in conversation with the vicar's wife. 'I recognise the name. You have a daughter,
I believe?'

Colonel Fairfax smiled. 'Indeed I have. Betsy!' His
parade ground bellow gave his daughter no choice but
to look their way and, when he beckoned, to come over
for an introduction.

Daisy smiled at her as though she had no previous
knowledge of the girl, let alone that she'd seen her hanging round Ben's neck like a limpet. But Miss Fairfax
herself could look neither of them in the face as she
made her curtsey. Daisy's only sign that this was not
in fact their first meeting was the way she clung to his
arm in a manner he couldn't help feeling was a touch
possessive. She kept hold of his arm all the way back
down the village street, nodding and smiling at all the
locals who came to bid her good morning as they went.
For show, of course. It was extremely foolish of him to
wish that she might be doing so out of affection.

'Phew,' she said, once they'd reached the safety of
their own grounds once more. 'I am glad you came with

me. I wouldn't have wanted to face that on my own.'
She gave a mock shudder.

He patted the hand she had tucked through his arm,
then left his hand there, so she would have to tug hard
to release hers. He wasn't ready to let her go just yet. He
was enjoying having her so close far too much to relin-
quish the pleasure of the slight warmth that penetrated
through the sleeve of his jacket. The barely percepti-
ble brush of her skirts against his legs as they walked.

'On reflection,' he admitted, 'it might not have been
so bad had you been on your own. You might have instead met with a great deal of sympathy, for having
been married for money...'

'When I am so notoriously top-lofty about the company I keep,' she added.

'The Fairfax females have clearly been busy,' he
growled. 'Did you see the pair of them prattling away
with Mrs Knowles before the woman came and spoke
so disrespectfully to you?'

'I did.'

'They are what passes for society in these parts,' he
explained. 'So it is obvious that it was they who tried
to malign you in her eyes. For I cannot see how anyone
could have written such unpleasant things about you,
as the vicar claimed.'

'Oh, I can,' she said, flushing slightly, 'if those friends
to whom she wrote were in London for any part of the
Season. I didn't exactly...cover myself in glory, did I?'

He wished he was a bit better at saying clever, sooth-
ing things. This was just the sort of situation where a
cleverer, smoother man would have been able to pour

oil on the troubled waters. Whereas anything he said would be like pouring oil on a naked flame. Because it was true that Daisy had not shown herself to advantage in polite society. Anyone who didn't truly know her might well have thought she was...top-lofty, she'd appeared so cold and withdrawn.

At his side, she heaved a sigh. 'Your silence speaks volumes,' she said. 'And you are right. I behaved very badly. Rather often. Although, in my defence, I would like to explain that at first I did try to make friends. I had never had any before I went to London. Well, you know what it was like at the Priory. A haven for males of all ages, but not exactly the kind of place females would stray into, if they had any sense. Besides which Father actively discouraged females from penetrating the fortifications he'd thrown up around his sons. In case their presence led to...lewd behaviour, I suppose.'

He'd never seen it like that before. But it was true. Daisy's father seemed to have a deep-seated mistrust of females. He'd lectured all his sons on the perils of *lewd beh*aviour, as Daisy put it. And even given *him* a lot of advice about avoiding having casual relations lest it lead to disease.

Daisy might well have become very lonely, and miserable, if she wasn't such a self-sufficient kind of girl. Or if she hadn't found so much solace in her books.

'There were several girls, in London,' Daisy continued, 'who...who pretended they liked me, and wanted to spend time with me. But it didn't take me long to discover that I was just a means to an end. That their interest was in James, and his title. They thought he was a marital prize, you see, for whom any amount of trouble was worth taking. Even to the point of attempting to befriend an awkward, rustic female with whom they had nothing in common.'

Awkward and rustic? He glanced at her sharply. She'd said that with such bitterness, as though somebody had said that to her. Or about her, within her hearing. Lord, but he knew how that felt...overhearing words intended to wound.

'Well,' she continued, with a defiant tilt to her chin, 'after falling for that sort of approach a couple of times I started taking all friendly advances with a hefty pinch of salt.'

He frowned. 'Surely there were girls there with whom you could have...'

She shrugged. 'Possibly. But after a week or so of being courted because I was a way of getting close to James, I... I suppose I threw up my own set of fortifications. And froze everyone out.'

She'd never looked all that happy during her Season. Jasper had said it was because she was shy. But it sounded as though the truth was that she'd kept on getting hurt. And had sealed herself up from risk of it happening too often. And he didn't blame her. He did the same himself.

'I spent so long looking forward to my Season and hoping it would be... I don't know, fun, I suppose. And then after only a week or so all I wanted to do was go home. Where at least, even if I didn't have any friends, I had...'

'Yes?'

'Well, my books.'

'Ah, yes. That was the first place you went, wasn't it? The library. I should have known.'

'And there was Jasper, feeling sorry for me and egging you all on to take pity on me too, and propose...'

She started to walk a bit faster. Anger was driving her, he supposed. Which was typical when she'd just given him such a golden opportunity to explain that he would never have proposed to her out of pity...

'And all that rot,' she said, swiping at a clump of nettles with her parasol, causing a flight of butterflies to erupt into the air in alarm, 'about Lord Martlesham not coming up to scratch...'

'What? But I thought...we all thought...that you were smitten with him. You certainly favoured him above all your other suitors.'

'Other suitors? What other suitors? The only men any of my brothers allowed anywhere near me were their own friends. Boys I had known all my life, and grown to heartily detest!'

Well, that told him, didn't it?

'I mean,' she added hastily, 'not you, Ben, of course. You never joined in those beastly tricks the others delighted in playing on me, did you? Not after the summer of the collar bone.' She looked up at him as though she'd never really seen him before. 'And you never gave away any of my hiding places, which helped me get out of any number of nasty situations. But the rest of them...' The considering look she'd given him vanished as she shuddered in remembrance of what to his friends, had seemed like just high spirts. Horseplay. Fun.

He gazed at her flushed, angry face, wondering. Did she mean, by what she'd said, that she…liked him? No, no, the best he could assume from what she'd just said would be that she didn't heartily detest him. But at least it put him slightly ahead of all the other males she knew.

Except Lord Martlesham. She still hadn't finished explaining about Lord Martlesham.

'Lord Martlesham,' she said, after they'd walked in silence for several yards, his brain seething with so many questions he wanted to ask that he didn't know where to begin, 'just sort of…pushed past my brothers. Defied them. For a while, I looked upon him as a…knight, a champion. Running the gauntlet of their disapproval because he…'

She shook her head. 'Well, he clearly did like me. Or at least, my pedigree, and my fortune. Because he did propose, in the end. But by then it was too late. I'd seen through him, too,' she finished morosely.

Seen through him? 'No, Daisy, I'm sure he didn't only propose because of your wealth, and your title. You are…' So beautiful.

She gave an inelegant snort. 'When he saw me behaving like an icicle? Being a complete…' She shook her head. 'I don't have the words to describe my behaviour. Not words I can utter on a Sunday, anyway. But he couldn't possibly have wanted to marry me because he *liked* me. I mean, what sort of man could possibly fall in love with…with, well, a walking icicle? Which was what I must have seemed like to everyone, if persons I have no recollection of speaking to have written to people I never expected to meet about how top-lofty and unapproachable I am? I didn't like the person I became in London, so how could Lord Martlesham? No, it was very apparent he was only interested in my…my pedigree, for want of a better word. But…' she drew a deep breath '…the thing is, none of that mattered in the end. Because I saw him talking to James one night, and it was as if the scales fell from my eyes.'

'I am sorry, but I don't understand…'

'No, and it isn't easy to explain.' She walked for a few moments, her head down, the only sounds the *frip-frip* of her skirts as she strode through the long grass and the murmur of the servants who were dawdling along behind. 'You see, when I met him, he seemed so…elegant, and charming, and cultured. He said all the right things to me and behaved with total correctness. And he was so handsome, too. I started thinking that he was different. Just like a hero out of a book,' she said dreamily.

'And then, one night,' she said, with a shake of her head, 'I saw him standing next to James, and they were laughing about something. Some shared joke, I suppose. And it hit me. James looked charming, and elegant, and civilised, in his evening clothes, too. And when he was in a ballroom, he behaved properly.

'But I knew it was only a façade. A façade, I suddenly saw, that Lord Martlesham was putting on as well. And then I looked around at all the rest of you. And how you *all* pretended to be civilised beings when you were in a ballroom. And I knew, I just knew, that Lord Martlesham wasn't any different at all. I knew that when he'd been a boy, he'd pushed girls into ponds, and got into fist fights with other boys, and revelled in rolling about in mud and getting black eyes and split lips. And that he probably still went to mills, the way you all do, and cock fights, and all those other horrid pastimes that so thrill my brothers.

'That he was, in short, merely an…an ape in elegant clothing. Who would be far happier swigging from a brandy bottle and swinging from a tree branch than reading a book or conducting a meaningful conversation. And so, when he asked me, in an extremely lukewarm fashion might I add… I couldn't. I just couldn't. And, oh, he was so cross with me. And Father accused me of leading him on, which was, to my shame, perfectly true… And said he wasn't going to waste any more of his money or his time hanging around London just for me to turn my nose up at any more matrimonial prizes…'

He stepped in front of her and caught her by the upper arms. 'Daisy, I am so sorry. I had no idea. I thought you… I really thought you liked him.' It had been eating him up inside. But she wasn't hankering after Lord Martlesham. She wasn't mourning an unrequited love. On the contrary, she'd spurned the man because all of a sudden he'd reminded her of an ape! A lukewarm ape, at that.

This meant he didn't have a rival for her affections. Even if she did resent the fact she'd had to marry him, she wasn't pining for any other man. And what was more, he recalled, a lot of the anger she'd displayed on her wedding day hadn't been directed at him at all.

It had been the slugs.

'I still don't understand why your father had to re-move you from London, though,' he said, since he didn't think it would be appropriate to throw back his head and let out a yell of triumph when what she'd told him had clearly made her very unhappy. 'Surely there was plenty of time for you to meet someone you could...' He swallowed back the word *love*. He couldn't bear to think of her loving anyone else. He didn't know how he could have even got to the verge of saying it.

Except he wanted her to be happy. He'd thought so far that he would never be able to make her happy. That there were too many factors ranged against him. But it turned out that some of what he'd thought he was up against had only been a case of a fleeting infatuation, and slugs, after all.

And she'd also just admitted that she didn't detest him as heartily as she detested every other male she'd ever known.

He was, by default, the clear front runner.

'It would have been no use staying in London,' she said, gazing up at him mournfully, while out of the corner of his eye he noticed Vale and Marcie taking a wide berth as they passed by. 'Father was right. I would never have been able to agree to marry any man I'd met under those circumstances. I wouldn't have been able to trust him. Marrying you, the way it all happened, was probably the only way he would ever have got me off his hands.'

Got her off his hands? How could her father have made her feel as though she was a burden to be got rid of like that? Damn him!

'I'm just sorry *you* are lumbered with me now,' she began.

'Lumbered with you? Daisy, I...' He sucked in a deep breath as he considered what to say. And breathed in her scent. And then he became aware of how close to each other they were standing. And how she was gazing up at him with sorrow and trust in her eyes.

And how much he wanted her.

And how long he'd wanted her.

And that he had no rival.

And that she was his wife.

And he couldn't behave like a gentleman any longer.

He pulled her close and kissed her. Rather clumsily, because he wasn't used to kissing beautiful women. Or any women, come to that. And because he'd seized the chance before he could think better of it and talk himself out of it.

She gasped in surprise.

He braced himself against the moment when she pushed him away or slapped his face.

But it never came.

Instead, she went pliant in his arms, and tipped her head to one side, so that their noses were no longer getting in the way. Which meant that he could kiss her more deeply. More thoroughly.

With predictable results. He became so hard, so swiftly, that it was almost painful. All he wanted to do was push her down in the long grass and make her his.

He groaned. He could just imagine what would follow if he slaked his lust, like an animal, outdoors, with a girl who'd just told him she thought men were all savages. He'd confirm her opinion. He'd never be able to get anywhere near her, ever again.

She might even hate him if, in his haste, he hurt her as well as humbled her.

He had to draw back. He had to.

Chapter Sixteen

It was one of the most difficult things he'd ever done. Physically.

But when he looked down into her face, half dreading what he might see there, he was glad he'd stopped, even though he wasn't sure how he'd manage to walk home with so much of his blood throbbing between his legs.

Because she was looking up at him in wonder. As though…as though…

'Ben,' she breathed, on a whisper. 'Does that mean… that you *do* want to make our marriage work? Now that you've had time to think it through?'

'Yes,' he grunted. Amazed that he could even form one word, containing as much as a whole syllable, when the most primitive part of him was stealing so much of his ability to behave like a decent human being.

She beamed up at him. 'Oh, I'm so glad,' she said. 'I really do think,' she added, somehow turning him so that he was at her side, before steering him along the path they'd trampled through the grass on their way to church, 'that we can do a lot of good together.'

He stumbled along at her side, his whole body throbbing with the way it had felt to hold her in his arms, her whole body pressed up against his, her hands upon his shoulders, her lips moving, in sweet response, beneath his own. He could hear her chattering on about plans for transforming the houses in the village, creating jobs, and sending messages to the villagers who'd already left, letting them know that things would be different. While all he could think about was that the first time he kissed her should have been in a rose arbour, or at a ball, with music playing in the background, not in the middle of a field on the way back from church.

After a few minutes of admiring the animation in her lovely face while she shared her ideas with him, his head began to clear. And two things dawned on him. The first was that all her happiness centred on what they could achieve together, in the district, with her money, and that she really seemed excited by the prospect that she could be useful, instead of merely decorative.

The second was that although she hadn't been repulsed by his kiss, she hadn't enjoyed it so much she'd wanted to have another one. When he'd broken off before he plunged into the abyss of unforgiveable behaviour, she'd neatly manoeuvred him so that they were now walking side by side, rather than standing face to face.

'Don't you think?' She was smiling up at him in an expectant way, as if waiting for his answer. He rapidly reviewed the things she'd been saying while he'd been wrestling his body back under control. Things that had filtered through, to an extent, or he wouldn't have been aware of how excited she was to be able to do something constructive with her dowry.

'I have had some thoughts of my own,' he decided to tell her. 'Since we came here I have spent a great deal of time riding the estates, and talking to what tenants there are left, and seeking their opinions.' Much of which he could not repeat, or not to her, anyway.

'The tenants who have stayed on,' he continued, 'are the older ones, or those who cannot face the prospect of moving to another town and looking for work that would prove to be arduous.' Or a few outlying farmers who were too belligerent to meekly move out, even after being threatened with eviction for refusing to pay the ridiculously high rent increases the Fourth Earl had attempted to impose. Those who'd met him with shotguns in their hands and desperation in their eyes, swearing they'd as soon hang for murder as see their families turned off the land and out of their homes to starve for no good reason. But he wasn't about to tell Daisy about them and cause her any alarm. He'd reassured them he was cut from a different cloth from their previous landlord. Which none of them found hard to believe. At least, none of them had actually shot him, had they? 'Which means there is a real scarcity of men to do the heavy work in the village or the Park, such as repairing roofs, and walls, and fences, or digging drainage ditches or even mowing this meadow until it resembles the lawn it once was.'

'So we need to get strong, able-bodied men to come here, then. How do you think we might do that? Do we advertise in London? Or...'

'No. I was thinking of contacting the regiment. Many ex-soldiers find it hard to find work, especially if they are disfigured.'

She frowned. 'But I thought you said we needed to find able-bodied men. Oh, not that I am against trying to help wounded ex-soldiers, it is just...'

'Well, we would have to select men who can do something. Men who are, also, desperate to find any kind of work, and prepared to live anywhere. We could offer a married man with children one of the houses in the village that stands empty, in return for repairing it, and...a few light tasks on the estate...'

They began to discuss various enterprises, and by the time they got back to the house they had created, in their imaginations, a sort of workers' paradise.

'I don't suppose any of it will come to pass,' he said heavily as he opened the kitchen door for her to go through.

'I don't see why not,' she said, over her shoulder as she went inside. He half closed his eyes, breathing in the scent of her, leaning in to catch every last atom of it. 'You are too inclined to look on the dark side, Ben.' Of course he was. He'd seen it. In fact, he'd seen little else.

She tipped her head to one side. 'I swear I could count the number of times I've seen you smile on the fingers of one hand.'

'As many as that?'

She shook her head in mock reproof, before undoing the ribbons of her bonnet. And proceeded to tease him, all the way through the meal that Mrs Green and Sally had stayed behind to prepare.

He had no idea how to react. On the one hand, it was wonderful that she was talking to him for the first time, properly, since they'd married. On the other…why, oh, why wasn't he the sort of man who could respond to her playful banter in kind? Who was less serious? Who could smile easily, and laugh and make jokes?

He could barely eat the wholesome food Sergeant Wilmot had dished up, he was in such turmoil. He was either shaking with the force of waves of desire that kept sweeping through him every time she smiled at him playfully. Or he was drowning in despair at the casual way she'd suggested they ought to spend her money doing good to other people, since they couldn't be happy with each other.

And then he'd remember the softness of her lips under his own, the curves of her slender body where he'd held her tightly, and he'd have no idea what everyone else at the table was laughing at.

And then, all of a sudden, Vale was getting to his feet and saying that, yes, he had no objection to starting out now, and Wilmot was standing up as well, and saying he'd give him a hand.

'On a Sunday?' Mrs Green was the only one who seemed to object to whatever it was that the two men had decided to do. Which was ironic since she'd chosen to stay here cooking their dinner rather than going with them to church.

'Well, it's a lovely afternoon,' said Vale. 'And all

we'll be doing is strolling around the orchard, seeing what can be salvaged. Won't be doing any lifting today.'

The furniture. They'd made some plans to rescue some of the furniture the late Earl had been so determined to deny him.

Daisy cleared her throat. 'I thought, if you don't object,' she said to Ben, 'that while Vale and Wilmot and Marcie and Sally take a walk through the furniture orchard, we could take a look around the stables and other outbuildings, and see which ones we could use for storage, and which could be turned into workshops.'

She was proposing they spend the afternoon together? Without Marcie and her footman dogging their footsteps? 'I don't object,' he said swiftly. And basked in the warmth of the smile she turned on him.

'You don't think,' she said, once the men had gone to the orchard, and they were on their way to the stables, 'that I am being silly? I noticed that you didn't say anything about the suggestions I made at lunch. And although I am grateful that you didn't pour cold water on them in front of the others, I would truly appreciate it if you…prevented me from making a colossal fool of myself.'

He didn't like the way she assumed he'd think her ideas foolish. But on reflection he supposed he hadn't said anything to make her think otherwise. It was about time he made more of an effort to speak up. He had to get over the feeling that he wouldn't be able to form three coherent words in the correct order whenever he was near her. She wasn't an unattainable goddess, who'd turn her nose up at him and stalk away or mock him for his clumsiness any longer. She was his wife. And she *wanted* to know what he thought. She'd asked him, hadn't she?

He cleared his throat. 'Getting the furniture under cover before it deteriorates any further is not a silly idea at all. I should have thought of it myself.'

She breathed out on what sounded like a sigh of relief.

'The truth, I suppose,' or part of it, anyway, 'is that there is so much neglect and deliberate damage to undo that I haven't known where to start. The more I have discovered, the bigger the task seems, and therefore the more impossible to achieve anything at all.' Although he had made some headway with some of the tenant farmers, hadn't he? He'd managed to persuade them that he had no intention of evicting them, or keeping the rents at a level they couldn't afford to pay, or prosecuting them for turning their weapons on him.

'Perhaps,' she said as they reached the stables, and she peered into an empty stall, 'some of those wounded ex-soldiers might have skills in carpentry, or furniture restoration, or something of the sort.'

'Hmm.' That was a possibility. He'd never ceased to be amazed at the skills the men serving under him had displayed, even though they'd preferred to put them to some nefarious ends. 'And some of the wives would have no trouble digging ditches or climbing up on roofs to repair the thatch. Army wives are a tough breed.'

She turned to him, and giggled. 'Oh, dear. It sounds as if we may be on the brink of creating a totally revolutionary settlement, where the men will sit inside sewing and baking, while the women go out digging ditches!'

'You would like that, wouldn't you?' He stepped to one side as she made to leave the stall, blocking her path. 'You would like to overturn the dominance of men.'

She looked up at him thoughtfully. 'I had never really thought about it. Not in that way. I mean, I have resented my father and my brothers sometimes, but...'

A shaft of sunlight was caressing her hair, making it glow like a million candle flames. She was so beautiful she took his breath away. And all he'd have to do was put his arm out, and he could pull her in and he could kiss her again. And she wouldn't object, not to judge by the way she'd responded earlier.

So he did. And she didn't. Instead, she melted against him, put her arms round his neck and moved her lips against his. Which she hadn't tried to do before. As if...

'Has no man ever kissed you before, Daisy?' He couldn't believe it. She was so lovely, every man in London must have tried to get her alone.

She shook her head with a little grimace of distaste.

'I have never let any male get me into a situation where it might be possible,' she said. 'Urgh.'

And yet she hadn't objected to him kissing her. Had just tried, shyly, to kiss him back.

And had been furious that he hadn't gone to her bed on their wedding night.

His heart thudded thickly. Tonight, he promised himself. He was going to give her the wedding night he had not dared to attempt before. Even though she'd predicted they might never be happy together, right now her body was his for the taking. She could not be telling him more clearly, without coming outright and saying it, that she wanted to know what it meant to be a married woman. Even if the husband she'd ended up with was him.

And he was more than willing to oblige.

Daisy's heart was thundering so hard she was surprised Ben couldn't feel it. And she was shaking. Because she'd done it! She'd managed to get him to kiss her. Not once, but twice!

She wasn't a total failure as a woman after all. She did have what it took to make a man…desire her. Enough to kiss her, anyway. The first time had been hard work. She'd racked her brains to recall the things Mother had advised her she could do to bag the man she'd set her sights on, and had come up with the ruse of clinging to his arm and shamelessly pressing her breast against his upper arm. Because Mother had said that breasts were a woman's most potent weapon. During her London Season she had observed that men did, indeed, look at them far more than they ever looked at her face. And it had made her wish to keep them covered up at all times. But with Ben…

And then she'd shared things with him she'd never told anyone else. Aroused all his protective instincts. And looked at him with what she hoped was a sort of feminine helplessness, as though he, and he alone, could save her.

But this time all she'd had to do was smile at him.

Right into his face, after acting as though she was interested in every word that dropped from his mouth. Just as Mother had said.

Although it hadn't been an act, really, had it? She had come to trust him enough to share things with him she hadn't shared with anyone else. Because it was Ben. Ben who never uttered three words if he could express what he meant with a sarcastic grimace instead. But when Ben did decide to talk, the things he said *were* interesting. He never wasted his breath saying anything unless he had something worth saying.

She sighed happily as she recalled the things he'd said about her ideas. He hadn't dismissed them, saying she didn't know what she was talking about, the way Father would have done. Or laughed at her and tweaked her nose, the way her brothers would have done. Instead, he had, in his turn, shared his own thoughts with her.

He made her feel…he made her…

'Ben,' she sighed up at him. He really did seem to like her, as a person. Or he couldn't have shared his thoughts with her, could he? He was usually so quiet, so withdrawn.

'Daisy,' he grated, and pulled her roughly up against his chest, again. And devoured her mouth as though he was starving. To her surprise she felt something that hadn't been there before. Something like a pipe, pushing against her stomach. She knew, in theory, what it was. Her brothers were always making crude jokes about flagstaffs and suchlike. But this was the first time a man had had that reaction because of her.

It had taken a week, and a great deal of determination, but she'd done it. She'd got Ben to see her as a woman, not a silly, petulant child.

She felt like thanking her mother for all the tips she'd given her about drawing a man into her net. And apologising for the way she'd behaved when Mother had been giving her that advice, declaring she'd never stoop to such tactics. And why would she, when the last thing she wanted was a husband?

Ah, but it was different now she *had* a husband, wasn't it? Especially since she didn't want that other woman to give him what he ought to be getting from his wife.

Chapter Seventeen

Ben paused on the threshold of what had once been the Fourth Earl's room, a lifetime of knowing he had no right to walk in here seizing him by the scruff of the neck. But after only a moment or two it began to relax its grip. Because this was not the Fourth Earl's room any longer. The Fourth Earl was dead.

And Daisy had made it her own, by moving some of the heavier, darker furniture out, and moving what was left into new positions. There was no longer a shaving stand by the window but a dressing table, covered with all sorts of feminine paraphernalia. Bottles, pots, brushes, and so forth. And it smelled of her. That light perfume that never ceased to make him slightly giddy with desire.

But, best of all, she was sitting up in the ancient four-poster bed, smiling at him, even though she'd looked slightly surprised when he'd first opened the door.

She was his wife, he reminded himself as he closed the door softly behind him. He had the right to get into the bed she'd made her own. No, more than that, she *wanted* him to give her the wedding night she'd accused him of denying her, when he'd assumed he had been sparing her an ordeal.

His heart pounded as he stalked across the room, his eyes fixed on her lovely face. Although he was aware that her legs were decorously covered by sheets and a coverlet. He'd taken in every detail of her while he'd been standing in the doorway, assessing her reaction to his approach.

She was wearing a blue silk gown so fine that he could see the shadows of her nipples through it. Nipples he wanted to take in his mouth and suckle.

He reached the bed and pulled back the covers. The silk nightgown was rumpled round her calves, revealing her slender feet and delicate toes. Toes that looked as though some great master had carved them out of marble. He might have known she'd have perfect feet. Everything about her was perfect. And he wanted to see…everything. Every exquisite inch of her. Even if her heart never belonged to him, this, this much, was his…

'I want to see you,' he heard himself grate. And was immediately shocked that he'd voiced that thought aloud.

But Daisy didn't seem to mind. Because, albeit shyly, her fingers went to the ribbon ties at her bosom and began fumbling them loose.

'All of you,' he admitted, greedily. If this night was all he ever had of her, he was damn well going to make the most of it.

'I suppose that's fair,' she said threadily. 'After all, I have seen you. Without asking permission. I...' She faltered into silence, blushing as he pulled his shirt over his head and shucked off his breeches.

Growing impatient with the time it was taking her to undo her gown, he replaced his hands at her neckline, and just ripped the flimsy garment, all the way down, so that it spread to each side of her pale, slender body like the wings of a butterfly.

She gasped. Her hands fluttered to her breasts, as though to cover them. Then to the triangle of pale curls where her thighs met, as though unsure what she was most determined to protect from him.

He could not move to prevent her. He could not move a muscle. She was every bit as beautiful as he'd always known she would be. A goddess of alabaster and gold.

No, not a goddess. He'd learned that much since marrying her. Or at least she was a goddess with feet of clay. She had a temper, and could be cutting when provoked. Although weren't the goddesses of myth prone to wreak vengeance on mere mortals who'd offended them?

And the only way to appease them was to worship them. Which he fully intended to do. And it wasn't blasphemous to think of this, what he was about to do, as an act of worship. Hadn't he, at some point in the marriage service, vowed to worship her body with his own?

He knelt beside the bed, the way a mere mortal should when approaching a goddess, reached over to take her foot and then kissed every single one of her perfect little toes. He stroked the arches of her feet, before encircling her ankle with kisses, while his hand slid up her calves.

He could feel muscle beneath the velvety soft skin he was caressing. Muscles that told him she was not weak, or delicate, though she was so slender. He could feel them bunching and trembling as she shifted her legs restlessly. Impatiently? Lord, he hoped so. But he wasn't going to rush this. Even though she'd told him she wanted this, and had welcomed him to her room, her bed, with a smile, he was determined to make absolutely certain her body was ready, too.

He would wait until her legs were not just shifting but opening, inviting, needing him to move between them. Until she was beside herself with desire.

Thank God he hadn't come into this marriage *pure*, as her father had hoped. Thank goodness he had some experience of how to work his way round a woman's body.

He climbed onto the bed, and took her hand, the one she was using to cover her breasts, and raised it to his mouth. And he kissed each finger, the palm of her hand, her wrist, the soft skin on her forearm…

'Ben,' she whispered.

Which made him raise his gaze to her mouth. And then lower his head to hers. While he kissed her he came down next to her, using his free arm to wrap round her waist so that he could feel the whole length of her pressed close to the length of him. It was almost too much. His need was so great that he almost came to a spend right then, just at the feel of her soft thigh against his own.

He moved back so that there was an inch or two of air between them, so that it didn't finish before it even began. He'd already waited for years, without any hope that he'd ever reach this place. He could wait a few minutes longer. No, however long it took. As he'd already vowed. For there would be no pleasure for him if she wasn't with him all the way. In this, physical act, if nowhere else.

So he began by tracing the outline of her breast. With his hand first, and then his mouth, suckling gently, breathing in the scent of her skin now, as well as the floral scent she used.

And then, as he'd promised himself, he worshipped every inch of her glorious body. Learning as he went what she liked. So that he could arouse her.

She was responsive. Beautifully responsive. She came to a peak of pleasure twice before he could no longer hold himself back. Before he finally laid claim to her, making her his wife in deed. By taking his own pleasure deep inside her in a release so powerful he shouted aloud in triumph. Before being torn by a wave of emotion so raw he almost wept with it.

Instead, he buried his face in the pillow, next to her face, lest she see how she'd unmanned him.

Daisy gazed, in awe at the man who lay half-sprawled across her, his ragged breathing gradually slowing. She had never, in all her life, imagined that a man could make her feel so...utterly amazing.

So amazing she could actually see the point in marrying, if this was what it was all about.

And to think that it was Ben who'd brought her to this place of…she wriggled…utter contentment. She wanted to hug him, although it was evident he was sliding into sleep, from the way his body was slackening and his breathing growing deeper. And she didn't want to disturb him. It would seem ungrateful, after all the work he'd put in.

A little smile tugged at her mouth, though, as she recalled the way he'd looked at her as he'd stalked across the room to the bed. The intent look on his face. Although she hadn't been able to resist taking a swift glance at the rest of him once he'd pulled off his shirt. It was true that she'd seen him before, but that had only been from a distance, and by moonlight.

Later, when they'd been in the boat, she'd had to keep her eyes firmly fixed anywhere but on him, in case he thought she was…admiring all those muscles. But she had no longer cared if he did think she was admiring his muscles. It was a completely different situation, with him deliberately removing his shirt and standing over her. The sight of his firm, powerful body had made her mouth run dry. He was different, she'd noted, with the tones of his skin and hair warmly lit by candles. And he was no longer just one of her brother's friends either.

The thought of what was about to happen had made her fingers clumsy. Which had made him lose his patience with her. Though not in a bad way. On the contrary, it had been terribly thrilling when he'd just taken hold of the gown and torn it in two. It had made her feel…irresistible.

Oh, dear, though, she'd have to explain the torn gown to Marcie in the morning.

Well, never mind, they'd probably have a little giggle about it. That was what had made her insist on promoting Marcie, after all, wasn't it? The fact that she had that irreverent sense of humour.

Ben was almost certainly asleep now. But Daisy was still too full of awe, and shock, though it was a pleasant sort of shock. More than pleasant.

Though Ben, slack with sleep, was rather heavy. And the sweat that was cooling on her skin made her want to pull the covers over herself.

'Ben,' she whispered, giving his shoulder a little nudge.

He mumbled something indistinct.

'Ben,' she said again, a little louder. Then nudged him more firmly.

He turned his head into her neck and breathed deeply. 'Daisy,' he murmured.

'Yes,' she said firmly. 'And I'm not a cushion. Could you just…' She gave him a harder shove, managing to dislodge him sufficiently to be able to grab the edge of a sheet, which she drew up over them both, before settling down next to her husband.

Her husband. She sighed. She was a married woman now. Properly married. And even though it was the last thing she'd wanted just a few weeks ago, right at this moment she felt as though she might be one of the luckiest women in England.

Chapter Eighteen

Ben came to with a start. He was half-sprawled across Daisy, who was lying flat on her back, looking most uncomfortable, and clearly cold. Well, what else should she be when he'd managed to get all the covers wrapped round himself?

God, he was a selfish bastard. Her first time, and instead of checking to make sure she was fine after her initiation into marriage, what had he done? Passed out in a surfeit of sexual pleasure. And then, in his sleep, stolen all the covers from her, leaving her chilled and… *vulnerable*.

He sat up, untangling himself from the sheets and draping them carefully over her body. Catching sight, as he did so, of the remains of her nightgown. Lord, if she hadn't hated him before, she must surely do so now. He'd been so greedy for her he'd ripped it from her body like some…marauding soldier after conquering a besieged citadel. After all those nights he'd spent comparing her to a city he was preparing to besiege, perhaps it was no wonder.

But what damage might he have done? Daisy had *told* him she thought men were savages, cloaked by only the flimsiest veneer of civilisation. And he'd just proved her right.

He slid, crablike, from the bed, fumbled for the clothes he'd cast to the floor last night and fled from the room without stopping to put them on. It was not yet fully light outside. The servants wouldn't be up and about yet. So he wasn't going to shock any of them by wandering naked along the corridors.

He ran down the stairs, making it to the relative safety of his study, which was also his bedroom, without running into anyone. He went straight to the desk, where he'd been putting out a pitcher of water every night, took his washcloth from the top drawer of the desk where he kept it, and swiftly cleansed himself.

But it wasn't enough. He needed to…to get outside. Somewhere he could be on his own. To mull over what had happened, what he'd done, and come to terms with it without having to deal with anyone else.

And work out how he was going to face Daisy, after the way he'd…used her.

Daisy woke feeling a bit cold. And a bit sore. And a bit confused. She'd been so lovely and warm all night, with Ben's large body next to hers. But now the space next to her was cold.

She rolled to her side and couldn't help smiling when she saw the imprint of his head in the pillow. She leaned into it, sniffing the scent he'd left behind. Her smile grew wider still when it struck her that before leaving he'd draped the covers, the covers which he'd hogged to himself while asleep, over her so that she wouldn't get cold without him to snuggle up to.

Ah, Ben! He was so sweet. So considerate.

She rolled onto her back, and raised her arms over her head, stretching her whole body. A body that felt somehow different today. A body that she would never be able to think of in exactly the same way after what Ben had taught her about it last night.

The sun was shining again today, she could see through the chinks in the curtains. It was going to be another glorious day.

She got out of bed and rang for Marcie, her mood so sunny that she didn't care what the maid might say about her ruined nightgown. She had plenty more, after all. Ben could rip one off her every night as far as she was concerned. And when he'd gone through what she had she'd just buy some more.

She was still smiling when, later, she reached the kitchen. Which was empty.

'Where is…everyone?' She meant Ben, of course, but wasn't going to give herself away by appearing so keen to know exactly where he was and what he was doing when so far she'd taken such pains to snub him. She might feel very differently about him, and about herself, too, but she had no intention of turning into one of those women who trotted about after a man like some spaniel at the heel of an adored master. The way Mother so often did with Father. She suppressed a shudder. That would never happen to her. Apart from her own determination to never sink to that level, Ben was nothing like Father. Or...or any other male she'd ever known.

He was unique.

'They've all had breakfast hours ago,' said Mrs Green from her place at the stove where she was stirring something in a big, blackened pot. 'All except His Lordship, who never showed at all. Gone off somewhere, his man reckons.'

'Gone?' A chill flooded her, replacing all the glowing warmth in which she'd been basking ever since waking up. Gone where? Gone out on some business about the estate? Or just...gone?

Now that she considered his behaviour last night, there had been something grim about the way he'd paused on the threshold of the room, looking around it, looking at everything but her. And then something determined about the way he'd stalked across to her bed. And now she came to think of it, although he'd taken her to heights of delirious pleasure, several times, he'd only experienced such a peak once. And had then, instead of hugging her, or speaking to her, or reassuring her, fallen straight to sleep. As if the effort of giving her the wedding night she'd practically demanded of him had exhausted him.

Had her needy behaviour, her downright lustful response sickened him so much he could not bear to look at her this morning?

'Thought you wasn't coming down for breakfast,' said Mrs Green, her spoon poised in mid-air. 'I can fry you some eggs if you like...'

Her stomach roiled at the mere mention of them. 'No, thank you. Just…some bread and jam will be fine.' There was always plenty of fresh bread about. And she could eat it swiftly and leave the kitchen without having to attempt to make any sort of conversation whilst worrying that Ben might have been so disgusted by the way she'd…rolled round the bed, moaning and sighing, and running her hands all over his back, and, yes, at one point when all her senses had deserted her, digging her nails into his buttocks like one of the sort of women Father was always warning her brothers to avoid like the plague, that he'd gone. Left not only the bed but the house.

Oh, no. Might he have even completely gone? He'd talked about leaving, hadn't he? She'd assumed he'd changed his mind, and decided to stay, but could last night have changed his mind back again?

'Vale,' said Mrs Green, turning back to her pot, 'has started carrying what furniture he thinks can be mended into the barn.'

'That is good,' she said absentmindedly, slathering butter onto a slice of bread. 'I'll take this out and go and see how he's getting on,' she added, it suddenly occurring to her that the stables were on the way to the barn. And while she was passing she could see if Ben's horse was still there. Which she had to do, as soon as humanly possible. And it would save a lot of time if she ate her bread and jam on the way rather than sitting at the table as though she had all day.

Heart lurching, she tried to make it look as if she

hadn't a care in the world as she made her way to the stables.

It was such a relief to see his horse in its stall that she could have kissed it. Because if the horse was there, then Ben was still about, *somewhere*. She just had to find him.

And...say what? Demand to know why he'd left her bed, rather than hug and kiss her in the morning, the way Mother said a man did when he was pleased with his wife?

The alternative, though, was to avoid him. And she'd already done far too much of that so far in this marriage. If they stood any chance of building a lasting, solid relationship, one of them was going to have to grasp the proverbial bull by the horns and discuss what they'd done last night. Or at least, she amended, feeling a flush sweep her entire body, discuss what it meant to them. Clear the air.

Because there was something amiss. A man didn't sneak out of his wife's bed the morning after making her his own and hide from her, and, more importantly, skip breakfast, unless there was some sort of problem. And it wouldn't be a case of trotting after him like a spaniel. Because she wasn't going to roll over and beg him to...well, beg in *any* fashion. She was going to... to stand up for what she wanted, that was what she was going to do. And that meant talking about things. She'd learned that much already during the short time they'd been married.

Another thing she'd learned during the days she'd been intent on avoiding him so that she hadn't *had* to talk to him was his daily routine. About this time in the mornings he usually dealt with his correspondence and other paperwork in his study. So that would be the most likely place to find him. If he really hadn't left her.

She could go and peep through the window to check, a cowardly part of her suggested. But that would smack too much of the behaviour of that other woman who'd come sneaking around Ben. And she was not going to descend to that level. She had every right to go and speak to Ben whenever she wished! He was her husband. So she strode back into the house, made her way along the corridor to his study and knocked on the door, waiting, this time, for his deep voice to reply, before pushing it open. He may be her husband, but she had learned her lesson the last time she'd burst in here. Not that she expected him to be kissing another woman today, not after what they'd done last night. Or even the same one. No, not at all. Because he'd explained it all to her. And she'd believed him. It was just…

'Yes?'

Her knees went weak with relief. He was there. Going about his business as usual. Perhaps it was only in her head that there was a problem.

Or was it? A man didn't skip breakfast for no good reason.

Timidly, she pushed open the door and stepped inside. Ben was sitting at his desk, papers and writing implements strewn about, and his thick, dark hair in disorder as though he'd been running his fingers through it. The way she had done last night when he'd been trailing kisses down her stomach…

The thought made her blush. It was all she could do
to look him in the eye. And when she did, it was to see
a wary expression in his.

Wary? Why should he be wary?

Although…she had flounced around in a strop for
the first few days of their marriage, hadn't she? And
made him think she was angry with him…which she
had been, though not at first…

She drew a deep breath. Yes, it was past time they
cleared the air.

'Good morning,' she said. 'I hope I am not disturb-
ing you?' The way she had done last time she'd come
in here and caught him with that woman draped round
his neck. Perhaps it was not wise of her to remind him
of that moment because his shoulders tensed up. And
the quill pen, which he was clutching in his fingers,
twitched as though he'd suddenly gripped it more tightly.

'Not at all,' he replied politely, his face devoid of
expression now.

Oh, Ben. She'd really put him through the wringer,
hadn't she? So it was up to her to reassure him that she
hadn't come to start a fight.

'Mrs Green said you didn't have any breakfast. Shall
I bring you something? Some bread and jam? Coffee?'

He blinked. The pen fell from his fingers, making an
ugly blot on whatever it was he'd been writing.

'Oh, dear,' she said, shutting the door behind her
and approaching the desk. 'I did not mean to, er…' She
peered into his face, trying to work out what he might
be thinking. As usual, though, it was impossible to tell.
Although it never looked as if it was anything good.

During his teen years he had perfected the art of keeping a cynical, if not downright morose expression on his face nearly all the time.

He drew in a deep breath. Sat up straight. 'I am at your complete disposal. Whatever you have to say,' he said, reaching for some blotting paper and dabbing at the document, which meant that he wasn't looking at her at all any longer, as though he was unwilling to meet her eye, 'I will...' All of a sudden he got to his feet. 'I beg your pardon, I should have...the moment you came in... Forgot my manners...'

'It doesn't matter.' He was plainly so agitated she forgot her own nerves in an overwhelming urge to soothe him. 'I can see that I surprised you. Though I cannot imagine why. I am your wife after all. It is my job to make sure you have breakfast, isn't it?' Although she had never done so before. It had never crossed her mind to wonder if he'd eaten. Oh, but she had been such a bad wife so far. No wonder Ben didn't know what to make of her coming here today.

'I just...' She trailed her finger along the edge of the desk. Now it came to it, it wasn't so easy to broach the question of why he'd fled from her bed and given every appearance of a man who was avoiding his wife.

'Actually, I am glad you've come,' he said. 'Because I need to apologise.' He stood straighter. 'And it is better to do so here, where nobody can overhear.'

'Apologise? What for?'

'For last night.' His face darkened. 'I was not...that is, I did not...' He ran his fingers through his hair. 'Dammit, Daisy, I shouldn't have...'

'Got up and left me? Sneaked out in the dark?'

'What? No, not that. I mean, I couldn't face you in daylight without…' He made a gesture that somehow made her understand he was talking about their state of undress.

'Why could you not face me in daylight? Did I…? I did wonder if I'd done something wrong…'

'You? No! *You* did nothing wrong. It was me. I was utterly selfish. I behaved like a brute, ripping your nightgown…'

Her nightgown. He was ashamed of having ripped her nightgown off.

A smile tugged at her lips as a giddy sensation of relief fizzed through her.

'Actually,' she admitted, 'I found that rather…thrilling.' Because she could absolutely not let him think she hadn't liked it when she'd been going over that moment over and over again this morning as she'd been getting dressed, mentally planning a shopping list to replace items she sincerely hoped he was going to rip off her on a regular basis.

'You…' He sat down heavily. 'Thrilling?'

'Yes. But the way you…vanished in the middle of the night made me wonder if something I had done had given you a disgust of me. I mean, I wouldn't blame you. I behaved so childishly when we were first married. And then the moment you came to my bed I… well…' She could feel the blood rushing to her cheeks, but she was determined not to give up, no matter how embarrassing this conversation was for her. 'I wasn't very ladylike, was I?'

'You...' He got up, came round the desk, and grasped her hands. 'You did nothing wrong. You were perfect. More than I deserved. Especially since I know I was not the man you wanted to marry.'

'I didn't want to marry anyone, Ben. I just wanted to stay in my library, reading my books, and for everyone to leave me alone.'

'Yes, I know,' he said, raising one hand to his mouth and kissing the knuckles. 'And I am so sorry that Walter and Horace forced us into a situation where you had no choice in the matter. To have to marry me, of all men...' He trailed off, shaking his head ruefully.

'Of all men? What do you mean?'

His eyes flicked to one side. Then he gestured to his face. 'Well, for one thing I am so ugly. Oh, I know I have always looked like a frog,' he said, referring to his rather wide mouth, she supposed. 'But since Salamanca I have looked like a frog that has been dropped in a tub of acid,' he said bitterly.

'Oh, Ben, you should know me better than to believe my opinion of you is based on how you look.' She stroked his face, gently tracing the scars that puckered the left side of his cheek. He shut his eyes, breathing in on a gasp, as if he couldn't believe she would voluntarily choose to touch his scars.

Goodness. She had never considered before that other people might have insecurities because of the way they looked. She hadn't thought it mattered to men. Beauty was a factor for women to consider, but men...

'But if you must know, you have never looked any uglier, in my opinion, than any of my brothers' other friends.' No, that wasn't enough. She sounded as if she was confirming his belief that she must think him ugly. She needed to nip that thought in the bud right now. She couldn't say that it didn't matter. He wouldn't believe it. She had to tell him something that he could believe. Hold onto. 'In fact, when I saw you in London, in your uniform, I thought you looked very…manly.'

'Manly?' He looked into her eyes with suspicion, as if half expecting her to declare he was a fool if he could believe such a thing.

'Yes. The first time I saw you, at the Danverses' ball, my heart fluttered.'

'It did not.'

'It did.'

'But…if… Then why did you never smile at me? Or give me some sign…?'

'I do have my pride, you know. It is not my style to cast out lures to men who make it blatantly obvious they are not interested. Which you did. In spades. You made no effort at all to come and speak to me. And when Jasper practically forced you to do so, you looked so grim. As though you would rather be anywhere else than at my side…'

'No, no, Daisy, you have it all wrong. I was…so worried that I'd react…that is, here, feel this.' He pulled her in close. 'This is the way I always react whenever I see you.' And now that she was a married lady she understood exactly what he meant. She could feel his reaction, pressing into her belly.

'Oh,' she said, picturing *that*…straining against a

pair of skin-tight evening breeches. 'Oh,' she said again, smothering a giggle.

'Precisely,' he said grimly. 'I couldn't risk disgracing myself in a ballroom. Embarrassing you. Offending your brothers. So I had to keep thinking of all the most unpleasant things I could to get it to…stay down.'

'I… I would never have guessed. I didn't think you even *liked* me, let alone…'

A pained expression came to his face. 'Like you? I more than like you. You have been my ideal woman ever since that summer I broke my collar bone.'

'No. That cannot be.' She pulled back from him and looked at him with suspicion now. 'The next time you came to stay, you barely spoke to me. You positively avoided me.'

He lowered his head. Gave it a small shake. Swallowed. 'I…' He lifted his head. 'I could not just take up where we left off…because I…' He whirled away from her. Thrust his fingers through his hair. Turned back.

'I was covered in spots,' he said. 'Don't you remember?'

'Spots.' He'd crushed her girlish heart, made her feel as if she was nothing to him, that he was only interested in being friends with her brothers, and not her, because he'd had *spots*?

'Ben, everyone has spots for a year or so. It is part of growing up.'

'Not like mine. My face looked like a…a pigsty after a rainstorm. Pitted and pustulant. Whereas your skin was always…' he scanned her face with a kind of admiration, tinged with jealousy, that filled her with equal parts exasperation and fondness '...perfect.'

She sighed. 'My skin was most certainly not perfect. There were a few years when I had to bathe my face several times a day in a mixture of rosewater and witch hazel.'

His eyes widened.

'Even during my Season, there were occasions when I had to resort to rice powder, to conceal the occasional blemish that popped up.'

'You...used cosmetics?' He looked stunned.

'Don't make it sound as if I am some sort of...scarlet woman,' she snapped. 'Every female needs a little help sometimes to look her best.'

He frowned. 'So what was all that about not trying to lure men into a matrimonial trap, then?'

'I didn't powder my face in order to lure anyone anywhere! I just...didn't want to disappoint my mother. She was so...proud of me being hailed as the beauty of the Season. She worked hard behind the scenes to make sure nobody could steal my laurels. And I...' She didn't know how she could make him understand. 'I enjoyed being the focus of her attention for once. All my life she's always been so focussed on my brothers and all their scrapes that I always felt like second-best. No, make that sixth-best,' she added bitterly.

He looked relieved. 'I knew you couldn't have a single ounce of vanity, not even though you are so beautiful.'

He thought she was beautiful?

Daisy experienced two emotions, very strongly, at

the same time. One was a thrill of pleasure at hearing this man, with whom she was going to live for the rest of her days, declare that she was beautiful.

The other was a definite twinge of disappointment. Because her so-called beauty was the only thing that any male she'd ever met had thought gave her value. Her father, for instance. His only consolation in having a daughter, he'd said more than once, was the fact that she'd inherited his looks, rather than her mother's. Which was so hypocritical, considering the way he kept on insisting, to her brothers, that they needed to beware of judging a woman with their eyes...

'But, anyway,' he continued, his jaw jutting as though he was summoning his resolve to say whatever he had to say next, 'it wasn't just the spots. I...' He did that looking away to one side thing, as if he was finding it hard to admit to whatever it was he was going to say next. 'Well, you know there is a sort of unwritten rule about a fellow's sisters. A man doesn't trifle with the sister of his friend. It just isn't done.'

Ah. Now, that she could believe. It explained the way her brothers had reacted when they'd discovered Ben naked in the boat with her. Even though Jasper had been the one to urge his own friends to try to save her from the dire fate of spinsterhood, they'd behaved as though he'd broken some mysterious masculine code of honour.

'Which was what made it so shocking when Jasper told us all to...'

'Do whatever it took to get me to the altar,' she finished for him.

'None of us knew how to deal with it, I don't suppose. We couldn't suddenly admit that all along we'd thought you...attractive. It would have meant admitting that we'd been secretly lusting after the sister of our friend.'

Lusting? Surely not! 'Walter and Horace made it very clear what they thought of me,' she reminded him tartly.

'I am sure they didn't mean it. I think they were saying those things by way of excuses because they thought they had no chance of winning you, no matter what they did. Not after the silly ass ways they'd tried to gain your attention when they first began to...'

She frowned. 'What? What are you trying to say?'

'Daisy, a lot of those pranks the fellows played on you,' he said patiently, 'were clumsy attempts to get you to notice them.'

Chapter Nineteen

'What? They thought I would enjoy discovering beetles in my teacup? Or slugs in my shoes? Or having live fish flung at me?'

He shrugged. 'What can I say? We couldn't just... flirt with you, could we? Not with your brothers watching us all like hawks.'

'My brothers were among the worst offenders,' she protested.

'Your brothers made sure you didn't get tangled up with unsuitable males before you were old enough to know how to handle them,' he corrected her gently.

She frowned. Re-examined their behaviour in the light of what Ben had just said. And saw that, indeed, their pranks had been much, much worse when their friends had been staying at the Priory. That they'd made sure she'd never wanted to be in any of the public rooms or anywhere that she might be vulnerable when the savage hordes, as she'd always thought of them, descended.

They had been...protective.

Which was in keeping with the way they'd been during her Season, she suddenly perceived. They hadn't suddenly changed their attitude to her, they'd just adapted their behaviour to fit the changed circumstances.

And then something else struck her about what he'd just said.

'You wanted to…flirt with me? When you came to the Priory covered in spots?'

He swallowed, looking guilty.

'I would have been content,' she said with exasperation, 'to just sit and talk to you sometimes, the way we did the summer before.' Instead, whenever she'd approached him he'd ducked his head and looked at her feet, then blushed scarlet and perhaps grunted before beating a hasty retreat.

'I wouldn't have known what to say. You kept frowning at me and making yourself scarce whenever I came near. I was so sure that my spots disgusted you…'

'No, I was hurt and angry because you made me feel that it was my brothers you liked, and not me. I had been looking forward to your return, practically counting the days, and then…' She grimaced.

'You had been looking forward to my return?'

'Well, yes. It was often very lonely, you know, being the only girl among that pack of boys. And I thought at last I would have one friend amongst the hordes. One person to whom I could talk about the books I'd been reading. But…you never really liked reading, did you?' she finished sadly.

'That's not true. That summer you showed me that

I could take pleasure from many things I'd never considered before…'

He'd always been a rather morose boy, she reflected. As though he truly hadn't known how to find any pleasure anywhere.

'Yes. I certainly taught you that books had their uses. To hide your hands at cards, to be specific.'

'No, that was not all,' he said earnestly. 'After that summer, even though I never plucked up the courage to talk to you on my own, I was never lonely, the way I'd been before. Books became my companions. The way you promised me they would be.

'I always had a book on the go wherever I went, especially during my years in the army. I…didn't always like the thoughts expressed in all of them, it's true. Found some of them dashed hard going. But what I discovered was that many other men, better educated and wiser than me, had contemplated the same things as me, and reached conclusions they expressed with far greater eloquence than I ever could. Thoughts that I had never dared voice aloud, thinking I was the only man who thought them. It made me feel that I wasn't so very different from everyone else after all. And I had you to thank for it.'

He bent and kissed her hands again, one after the other. 'It wasn't your beauty that bowled me over, to start with. That came later. It was the kindness you showed me. I couldn't…accept, at first, that you had no ulterior motive for coming in and…'

'Reading at you,' she said with a smile.

He nodded. 'I was surly and suspicious, wasn't I? I'm

so sorry for that but, you see, nobody had ever just…
been kind to me, for no reason, not like that, and I…'

'Nobody?'

He shook his head.

And she believed it. Having seen the wreckage that
had been left in the battleground that had been his parents' marriage, she could see exactly how one small
boy could have become a casualty. Why, even back
then it had been clear that his parents were, at best, indifferent to him.

'You opened a door into a world I would never have
discovered had you not visited me, day after day, and
persisted until you'd found a way to cheer me up. That
was what first made me…admire you so much.'

Something surged through her then. Something she'd
never felt before. A sort of wild exhilaration. Because
Ben was saying that it wasn't the way she looked that
had made him develop feelings for her. It was because
of something she'd done. Something she was.

He valued her as a person.

Nobody had ever valued her as a person before. To
her father she was the runt of the litter, the girl her
mother couldn't be blamed for producing, considering she'd given him five strapping sons as well. To her
mother she'd been a way to re-create the disappointing
season she'd experienced as a girl. To her brothers…
well, she wasn't sure what they thought of her, although
Ben had just convinced her they had always been protective of her, in their own, peculiar fashion.

'Oh, Ben. You don't know what that means to me.

And then, to know that something I did helped to make your time in the army less of an ordeal...'

She gazed at him in wonder.

'Daisy,' he grated. 'Don't look at me like that. Or I will have to...'

She didn't have to wonder what he'd have to do for more than a second. Because he gave a strangled groan, pulled her close and kissed her.

'Daisy,' he panted after a while. 'We can't. Not here...'

He was breathing heavily. So was she. And somewhere through the haze of...lust that had her in its grip his words began to make sense. She had never thought of...the marriage act as anything other than something that happened in the bedroom. In the dark. At night. But the feelings that were ripping through her, just because he'd kissed her, were compellingly strong even though it was daylight and they were nowhere near a bedroom.

'Do you mean to tell me,' she said, feeling very let down, 'that I am going to have to wait until tonight before we...finish...*this*?'

'I...' He looked torn. 'Anyone might come in and see us. It wouldn't do to expose you to...'

'I suppose you are right,' she admitted reluctantly, leaning her forehead against his chest and breathing in deeply. Which didn't help because she got a lungful of him. His scent. Which was now, it appeared, inextricably linked in her mind with bedroom activity. 'It would be more sensible to restrict ourselves to the bedroom. With the door locked and the curtains drawn.'

'Are you telling me,' he grated, 'that you'd be willing to...right now?'

'It is not a question of *willing*.' She wriggled against him. 'It is more the fact that when you kiss me like that, and let me feel what you have in your breeches, I... I...' She looked up at him. 'I don't feel,' she admitted, 'as if I *can* wait until tonight.'

Ben let go of her so suddenly that her heart sank.

It rose again when she saw him stride to the windows and draw the curtains closed, plunging the room into a dappled twilight from where moth holes punctured the shabby material.

'You could actually consider this as a bedroom,' he told her as he practically ran to the door and turned the key in the lock. 'Since I have been sleeping here.'

'You have been sleeping here?' She looked swiftly around the room. 'Where, exactly? There is no bed.' But his trunk was there, by the wall next to the fireplace, his sword propped up against the mantelpiece. She'd wondered where it had gone when it had vanished from her room after that first night. But she'd been determined not to ask what had become of it. Like so many of the other questions she'd had, she'd refused to let him, or anyone, suspect she might be interested in anything he did.

'In the corner, over there,' he said, pointing briefly before taking her in his arms again.

'Oh, dear. That cannot have been very comfortable.'

'I am a soldier. Was a soldier,' he amended. 'I have slept in far worse places. At least I was out of the rain and had the hearthrug to soften the floorboards.'

'I made you feel you could not sleep in your own

bed,' she said, appalled at her selfishness of the first days of their marriage.

'No, Daisy, don't feel guilty. The marriage was... You didn't want it. You needed time to get used to it. Used to me. I didn't want to make you...'

She didn't want to talk any more. Talking had served its purpose. Had drawn them closer. But now it was making those wanton feelings fade. Making her wonder about the wisdom of what they had been about to do. Allowing all the lectures she'd had from a series of governesses about ladylike and proper behaviour flood to the forefront of her mind.

In fact, if they went on talking for much longer, she would change her mind altogether, citing the need to go and arrange furniture in the barn with Vale or something of the sort.

She couldn't have that. Not after finally managing to prise Ben's thoughts from a mouth that he usually kept as firmly closed as a...as an oyster.

So she walked up to Ben and plunged her fingers into his luxuriantly thick hair, before stopping his generous mouth with a kiss.

It was all the hint he needed that she'd had enough of talking for now. He kissed her back. Took over the kiss. And the position in which they were standing. He backed her up to the desk, lifted her onto it, and reached down to gather her skirts in his hands.

'Are you sure about this?' he panted into her neck.

She wasn't sure of anything but the feelings surging through her, feelings that doubled when he breathed so hotly into her neck like that.

'Ben,' was all she could moan, wrapping her arms round his neck and lifting her legs so that he could push her skirts up and step between them. It was all the encouragement he needed. He acted swiftly, with a flattering lack of patience, fumbling his breeches open and simply…taking her. Passionately. Holding her close to him with one arm round her waist so that his powerful thrusts didn't push her right across the desk.

'Ben,' she squeaked, on the verge of laughter now, it seemed so…well, naughty. To be doing this, on a desk, in the daytime. With all those important papers virtually under her bottom.

'Ben,' she said again, more on a moan as rational thought started to become impossible.

'Daisy,' he panted. 'Daisy.'

And then it was all either of them could do to breathe under the onslaught of the flames that engulfed them both. It was so intense she felt a scream working its way up her throat. She pushed her head forward and bit into the cloth of his jacket at his shoulder instead, because the last thing she wanted was for anyone apart from him to hear her expressing herself in such a very… basic way. Because they'd know what they were doing.

Ben threw his head back and moaned a second later, as though her release had triggered his own.

And then they just stayed, fused together, panting for a few more moments.

She couldn't believe it had happened so quickly.

'I can't believe we just…'

'I'm sorry,' said Ben, withdrawing. 'I shouldn't have…'

She grabbed him round the waist and stopped him from going anywhere. 'It was wonderful,' she said sternly. 'Don't apologise for showing me that…well, so much pleasure. I never dreamed… I… I wasn't complaining. Ben, you have got to stop apologising all the time,' she said, looking up at him with a frown, as she realised that was what he did. He always assumed that she was going to be cross with him. Or not want him.

'And,' she added, 'you have got to stop sleeping on the floor in here.'

'I…' He looked deep into her eyes. His face flushed. Or perhaps it was just reddened from the exertions of a few moments ago. 'If I sleep in your bed, I don't think I will be able to keep my hands off you. Not now we've…'

She couldn't help smiling. 'Good. I don't want you to keep your hands off me. Not when they can make me feel so marvellous. Besides, now I come to think of it,' she continued as something like a flash of inspiration opened her eyes to something that had always puzzled her, 'my parents always share a room. Even when they were in London they didn't have separate bedrooms. And they seem far happier with each other than any other married couple I know of.'

It had been a shock when she'd gone to London and seen the way others of her class conducted their marriages, to see how many couples appeared to actively dislike each other. And the gossip mill was always turning with the tales of who was getting up to no good with whom. And speculation ran rife about whose children were fathered by which of a woman's numerous lovers.

She didn't want to have that kind of marriage. What was termed a fashionable marriage. She wanted...well, the closeness that her own parents had, if not the exact same sort of relationship.

'It's down to more than just sharing a bedroom, Daisy,' said Ben gently. 'Your father loves your mother, and she loves him back.'

Daisy considered that statement. No matter what she thought of the way Father treated Mother, the truth was that they were both happy with each other. She supposed Father did love Mother, in his way, even though he was always telling her she wasn't pretty. And Mother loved him back, even though he had a temper, and was autocratic, and often unfair. She knew that neither of them had ever been unfaithful to the other. She knew that because Father was always boasting to his sons about it and urging them to follow his example. It wasn't just about keeping free from diseases, she began to suspect. It was about so much more. It was about trust. Building trust. And showing the other person that they were special.

'You truly believe that my father loves my mother, even though he doesn't think she's beautiful?'

'Oh, yes,' he said without a moment's hesitation. 'It's as plain as a pikestaff. He loves your mother because she is such a...good-hearted woman. She...well,' he said, nuzzling her nose with his own. 'She was more of a mother to me than my own ever was. It wasn't just your brothers that made me look forward to my times at the Priory.'

So Ben liked her mother, as well as her brothers.

The temptation to become one of the family and have the mother figure he'd clearly lacked in his own home must have been overwhelming. Well, clearly he had been overwhelmed because he hadn't argued the case for not marrying her for long, had he? What with his longing to be part of her family, and the extremely generous dowry…

No, no, she wasn't going to yield to the temptation to feel sorry for herself because of the route she'd travelled to reach this point. The point where they both wanted each other so much they couldn't wait until nightfall. This, between them, was real, and precious, and she wasn't going to allow anything to spoil her pleasure in it.

'I am going to ask Vale to move your trunk to my room. To *our* room,' she amended.

'But,' he said, his brow wrinkling, 'what if I want… and you…?'

'If, for any reason, I don't want to do…this,' she said, wriggling her bottom, 'I shall tell you. And we can just curl up together and keep each other warm.'

Although over the next few days that never happened. He only had to climb into the bed next to her to make her wish he'd do all those wonderful things that made her feel such pleasure. Some nights she was the first to reach for him. Just to make sure he knew that she was willing. Because there was still that air of restraint about him. Not just at night but during the daytime, too. She would have thought he would have felt like singing all day long, the way she did, after discovering how wonderful it could be to share the pleasures of the marriage bed. But he never even smiled at her during the hours of daylight. Instead, he would watch her gravely. With an air almost of suspicion. As though he was waiting for her to say she'd had enough and give him his marching orders.

She sighed as she slipped her arm through his the next Sunday as they prepared to set out for church for the second time. This time with not only Vale and Marcie fell in behind them but Sally and Wilmot too.

Why, she wondered, as the vicar climbed into the pulpit, couldn't Ben just enjoy being married to her? Why was it so hard to...to *read* him?

Because he wasn't a character in a book, that was why. She didn't have the benefit of an author to tell her what was going on inside his head. She picked at the seam of her glove. It was possible, she supposed, that she'd spent too much time growing up reading about fictional people, instead of paying attention to the ones living closest to her. For she'd learned more about her family since she'd been married to Ben than she'd ever observed from living with them for seventeen years. So if she wanted to understand *him* she'd have to...well, the only way she could start to guess at what he might be thinking, or feeling, would be by closely watching the things he did, and paying attention to the things he said.

As the Reverend Knowles droned on through a sermon that had nothing to do with anything that interested her, she started mulling over all the things she knew about Ben. And re-examining all the conversations they'd had to see if she could somehow find the key to understanding him.

He'd always been prone to look on the dark side. Even as a boy, he hadn't had the same carefree attitude of her brothers' other friends.

He hadn't been loved, though, had he? When he'd broken his collar bone she'd been shocked, as had her parents, that *his* parents had not immediately come to take him home. They hadn't even enquired as to his health. And now she'd learned that her mother had been more of a mother to him than his own had. Nobody had ever just been kind, without an ulterior motive, he'd said.

She hadn't exactly given him a very good impression of a doting wife so far, either, had she? She hadn't spoken to him at all for the first few days of their marriage. And now, all of a sudden, she'd turned about and told him she wanted him in her bed all the time. Was it any wonder he was behaving as though he was waiting for her to change her mind again and kick him out again?

Well, she'd just have to show him that she wasn't as fickle as she'd probably made him think she was, wouldn't she? Show him that she was capable of not being selfish and spoiled. By working hard on the estate, and being loyal and loving to him, too. Eventually, he'd stop looking as though he was waiting for something awful to happen between them.

Wouldn't he?

The congregation stirred, alerting her to the fact that the vicar was, finally, coming down from the pulpit. She smoothed her gloves and stood to sing the last hymn.

As the vicar intoned the dismissal, Daisy considered all those years Ben had spent in the army. They must have had an effect on him, too. When she'd seen him, in the Danverses' ballroom for the first time after the years he'd been away, she really had thought how manly he looked in comparison with all the other men there. And it hadn't just been due to his uniform. There had been many other men in uniform in London, but they'd just looked…gaudy in all that scarlet and gold lace. Ben, on the other hand, had looked…hard. And the scar on his face had made her wonder what being a soldier was really like. And once she'd thought about how Ben may have come by that scar, she'd started to notice soldiers begging in the streets, with only one arm or leg. And their faces, too, had been…hard. Wooden. As if they didn't dare let anyone see what they felt like.

Did they all have wounds to their souls, as well as their bodies? The pain of losing a leg or an arm must have a terrible effect on a person's mind. She recalled the one time she'd fallen over, on some ice, and broken her wrist. It had shaken her up. She hadn't cried but she hadn't been able to stop shaking for a long time after. And that had only been a silly accident.

And then there was the way he believed that anyone looking at his scarred face must think him ugly. Repulsive.

With all that going on inside, no wonder Ben was so often grim and taciturn. How she wished there was something she could do to help him…heal.

At last the churchwarden was opening the door, allowing the congregation to begin trickling out into the sunshine.

As usual, people didn't immediately set out for their homes but took advantage of the fine weather to gather in little groups around the church porch and along the path through the churchyard, sharing gossip and extending invitations.

She strolled down the path on Ben's arm, nodding to those she was beginning to recognise. And after a while they naturally parted company, he to converse with a cluster of men he informed her tersely were some of the tenant farmers, and she to chat with the village women, who were keen to tell her that they could do laundry, or fine needlework, or that their sons or nephews were skilled carpenters or glaziers, who might come back if pay and conditions were tempting enough.

They were both making their way, slowly, and separately, in the general direction of the lychgate when Miss Fairfax bounced up to her.

'Lady Bramhall,' she gushed, dropping a curtsey. Daisy blinked. It felt so strange to hear someone call her Lady Bramhall. But, then, this was the first time anyone had done so. But that was who she was now. Not Marguerite, the lonely girl, shoring up her own self-worth by clinging to an impressive name, or even Daisy, the butt of her brothers' practical jokes. She was Ben's wife now. That was who Lady Bramhall was. And even Miss Fairfax was obliged to acknowledge it.

She smiled at the girl, who'd unwittingly given her a rare moment of self-awareness. But the girl wasn't smiling back. 'You may think you are something special, but

you've won a hollow victory,' said Miss Fairfax a little
wildly. 'And anyway, now I'm glad you married him
before I got the chance,' she hissed, pushing her face
close to Daisy's ear. 'Because I've discovered that he
isn't what he seems. Mother says he isn't the true heir,
at all, and that everyone feels sorry for you because he
only married you for your money, and what's more, if
you weren't so rich, nobody around here would have
accepted him back either.'

Chapter Twenty

Ben couldn't believe how different everyone was with him this week at church. It seemed they all wanted to stop him and have a word. And not to grumble either. Word must have got around about Daisy's plans to spend her money restoring the fortunes of the village, he supposed. And they knew on which side their bread was buttered. Daisy and Ben were the ones who would be able to hand out jobs and authorise repairs to the cottages.

No matter what they felt about him taking up residence as the Fifth Earl, he was the one who was going to make it possible to undo the damage the Fourth Earl had done. Even the most belligerent farmers were prepared to give him the benefit of the doubt.

The women were all clustering round Daisy, trying to get into her good graces, he could see. And she was dealing with them all with both charm and dignity. None of the coldness or haughtiness she'd displayed last week.

Until Miss Fairfax stormed up to her and spat something vile into her ear. At least it looked as if it had been, both by the expression on her face as she'd spoken and Daisy's recoil immediately after.

He cut the conversation with Farmer Brightwell short, made his way to Daisy's side, and took hold of her arm as he led her from the churchyard.

He waited until they were well up the high street before speaking.

'What did Miss Fairfax say to upset you?'

She glanced at him before answering. 'Something very silly and spiteful.'

'I could see that. What, precisely, was it, though? I don't want her upsetting you with her…well, lies, if that is what she did. You know that there was never anything between her and me…'

'Oh, no, that was not what she implied. No, it was… well, I didn't really understand it. Perhaps you can explain?'

His heart gave a lurch. Miss Fairfax wouldn't have… would she?

'What did she say?'

'Well, she said that my marrying you was a hollow victory because you aren't the true heir, and people only accept you because of my money.' She worried at her lower lip. 'Ben, what did she mean? Why did she say that you don't belong here? Is she…mad?'

His heart sank. He'd hoped she would never find out. That nobody would be crass enough to tell her. He might have known he would not have that kind of luck.

'She is not mad,' he said. 'Just…bitter. Possibly even

a bit vengeful.' That must be the only thing that could have driven her to tell Daisy what she had. Because it certainly wouldn't have bothered her had *she* been the one to have married him.

'So…she was just…making up some kind of…'

He gritted his teeth. He had to tell her. Confess. Because if she didn't hear it from him, she'd eventually worm it out of someone.

They'd reached the gate that led onto their land. The servants were well ahead of them, trampling down the trail they'd already worn through the long grass over the past week or so. He stopped walking, turned her to him, and gazed at her lovely face.

One last time. He had to kiss her one last time, while she could still look at him with such…trust and openness in her beautiful blue eyes. For once he told her the truth about himself she'd never look at him in the same way again.

He put all his heart into the kiss. Drank in her generous, trusting response to the man she'd married. The man she'd *thought* she'd married. The Earl of Bramhall.

But he couldn't put off the moment for ever.

'The truth,' he said, letting go of her, and turning away so that he wouldn't have to see her shock, 'is that the Fourth Earl was not my father.'

'Not your father? What do you mean?'

He ran his fingers through his hair. She was so… innocent. Had been brought up in such a…close-knit family, with such strait-laced parents, that she wasn't going to be able to work it out from hints. He was going to have to explain every last sordid detail of it.

'My mother conceived me at a time when it was impossible for the Fourth Earl to have fathered me.'

'She…she had a lover?'

'By all accounts, from that moment on she had numerous lovers.'

'Oh,' said Daisy. With no inflection in her voice that gave any clue as to what she might be thinking.

'So I am a bastard.'

'No…' she said thoughtfully. 'I mean, not technically. Your parents were married.'

'Yes, but the man to whom she was married was most definitely not my father. And he never let me forget it!'

She came up behind him and placed one hand on his back. 'That was extremely bad form. On his part. I mean, if your parents had a…*fashionable* marriage, then he had no business exposing her…um, indiscretion.'

He whirled round to look at her. Really look at her. He'd expected to see revulsion in her eyes. Withdrawal. But she just looked puzzled. A little cross perhaps. As she had every right to be.

'They didn't have a fashionable marriage in the sense you mean, where each partner takes lovers whenever they feel like it. It was a love match. Or so the story goes. My father was obsessed with my mother. To begin with.'

She frowned. 'So what went wrong?'

'I don't know. All I do know is that for some reason, during a spell when the Fourth Earl was away for an extended period on a mission abroad to some embassy or other, she took a lover. And the result was me. When he came back, he…' Ben shook his head.

'I always wondered why your parents appeared to be so neglectful of you,' she said, placing her hand on his arm. 'But it was wrong of them. Very wrong to take out their own sins on an innocent child.'

He examined her face closely. She appeared to be in earnest. There was nothing false, or contrived, or strained about her expression. As though she really didn't care about his parentage.

His heart swelled up with love for her.

'They weren't so bad,' he said. 'The Fourth Earl just ignored me, for the most part, until my older brothers died…'

'He made you eat in the kitchens, didn't he?' she blurted, looking outraged. 'You told me you were used to eating with the servants. Now I can see why…'

'No! He didn't *make* me eat with the servants. But he was always going on about how my mother might have had an affair with some male member of staff for all he knew, because she refused to name my true father, and in spite of all his enquiries he could never discover that any strangers of rank had visited this area while he'd been away. Which made him dismiss all the male staff, eventually, so she couldn't repeat the offence. After she died, he became so…abusive to me during the few times our paths crossed, like at mealtimes, for example, that I chose to eat in the kitchens with the servants since that seemed to be where I belonged when I was here. Which was as infrequently as possible…'

'Oh, Ben. No wonder you spent so much time at the

Priory. No wonder you became so fond of my own parents.' She caught her lower lip between her teeth again. 'I have always complained about them, and what I perceived to be their faults, but compared to your parents, mine were absolute paragons. I feel ashamed now for moaning about them so much. Or even at all.'

'Don't be,' he said, running his hands up and down her arms to comfort her. 'You weren't to know... I hid it from everyone. As much as I could anyway. Especially from you. I never wanted you to find out I am a bastard. That I wasn't fit to breathe the same air as you, let alone aspire to...well, when I didn't have the excuse any longer of an injury making it acceptable for you to converse with me...' he faltered, gathering courage to tell her the truth about the way he'd behaved all those years ago. 'You see, when you came and sat with me and played cards, people knew it was your choice. But what right, what reason could I give for approaching you and spending time with you when I was fit again?'

'You mean...it wasn't because of the spots?'

'Not only because of the spots. I'm sorry, Daisy, I used having them as an excuse to explain why I couldn't just act as if we could be friends. Because I didn't, even after we married, want you to learn of my deepest shame.'

Her eyes flashed. 'You have nothing to be ashamed of,' she said hotly. 'You were not responsible for how your mother behaved. Though...' A faraway look came to her eyes. 'Oh, well, now I understand the destruction your f... the Fourth Earl wrought in the Countess's bedroom.'

'Yes. He did that when she died. Then locked the doors and refused to let anyone go in and clear it.'

'And…the rest of the house? When did he start to lay waste to the rest of it?'

It was strange, but now that he'd started talking about it, it was something of a relief. She didn't seem at all shocked by the discovery that she'd married a bastard. And once he'd got it all out in the open he wouldn't need to worry about what she might be thinking of the state of the Park any more. He wouldn't feel as if he was keeping secrets from her.

'After both my older brothers, his true sons, died, he was beside himself with anger to know that it would all come to me. Particularly since he'd taken steps to make sure it wouldn't. That is, he had hoped that buying me a commission and sending me into the army would bring a swift and hopefully brutal end to my existence.' She gasped as though horror-struck. 'Ironically, I soon felt more at home in the army than I ever had anywhere else. They accepted me on my merits, you see…'

She flung her arms round him and hugged him tight. Pressed her face into his chest, dislodging her Sunday bonnet as she did so.

He stroked her hair, which came straggling down in the process as he continued unburdening himself.

'He was particularly devastated when Paul, who was his second son, died, because he'd tried so hard to shield him from every breeze that blew. He was a bit…delicate, you see. And so the Fourth Earl got him into university and procured a curacy for him so that he could live in comfort for the rest of his days, if he weren't called upon to step into my older brother William's shoes in the event something happened to him.

'But within the space of five months first William was thrown from his horse and broke his neck, and then Paul took some fever from one of the poor parishioners he'd been visiting. And he saw that I, the despised bastard, the cuckoo in the nest, was going to inherit it all. Because legally there was nothing he could do by then. He'd never disowned me publicly because he was too humiliated by Mother's adultery, or so he said. And he…took to the bottle.'

'And burned all the books in the library, ordered the furniture to be burnt…'

'Gambled away what ready money there was and sold anything of value to fund that habit. All so that I would have nothing to inherit but debts and dilapidation.'

She pulled away and looked into his face, her mouth pulled into a tight line.

'He had nobody to blame but himself for any of it,' she said vehemently. 'He sounded as though he was extremely unstable. It wouldn't surprise me to learn that your mother had good reason to take a lover. He had probably been beastly to her. Well, it stands to reason, doesn't it, if he could behave the way you told me to an innocent child. I mean, why didn't he take her with him on this mission to some foreign embassy? If my father had been sent abroad on business for the Crown, he would have either taken Mother with him or refused to go.'

'I have no idea, Daisy,' he said, stroking the hair

from her face, then setting the bonnet back on her head. 'But it doesn't alter the fact that I am a bastard, and everyone around here knows it. If they didn't when I was a lad, they certainly did so after my brothers died. The Fourth Earl seems to have made sure of it. So that nobody would be in any doubt, when I returned to try and take over, that I have no right to do so. He must have done, or Miss Fairfax would not have been able to tell you so.'

'Of course you have the right to inherit! Good grief, Ben, how many third or fourth sons of the aristocracy can honestly say they know who their real father is?'

So she wasn't as innocent as he'd first thought. Though how on earth she'd learned such things…

'Well, perhaps so,' he admitted. 'But most of them can be certain that their father was a lord. Mine might have been a footman. A groom…'

'It doesn't alter the fact that your mother was a lady. Does it? Wasn't she the granddaughter of the Duke of Cransley?'

'She was…but how did you know that?'

'Oh, well, Mother had the *Peerage* out the moment marriage with you was first discussed. Traced your antecedents on both sides. Not that the paternal side is relevant now. But the point is,' she said, seizing his lapels and giving him a little shake, 'that you are, in-disputably, the great-grandson of a Duke. And, to be perfectly honest, now that you've told me all that stuff about the Fourth Earl, I'm jolly glad that none of his blood will run through the veins of any of our children. He sounds like a monster.'

'He…' All his life Ben had thought the same. But now he'd talked it all through, for the first time he was beginning to wonder if that was true. 'He was not a monster,' he suddenly perceived. 'Just a very sad, disappointed man, who let anger and bitterness rule him at the end of his life. I can remember him being…jovial sometimes when I was very little. Oh, not with me but with my brothers. He was a good and protective father to *them*…'

But now he was wondering how he would feel if Daisy were to take a lover and bear that man a child. Every time he looked at that child, he'd see the face of a man who'd taken Daisy to bed, and a pain would rip through him, a pain far worse than any physical injury he'd ever suffered on the battlefield. He just knew it.

'I think he must have loved her very much at one time,' he said. 'Or he could not have acted with such rage when she played him false.'

'We'll never know,' said Daisy pragmatically. 'And, anyway, it doesn't matter now, does it? We have *our* lives to live. *Our* marriage to tend to.' She placed one hand on his cheek, his scarred cheek, and smiled at him. 'But at least now that you've told me all that stuff about your conception I can understand you better. It must have been horrid growing up with all that hanging over you. I totally understand why you have never referred to the man as your father but always as the Fourth Earl. He didn't *deserve* that you should think of him as your father.'

Chapter Twenty-One

Horrid. What an inadequate word to describe what Ben's childhood had been like. Growing up in a family who not only told him he didn't belong but actively hated him, by the sound of it.

She tucked her arm through his as they began to make their way slowly back to the Park. At least her family were all fond of her, in their own ways. The fact that they hadn't ever treated her the way she had wanted them to treat her was *her* problem, not theirs.

Take her Season, for example.

At the time she'd thought her brothers had been interfering and insensitive, and had done all the things they'd done to spoil any fun she might have had if they hadn't been there. And ruin any chance she might have had to find romance, the way heroines in story books found it.

But now that Ben had offered her a different perspective, she could see that they'd been trying to keep men they considered fortune-hunters at bay. Or men they had thought unworthy in other ways, too, she supposed. Gamblers, or libertines...all of her brothers despised men of that ilk, and would never wish her to end up married to that sort of man.

So, whenever one of them had approached her, or looked as if they might, they'd pushed one of their friends forward so she wouldn't even have to *dance* with anyone they considered unworthy. Every ball she'd attended they'd roped in a good handful of their friends, even though none of them really wanted to be there.

Never, she would swear, had any young lady been so protected, in such an organised fashion by her older brothers. Because they all knew how badly young men could behave towards unprotected females, and they had no intention of letting anyone treat their Daisy with such disrespect.

She almost groaned. Even the nickname of Daisy, the name she had hated for so long, showed that in their own way they considered her one of them. Because they'd all given each other rather derogatory nicknames. If they hadn't cared about her, one way or the other, they wouldn't have bothered at all, would they?

Goodness, but all that thinking she'd been doing during the sermon had made her look at a lot of her past with fresh eyes. She could see now that she'd always wanted all her family to behave like characters in a book. But, of course, they hadn't because they were real people, not fictional characters, who had moods that affected their behaviour, and motives to which she was not privy. For there was no narrator to spell it all out for her. Or there hadn't been until Ben had opened her eyes. She glanced over at him.

In the face of what Ben had gone through, she had never had any right to complain. Her father might have acted disappointed that she was a girl, and not expected anything of her but to marry well, but Ben's father, or the man who had stood in the place of a father to him, had actively hated him. Hoped he would die rather than inherit.

She squeezed his arm as hard as she could. But it wasn't enough. She wanted to gather him to her bosom and rock him, the way she'd rock a child who was hurt. She wanted to weep for the poor, lonely, maltreated little boy who still lived deep inside Ben's adult frame, always braced for a rebuff, never daring to hope anything good might come his way...

No wonder he hadn't trusted in the youthful friendship they'd started to form. No wonder he'd pulled away. He'd been taught that he was unworthy to associate with 'decent, respectable' people. And so he'd assumed she'd change her attitude to him if she ever found out about his parentage. Even once they were married he had only told her the full truth when he'd been backed into a corner. He'd even made up the excuse that he'd been sensitive about having spots rather than come clean.

She stifled a sniff as a huge wave of emotion flooded through her.

But could not walk one step further. She had to fling her arms round his waist.

'Ben, oh, Ben, I'm so sorry,' she breathed into his

coat. 'I wish there was something I could do... I feel
so...inadequate.'

'What? Tears?' It was only when he brushed at her
cheeks with her thumbs that she realised that, yes, she
was crying.

'You should have been loved as a boy,' she told him.
'Every child should be loved. No wonder you have always been so...quiet. So disinclined to laugh, the way
other boys do. How I wish I'd been more...sensitive.
Seen that you weren't just grumpy but hurting...'

'But you did, don't you remember? That summer
when I broke my collar bone and couldn't join in with
the others, you came to me every day and kept on at
me until you'd lifted my spirits. You were so kind, so...
playful, such good company. That...that was when I fell
in love with you,' he said.

'You fell in love with me?' He loved her? Had loved
her all this time? 'That summer?'

He nodded, shifting from one foot to the other as
though he was embarrassed to admit it. But he wasn't
denying it. Or trying to laugh it off, saying he'd spoken
on the spur of the moment and hadn't meant it really.

Though, come to think of it, he had mentioned that
his *admiration* for her had started then. Only she hadn't
thought that he was using the word *admire* in place of
love.

'Because I took the time to cheer you up?'

He nodded.

'Not because of...the way I look?'

He shook his head.

That meant a lot to her. To know that he had always

looked beneath the surface, the surface that she'd been
told was the only valuable thing about her, to see something lovable in *her*. But for once she was not going to
put herself and her own feelings first. Well, it was about
time, wasn't it? She'd been selfish and spoiled for far
too long. Ben needed to know that she could see beneath the outer layer of him as well. To his heart.

'Ben, if you didn't fall for me because of the way I
look, surely you can believe that what I feel for you is
not affected by the way you look either?'

His face, which had been softening, closed up. Oh,
how could she reach him? How could she make him
believe that he was worthy of love? And then it struck
her that she had a brilliant example she could use.

'You can believe that my father loves my mother,
can't you? Even though he is always saying she is so
plain and homely? Because she has a good heart.'

'Yes,' he said thoughtfully. 'But that is different.'

'Why?'

'Because, well…' He ran his fingers through his hair.
'Well, for one thing, I don't have a good heart or a kind
nature. I'm a soldier, Daisy. A hard heart, that is, the
ability to plan and execute orders without sentiment
getting in the way, is part of what has made me a good
officer…'

'And yet now you are thinking about employing former soldiers. Ben, that isn't the behaviour of a man with
a hard heart. That is the behaviour of a caring, compassionate man…'

'Employing former soldiers was your idea,' he argued.

'No, it wasn't. It was yours, wasn't it? You talked

about contacting the regiment first…and you didn't even insist on only employing men you could get your money's worth out of.'

'But—'

She saw that she wasn't going to argue him out of his low opinion of himself. She was just going to have to show him how he made her feel. So she pressed her mouth to his. Licked at his lips, the way he'd already taught her he liked. And, just as she'd hoped, his reaction to her move was swift and powerful. He put his arms round her and took the kiss to another, deeper, more heated level.

It was as if he needed to drink her in. As if he needed to grab at her, at what she'd said, before it slipped through his fingers. So she didn't protest, or remind him that this was Sunday and they were out of doors. Besides, when he began to lower her to the ground, her knees were so weak, her heart was beating so fast that she didn't want to stop him. She just wanted to revel in the moment. Leap into the flames with him.

This…this thing that blazed between them was an elemental, living thing, she thought as he came down on top of her. The need of a male for a female. The need of a female for a male. No…more than that, it was not just nature having its way to perpetuate the species. It was the cry of two lonely souls needing love for what they were as themselves, with every fault laid bare to the other, and to know they were still accepted. Cherished.

No longer alone.

The bliss Ben brought her soon drove all other

thoughts away. She was a mass of sensation, of feeling. Of ecstasy.

Even when it was over, and they lay there in the long grass, panting and running their hands over each other as though each had to be sure that the other was still there, she knew that the effect would linger. Not just as a pleasant, rather naughty memory but as a knowledge that this pleasure would always be there for them to enjoy whenever they wished.

'Daisy,' he murmured into her neck. 'I should not have… In a *field*. After *church*. I…'

She hugged him fiercely. 'It was wonderful. And… out here, in the open, it makes me see that it is one of God's greatest gifts to mankind. This joy. This pleasure. And not just for our bodies but for our…yes, our souls. When you need me so much that you throw caution and propriety to the winds, it makes me feel…'

'Loved,' he said. 'You are loved, Daisy.' He turned his head to kiss her cheek. 'I love you.'

For the first time in her life she believed it. A man like Ben, normally so…controlled, so…undemonstrative, couldn't fling a woman down into a field and make love to her like he just had done unless he was driven by extremely powerful emotions. It took something extraordinarily powerful to crack through that façade of reserve of cynicism behind which he habitually hid. She stretched her arms above her head, feeling…irresistible.

'Here, let me tidy you…' he said, getting to his knees and pulling her up. 'We don't want everyone knowing what has made us late back from church.'

He began to brush at her skirts to remove twigs and

stalks of crushed grass. Went off to search for his hat, and her bonnet.

She eyed him with amusement when he brought them over.

'You have grass stains on your knees,' she said, pointing. 'And I wouldn't be a bit surprised if I didn't have some on my, er, behind, too. I don't think anyone is going to be in any doubt as to why we will be getting back so much later than the others.'

He flushed red. 'I am so sorry. I would rather cut off my hand than expose you to embarrassment.'

'I won't be embarrassed,' she said, even though she wasn't sure that was totally true. 'You are my husband. We are just newly wed. It is…natural that we… That is, it is a good thing that we are so…keen on each other that we cannot walk from church to our home without… That is…' She broke off into a peal of giggles. 'Oh, dear. You are correct. It will be a touch embarrassing. But it is also very flattering to me to know that I am so irresistible that you cannot behave yourself when you are alone with me. Especially after the way we started out. I think,' she said, with a glow of something that felt like hope welling up within, 'that we are going to make a success of our marriage after all.'

For the next few days, Daisy kept on feeling the same way. Ben took her to heaven every night and took every chance he could to snatch kisses and cuddles during the day, when he was certain nobody else could see them. He didn't seem anywhere near as closed up and grim looking as usual either. Once or twice she even saw the ghost of what looked like a smile hovering about his mouth.

And he kept saying the most flattering things. It was as if, now he'd admitted he loved her, he felt free to say things he'd kept hidden for years. Or perhaps it was relief that after he'd confessed what he'd felt was his deepest, darkest secret she hadn't pushed him away but had instead taken his side.

One afternoon he surprised her in the barn, just after Vale and Wilmot had brought in a rather dilapidated sofa, which looked as though chickens had been roosting on it.

'You cannot seriously mean to bring that atrocity back into the house,' said Ben, startling her, because she hadn't known he'd been there She turned, pushing a stray wisp of hair back under the protective scarf she'd taken to wearing when dealing with whatever finds came in from the orchard.

'It won't be an atrocity by the time I've finished with it,' she told him. 'Once I've had it re-upholstered and cleaned up, it will look as good as new, I promise you. Mother was always re-upholstering chairs and hanging new curtains to keep the whole of the Priory looking smart. It is amazing what a few yards of good material will do. It won't be long before we can show visitors into a room that would not disgrace any drawing room in the land,' she told him with pride.

He tipped his head to one side as he took another look at the sofa and the set of chairs that she'd told Vale to group near it so that she could see if she could turn them into a matching set.

'I can see you sitting on that,' he said, darting her an admiring look, 'once it is covered with a blue silk, to match your eyes. Any room would look…stunning with such a tableau…'

'Not silk, silly,' she said, swatting at him with the duster she had in her hand at the time. 'That wouldn't be at all practical. We will need something hard-wearing.'

'But something that will set off your beauty, too,' he said, with mock severity. 'That's an order.'

'Naturally,' she replied with a toss of her head. 'I shall hang the walls with silk, of a shade that will make me look like the jewel in your crown and have all your neighbours turning green with envy at what I have accomplished. Before you know it, this place will be the most elegant, fashionable dwelling in the county.'

'I don't doubt it,' he said wryly, before melting away on business of his own, no doubt. He always seemed to be busy. Well, he was. There was so much to do to get the estates profitable again. While she was equally busy transforming this sad, neglected house into a magnificent yet comfortable home.

Later that night, she was smiling as she brushed out her hair before going to bed. She'd never been so happy. Not just in her life now but in what she could picture of her future. With Ben.

As she laid her hairbrush down on the dresser, she caught sight of his reflection in the mirror. He was standing in the doorway, watching her, his face twisted in an expression of hunger, tinged with sadness.

She whirled round. But by the time she was looking at him, rather than his reflection, he'd wiped all expression from his features. But she felt the cold hand of foreboding squeezing at her heart.

'Ben, what is it? What has happened?'

'Nothing,' he said, his eyes shifting from hers.

'Ben.' She got up and walked across the room to where he stood. 'Don't lie to me. I can see that something is troubling you. Tell me. We can deal with it.' She caught at his hand. 'Together we can deal with anything.'

He lowered his head. Took a deep breath. 'I wasn't going to say anything tonight. But perhaps you are right. Perhaps it is best to get it out in the open.' He lifted his head and gazed at her mournfully.

Her heart began to beat hard. Whatever he had to tell her, it looked as though it was tearing him apart.

'I had hoped we could have one last night together, without…'

'Last night? What are you talking about? It sounds as though you are going to leave…'

He winced. 'I am.'

Chapter Twenty-Two

'What?' She dropped his hand. 'I don't believe this.' But in a way she did. She'd always known he couldn't possibly love her the way he said he did. Nobody could. 'I was beginning to believe that you love me,' she said bitterly.

'I do, Daisy, I do,' he said, taking hold of both her hands and squeezing them as though to show he meant it. 'That is why we must bid each other farewell.'

She snatched her hands away. Wrapped her arms round her waist. Bit her tongue because she thought she ought to just listen to his excuses before ripping up at him, telling him what she thought of men who would say just about anything to keep a woman sweet-tempered and willing.

Oh, why had she started to believe he was different from other males? That he was honest and kind, and... and *noble*. She'd done it again, hadn't she? Imagined motives for the way he behaved that fitted her notions of how she wanted him to feel. Instead of seeking out the truth.

Well, the only way she'd learn the truth would be if he spelled it out to her. Because she couldn't make any sense of what he was saying. If he loved her, why on earth would he leave?

'I think,' she said shakily, 'you had better explain. And you had better have a jolly good excuse for running off and leaving me after spending this last week or so making me believe...'

But she might have known he didn't really love her. Nobody else ever had. Ben had claimed he'd loved her since they'd both been in their teens, but that had been before he'd really got to know her. When he'd been dazzled by the exterior that all men agreed was attractive to the eye. Before he'd seen that as a person she was silly, and selfish, and had a temper...

And, yes, he might find her physically attractive, but, then, men did find women irresistible, until they'd had them, didn't they? Father was always telling her brothers to beware of such affairs. To wait until the attraction wore off, as it was bound to do, so that they wouldn't get mired in sin and sickness. Oh, dear. But this was going to the other extreme. Believing his motives were evil. And they weren't. They couldn't be. Ben wasn't a villain. A complicated, troubled man, yes, but not a villain.

'I had a letter from my commanding officer,' he said bleakly. 'He wants me back. You know that Bonaparte has marched through France, gathering support along the way, and that the Allies are banding together to try to stop him. Or perhaps you don't but, anyway, my regiment needs me. And…' He trailed off, spreading his hands wide.

'And you *want* to return to your regiment,' she finished for him, feeling as if he'd punched her in the stomach. 'You said so, right at the start. You warned me you were going to leave. I just…' She groped for something to sit down on as her legs turned the consistency of blancmange. 'I thought you'd changed your mind.'

'I… I did. I have.' He strode to the window, running his fingers through his hair. Then whirled back to look at her. 'But I had already written by then. I wrote the very day I told you I planned to return. When I thought we had no chance of making a go of it. When you weren't even talking to me, let alone permitting me to share your bed. And then, when you caught me with Miss Fairfax, I thought, I really thought, that was it. It was over.'

'You wrote…that day?' Before they'd come to this… understanding. This place of…togetherness.

She clutched at the bedpost. 'I… I see. Well, that makes sense, I suppose. That you wrote then, that is, but…' She frowned. 'Why does it have to be farewell, though?'

'Well, obviously, you can't come with me,' he said impatiently.

'It isn't obvious to me.' Unless he really did want to leave.

'Daisy, as your husband, I am supposed to look after you. And taking you abroad, into a situation that is unstable, possibly even dangerous, would be foolhardy in the extreme.'

'Foolhardy?' Oh, so he didn't think she was sensible enough to cope with life as an officer's wife. Because she was foolish.

'Yes, Daisy, foolhardy. I would never be certain that I could keep you safe, let alone housed in the kind of conditions you are used to. That you deserve. Bringing you here, to all this…mess,' he said, waving his arm around the room, although he probably meant the rest of the house and the estate, rather than just this one rather shabby bedchamber, 'was bad enough. But to take you to the theatre of war?' He shook his head. 'I cannot do it.'

'You…you don't think I could cope with living in billets? Is that what you are saying? Ben, I am not some hothouse flower. I am not a marguerite. My brothers started calling me Daisy because I am like a weed. I can thrive in the poorest of soil…'

'But you will be happier here. You said so yourself. That you are going to enjoy transforming the place and making it into a showpiece that will become the envy of every other family of note in the county. That you have found a purpose for the first time in your life. I cannot drag you away from all this…'

'I wouldn't be a bit surprised if that wasn't the reasoning that your father used when he abandoned your mother,' she said bitterly. 'That it was for her own good. And look what happened as a result.'

'Ah, but you are not like that, Daisy,' he said with a tender smile. 'It is not in your nature to take your vows lightly. Besides, I happen to know that although I look like a frog, you consider all other men to be toads. I don't believe any of them will even tempt you to yield, no matter how hard they might try.'

He was certainly right about that. The thought of even kissing Hairy Horace or Wooden-Headed Walter made her feel queasy. And as for wanting to see either of them with their shirt off? Ugh!

'I suppose I should feel grateful to learn that you've been listening to me and believing what I've said about my feelings for you not being based on what you look like. Or being affected by what you look like. But you know what? I'm not. I'm furious that you are using my own argument to prop up your excuses for…abandoning me!'

He shook his head and took a breath as though to argue the point.

'No, Ben,' she said, as he held up the first finger to indicate the first item on his list of excuses. 'If you really loved me, you wouldn't want to leave me behind. It would tear your heart out.' As the thought of it was tearing at her own.

'It will be painful,' he said. 'The parting. But I will always have these last two weeks to remember. The closeness we shared that I'd never dared dream of. That I never thought I'd ever be privileged to share with you. And it will be a comfort to know that you are safe and as happy as a marriage to me could ever have made you, with all the work you have here…'

'Fustian! We could keep on sharing that closeness if you took me with you. Why settle for just two weeks when we could have a lifetime together?'

He looked at the ground in front of her feet. Shook

his head. But just as she was on the point of completely losing her temper with him, something about his attitude sparked a memory. A memory of the way he'd acted as a lad, the visit after the broken collar bone, when he'd been too self-conscious about his spots to dare speak to her. But it hadn't been just the spots at all, had it? Deep down, Ben just thought he was unworthy of her regard. That he didn't deserve her loyalty, let alone her love. Back then, rather than expose his true feelings and risk her rejection, he'd walked away from her, pretending he didn't care.

Her heart sped up. If she wasn't mistaken, he was doing the same thing now. For all she knew, he actually *wanted* her to go with him. But he couldn't bring himself to believe they would be happy together for very long. And he'd rather remember two perfect weeks than live through the pain of them perhaps falling out with each other. He wasn't saying she wasn't able to cope with the rigours of army life at all. This wasn't about him thinking she wasn't up to the challenge. It was him, being afraid she'd get tired of him and leave him, which would hurt him far more than just leaving her behind with some rosy memories to keep him warm at night.

Yes, yes, because this was the man who'd loved her for years without telling a soul because he hadn't believed it was possible that she should ever care for him in return. He'd suffered in silence, watching other men court her, and had never dared to declare himself.

Because he'd been so abused as a child that he genuinely believed he was unlovable.

If it hadn't been for Walter and Horace, and that

drunken prank, they wouldn't even have had these two weeks. He'd have gone back to the army and she'd never have known…

'Ben, I am really cross with you,' she told him. His face settled into an expression that spoke of his acceptance that her anger was all he deserved. 'For thinking that I could possibly be happy here without you.' And for not even *trying* to believe in what they could have.

But, then, he simply couldn't, could he?

No. She was going to have to be the one to fight for this marriage. She was going to have to prove to him that he was worth loving. By refusing to let him walk away.

'I shan't be happy at all. I shall be miserable. And not just because I will be on my own again. But because you walked away from me. Deliberately. And don't think that I will be sitting here feeling sorry for *myself*,' she said, holding up her hand to silence him when he took a breath to argue with her. 'I will be worrying about what is happening to *you*. How can I be sure you are safe and well if I'm not there to see to it for myself? Who is going to make sure that you have enough to eat? And a proper bed to sleep in at night? With a roof over your head?'

'Yes, but, Daisy,' he said, coming over to her, 'those are the conditions I don't want you to have to endure.'

Ah. There was that irritating, masculine need to protect her, which had driven her brothers to behave in such an obnoxious fashion.

'What,' she said tartly, 'if you are injured in some battle? Who will look after you if I am not there?'

'Sergeant Wilmot is experienced in—'

'Yes, but he won't go back with you, will he? Haven't you noticed? He's fallen for Sally.'

'Sally?'

'The scullery maid. Whenever she is in the scullery, peeling vegetables, he's there, chopping them. If she's washing up, he's drying up. If she's out tending the vegetable patch he's out there with a hoe.'

'Well...' he frowned '... I can hire someone else...'

'Why would you want to do that when you have a wife?'

'Daisy,' he began, on an exasperated sigh.

'Don't you Daisy me,' she said, getting to her feet. 'If you go without me, I shall just jolly well follow you.'

'And abandon all your schemes for restoring the prosperity of the Park?' He shook his head. 'I don't think so. You are not the kind of woman to promise so much to the poor folk around here, only to let them down.'

'But anyone could continue that work, now that we've decided what wants doing. I could write to... to James, for example, to come here and carry out the plans we've already put in place.' James was showing signs of becoming rather frustrated with the lack of purpose in his life. Father would not let him implement any changes on their own land, saying he was not ready to hand over the reins just yet. And James didn't have the outlets available to other men of his rank. Father had given all his sons an abhorrence of gambling and whoring. And so he just drifted about from the house of one friend to another. And the number of those friends was dwindling, too, now she came to think of it. 'It would do him good to have something productive to do with his time.'

'Daisy, be sensible…'

'No. I won't,' she said. 'I don't care about the improvements for their own sake. I am happy doing them all because I'm doing them for you, can't you see that? I… I love you.'

He raised his brows. Shook his head. Took a step back. 'Look, Daisy, you might think you do, but this is just…panic speaking. Because you—'

'It is not panic speaking. I know my own mind. I'm not a child,' she said, stamping her foot in vexation. 'Why can you not believe that I love you?'

'Perhaps because you never said so until this moment. Even though I have said it to you many, many times.'

No, she hadn't said it before. Because she hadn't realised she did love him. Not until he'd said he was leaving, and the happy, shiny future she'd been imagining turned into a grey, bleak wilderness.

'I didn't realise I did love you,' she explained, 'until just now. When you said you were leaving and a pain went right through my middle.' She laid her hand flat on her abdomen, where she'd felt that pain slice into her. 'I don't want to stay here, fretting myself to skin and bone worrying about you. I don't want to live without you, Ben, not now that we've finally found each other, after all the years of…stupid misunderstandings.

'And if you…die…abroad…in some battle…' She sniffed. Had to dash a tear from her cheek. 'You have no right to put me through that, Ben,' she said angrily. 'If you really love me. No, Ben, I would never be able to survive that. Knowing I'd stayed here, in safety, while you went off on your own…to die alone…'

He put his arms round her. Cradled her head with one hand. 'Shh… Shh, now. Don't cry. I never wanted to make you cry.'

'Well, what do you think telling me you were planning to go away and leave me behind was going to do? Just imagine if it was the other way round? Could you stay at home managing this estate knowing I was off in danger somewhere?'

'Daisy, it's different for men. I'm used to the life. You are not…'

'No, but I could learn. And, oh, Ben, for the first time in my life I want to…seize life, and love, rather than just being content to read about it in books. To fight for what we could have together. Because of you. You have made me feel I belong, and have value, things I have never known before. Not only that, but for the first time in my life I *want* to follow a man wherever he goes, whether it's dangerous or not.'

He sighed. 'Daisy, I am not worth you putting your life in danger for…'

'Ben, you have got to stop thinking of yourself as worthless. You have as much value as any man. More than any man, for me. But…' she grabbed his lapels and gave them a little shake '…surely you believe that all men have equal value in God's eyes? You came to church with me. You believe in it all, don't you?'

'That's just religion, Daisy. And maybe I can believe

in the goodness, the impartiality of God. But when it comes to people, to real life…'

'People are idiots! All of them. All of us!' She slapped at her own chest. 'We look on the outer shell and judge others by clothes, and appearance, and rank, and wealth, and pedigree. None of which matter. Not really. What really matters is what's in here.' She laid her hands on Ben's broad chest. Right over his heart. 'You are a good man, Ben. The best. A man worth fighting for.'

She looked into his eyes, bracing herself for signs of masculine exasperation. Instead, she saw something she'd never seen in Ben's eyes before. It looked like the dawning of hope.

'You really do mean what you say, don't you? About me being your…your frog amongst toads…'

She had never said that, not specifically. But it sounded as if he was taking a step in the right direction regarding his self-esteem.

She nodded. 'My home,' she assured him. 'My love.'

'It…it isn't true,' he said slowly, 'what you just said, about this being the first time you have been prepared to fight for what you want.'

'Yes, it is,' she said hastily, feeling as though he was slipping away from her somehow.

'No. Don't you remember that night by the lake? When your brothers knocked me down? Instead of walking away, you leapt right into the fray, wielding your umbrella like a sword. You looked like some kind of avenging angel, all in glittering white, with lightning flashing across the sky as you tried to drive them off.' A smile tugged at his lips. 'You were magnificent. If I hadn't loved you before that night, I would have fallen in love with you right then. You see…' he frowned down at her hands, which he was holding between his own '…nobody had ever come to my defence, before then. Not me personally, I mean. In the army, when I was part of a unit, we all looked out for each other, but that was done to preserve the integrity, the strength of the unit.'

'Ben, what are you trying to say?' Was this some new line of reasoning he was going to use to try to convince her he knew best? That he was making ridiculous decisions for her own good?

He looked up into her face. His own twisted as though he was screwing himself up to say something he feared he was going to regret. And he took a deep breath.

'What I am trying to say is that, I suppose, as long as you bring your umbrella with you…'

She gave a whoop of joy. 'You mean it? You really aren't going to leave me behind?'

'You haven't given me much choice, have you?' he said, cupping her cheek with his hand and looking at her in a way that tugged at her heartstrings. 'I don't suppose I will ever be able to argue you out of it. Let alone think I could ever *command* your obedience…'

'Not a hope,' she said, hugging him. And then she kissed him hard, but briefly. 'Oh, Ben, thank you, thank you. You won't regret it, I promise. I will be such a good wife to you. Bandages,' she said, suddenly thinking of all the occasions she might need to nurse him. 'And medicines. I had better get in a stock of such things…'

He cupped her face in his hands. 'Not tonight. There is plenty of time to purchase such things. Tonight I want to share our last night together in this house as the Earl and Countess of Bramhall. As from tomorrow we will be Major and Mrs Flinders.'

'Major?'

He nodded. 'I bought promotion. I didn't use your money, truly, I—'

She placed one finger over his lips. 'I don't care if you did. And I don't care if you are a captain or a major or an earl, because to me you are… Ben. My Ben. Others can call you what they like. Or me. As long as, to each other, we are always just Ben and Daisy. Dealing with whatever comes our way, *together.*'

It was going to be an adventure, she reckoned, marriage to Ben. And one that would be better than any she'd ever read about in any book.

Because she was going to live it with the man who loved her and who she'd learned to love right back at her side.

'Very well, then, Daisy,' he said, smiling in a way she'd never seen him smile before. With pure joy. 'Let's go to bed.'

* * * * *